FOREVER AFTER

BOOK FIVE IN THE UNRESTRAINED SERIES

S. E. LUND

ACADIAN PUBLISHING LIMITED

ISBN: 978-1-988265-06-3

❦ Created with Vellum

S. E. LUND NEWSLETTER

Sign up for S. E. Lund's newsletter and gain access to updates on upcoming releases, sales and freebies! She hates spam and so will never share your email!

S. E. LUND NEWSLETTER SIGN UP

CHAPTER 1 : DRAKE

The days grew shorter in October and the hot humid Manhattan summer was replaced by cooler, drier air of autumn. I couldn't help but feel invigorated. With the equinox passed, I could feel the days shorten, the sun setting earlier and earlier, the long shadows cast by the buildings surrounding our apartment on 8th Avenue.

I loved autumn, especially the colors of the trees in Central Park. It reminded me of our wedding almost a year earlier, the one-year anniversary of which was fast approaching. I wanted to do something special for Kate, and show her how happy I was that I bumped into her in that bar so many months ago.

It seemed like yesterday that I was a going through my days at a frenetic pace, keeping busy at work doing surgery, playing with my band on weekends, and spending a few nights a week with my current submissive – whoever she was at the time.

Back then, I thought my life was full, but I was fooling myself.

I was lonely as hell.

Now, my life was truly full, filled with meaning, instead of meaningless things intended to keep me so busy I didn't know how lonely I was.

I had Kate, the love of my life. My soulmate.

I had Sophia, our child. A beautiful cherub of a baby, with pink cheeks and a bald head. She was quickly gaining weight and if you didn't know she was a preemie, you'd never guess. Kate was lucky that her breastmilk was rich and Sophia grew very quickly, putting on the weight she should have put on in the womb, before she was so unceremoniously removed from Kate's body.

I had my Fellowship on hold, so I could spend the year with Kate and Sophia, helping them both recover and hopefully thrive.

I had my practice at New York Presbyterian and although I was on a year's Leave of Absence, I could return once I felt that things were right with Kate and Sophia.

I even had Mersey, my Brit Invasion cover band. We took a brief hiatus so I could spend my nights with Kate and Sophia, but we were planning on reuniting again. We'd be starting a new season of performances at the local pubs in Manhattan and surrounding boroughs once Kate and Sophie were stable and I felt okay leaving them a few nights a week. Kate insisted that I at least keep up my music, considering I'd given up my Fellowship and practice for a year, and I finally agreed after much coaxing.

So it was that I stood at the window of the 8th Avenue apartment as the sun set and watched the sunlight glint on the windows of the buildings towering around us. In the bedroom, Kate and Sophia slept on our bed, Kate on her side facing Sophia and Sophia on her side facing Kate, having fallen off Kate's ample breast after a feed.

The two lay on the coverlet and slept and at that moment, I felt such love and contentment. I went over to the bed and crawled in behind Kate, spooning my body against hers, one arm slipping around her waist to touch Sophia. Lying there like that, I had to swallow hard and blink away moisture in my eyes.

Of course, at that moment, my cell buzzed on the nightstand. I didn't want to answer it, and let it vibrate away, but the sound woke Kate, who turned slightly so she could look at my face.

"Aren't you going to answer?" she asked, her voice sleepy, her eyes heavy.

"It can wait. I wanted to lie here with the two of you for a while."

She smiled and moved closer, kissing me softly on the lips. "We're glad you did."

I pulled her closer to me and kissed her more deeply, careful to keep Sophia in the corner of my eye. "I love you, Mrs. Morgan."

She kissed me back. "I love *you*, Dr. Morgan. What do you want for supper?"

I grinned and narrowed my eyes then squeezed her ample breast, tweaking the nipple between my finger and thumb. The feel of her heavy breast in my hand made my dick stiffen. I pressed it against her and kissed her neck. Then, I rolled on my back and carefully pulled Kate on top of me.

"Dr. *Morgan*," she said in mock affront. "In front of our child?"

I laughed and tickled her and she fought not to laugh out loud.

"Luckily, she's asleep," I said. "I love you so much I could eat you for supper but we could order in from *Quance*, if you insist on actual food. You love their ribs."

2

She poked me in the ribs. "You're always hungry."

"For you? Always."

We kissed again and I wondered when she'd be ready for sex. It felt to me like she responded, but not with the same interest she once did. I wouldn't push her. I'd let her signal her readiness. When she kissed me again, I thought maybe she was ready now, but then Sophia stirred on the bed beside us, no doubt woken by the sound of our voices.

Kate struggled out of my arms and sat up, lifting Sophia to her shoulder, deftly tucking a receiving blanket beneath her in case Sophie spit up.

"I have to burp her," Kate said, and patted Sophia's back while she rocked back and forth slowly.

I sat beside Kate and stroked her back while she burped Sophie. Little Sophie was still half-asleep, her eyes closed, her cheek resting on Kate's shoulder. Kate was wearing a sundress that had an easy to remove shoulder strap so she could feed Sophie whenever she needed it.

The domesticity of the moment was so quaint, I decided to take my phone and videotape it so I could show it to Lara when I saw her for lunch the next day. Although Lara wasn't a maternal person, she was interested in my relationship with Kate, and was always asking for pictures.

I picked up my cell and entered my passcode, only to see a notice of a new email from someone I didn't know, but the name was familiar. It was sent to my professional email address, so I frowned and opened it up.

Dr. Morgan,

I wanted to offer you the chance to respond to the article that's going into the weekend paper. One of my reporters has been researching your wife's assault and she's tracked down a few interesting leads. You may want to see what my reporter has written and prepare yourself. I don't usually give people much of a chance to respond but due to your delicate circumstances, I thought I'd be nice... I could do this over the phone but given that nothing is secure anymore, you can come down and we can talk in private. Take it or leave it.

Please call me at ...

It was signed Janice Peterson, Senior Cultural Editor, New York Herald Magazine.

That last line about preparing myself set me on edge, and I had a sense of gloom envelope me. That could only mean one possible thing: she'd dredged up some information about my past in the BDSM community. It shouldn't be much of a story, given I was considered a gentle Dom, not a sadist, and only interested in games of D/s with a little bondage thrown in, rather than S/M, but I didn't know what the average reader might think.

I had no idea who this Janice Peterson was, so I quickly googled her name and came up with a website for the paper. It was filled with gossipy pieces about local celebrities and Manhattan's elite. The paper's owners seemed to have a thing about bringing down wealthy businessmen and had written a few scandalous pieces about men caught *in flagrante delicto* with mistresses and their subsequent divorces.

I could only imagine what the editor would want to write about me. Either she thought I was a suspect or she thought I would soon be a newly divorced husband – both of which would be of interest to her gossipy readers.

"I don't like the looks of this," I said, my voice low.

Kate craned her neck around to see what I meant. "What is it?" she asked, her eyes wide.

I held out my cell, showing her the email. "The cultural editor at the New York Herald Magazine wants to meet me to discuss an article in a gossip column. She must be interested in doing a story on my scandalous past."

Kate frowned and rocked Sophia gently. "Oh, God, Drake," she said and shook her head. "As if you need that."

"I'm pretty much okay, I think. I've let Fred Parker know at NYU that I had a bit of a kinky past, and he was fine about it. Shrugged it off. Said he didn't care what went on in people's bedrooms, so long as it was legal."

Kate sighed. "Still, it's not going to be pleasant."

I nodded and took in a deep breath. "I'm glad I'm on a leave of absence for a year. If anything is revealed that is somewhat scandalous, it'll all blow over by the time I return to finish my Fellowship."

She nodded, but still looked worried. "I hope so."

I re-read the email. "She wants me to come and meet her tonight before the story goes to print. I guess I better go."

Kate frowned. "It's a bit late, isn't it?"

"It's for the online magazine and the news cycle is now 24 hours, so..." I checked my watch. It was close to 6:45. If I left then, I'd make it to the news room in thirty minutes. Her message said she worked until ten, so we had time to go over the draft so I at least knew what she was going to write and could respond.

"It was nice of her to give me a head's up at least," I said and slipped off the bed.

Kate frowned. "It would be even nicer if she minded her own business."

I grabbed my suit jacket from the chair beside the chest of drawers and slipped it on. "There's no privacy any longer. For any of us."

"I guess not," Kate replied and finished burping Sophie. She lay Sophie back down, tucked a rolled-up blanket behind her back so she didn't roll onto her back, and slid off the bed. She came to me and wrapped her hands around my neck.

"You're going to miss dinner if you have to go to the office. Why can't she send you a copy of what she's going to write and you can respond over the phone or something?"

I checked the email. "She says she usually doesn't give people much of a chance to respond but given my delicate circumstances, if I want to come down and speak to her, she's happy to oblige."

"That's big of her," Kate said with a harrumph. "She probably wants to seduce you because you're such a hunk."

I laughed out loud at that and squeezed her. "She said I should come down because nothing is secure anymore and so we could talk in private."

"Huh," Kate said and shook her head. "Riiight. She probably wants to blackmail you and force you to be her Dom or something."

"You are so suspicious," I said and kissed her. "I promise you I won't give in, no matter how she threatens me. I'm no one's Dom but yours."

I squeezed her and then tickled her, enjoying when she squealed with delight. Then, I kissed her more deeply, wishing I could stay home and have a nice soapy bath with her while we waited for *Quance* to deliver. So, while I had hoped tonight would be the night, unfortunately, Fate intervened and I'd have to leave my beautiful wife and sleeping child and brave the wilds of Manhattan at night.

"Go ahead and order from *Quance*. Get whatever you feel like eating," I said as I adjusted my tie. "When I come back, I'll have supper."

She nodded. "I wish you didn't have to go. I feel so indulgent getting you all to myself all day and all night."

"I wish I could stay, too."

I smiled and rubbed her back, kissing the top of her head. Then, I went to the hallway to get my keys. She followed me to the door and kissed me again before I left.

"Hurry back. And don't let the bitch give you any trouble."

"Don't worry," I said and smiled. "I can handle Ms. Peterson."

I closed the door behind me and made my way down the street to the parking garage where I kept my car. Manhattan traffic at that time of night was still busy and so I took as many alternate routes as I could to try to make it to Peterson's office quickly. I didn't want to waste my night with Kate completely. Finally, in about twenty-five minutes, I arrived at the building and found a parking garage about a block away. I handed the attendant my keys and walked briskly down the still-crowded street to the office of the Herald where Ms. Peterson was located.

I hoped that my sense of security wasn't false and that I could, in fact, handle Ms. Peterson.

CHAPTER 2 : KATE

W hen Drake left, I dropped the fake smile I pasted on my face.
It was replaced by a face that, when I glanced in the mirror, looked like a zombie instead of what should have been a happy new mother in love with her beautiful baby and wonderful, loving and very handsome husband.

Instead, I felt this low-level sense of doom hanging over my head – as if something bad was going to happen at any minute and there would be nothing I could do about it.

I hated myself for feeling that way, but it was the truth.

I was so damn tired all the time, I felt like it was all I could do to feed and change Sophie when Drake was busy. The rest of the time, I wanted to lie down on the bed, cover my head with a pillow and sleep.

I hid it from Drake because I felt so unappreciative of how lucky I was. I loved Sophia beyond all thought but often found myself crying at times for no reason. Anything could set me off – a television ad, a song on the stereo, a crazy video on Facebook…

I was angry that I couldn't be more thankful. Even though I loved Drake with a passion, I felt so tired all the time, that I didn't feel like doing anything but sleep and look after Sophia.

On top of it all, I was also worried about my father, who fell the previous week and seemed to be having small strokes.

Concerned, I picked up my cell and called his number. After a half dozen rings, Elaine answered, her voice quiet.

"Hi, Katie, how are you, dear?"

"I'm fine," I said softly, although it was a lie. "How's my dad? Can I speak to him?"

"He's sleeping in his chair," Elaine replied. "He had a trip to the hospital today for a CT scan to see how things are and he's tired. It's always such an ordeal getting him there and back, now that he needs a wheelchair to get around."

"He needs a wheelchair?" I said with alarm, my body tensing. "When did this happen? He never said anything..."

"He didn't want to upset you," Elaine replied. "He doesn't have enough strength in his left side anymore and was starting to lean too much to one side. His doctor said that your father should use a chair or stop going out. If he fell again, he could harm himself because he isn't strong enough to protect himself from the fall."

"Oh, God," I said and rubbed my forehead. "I wish I'd known. I would have wanted to go with him to the hospital."

"You can't worry about him, Katie. You have enough on your plate with your own recovery and with Sophia. Not to mention the investigation."

I closed my eyes, brought back once more to the ongoing investigation into the accident – or should I say, attempted murder. Both Drake and I had been interviewed at the hospital but not since Sophie came home. I told the detectives that Lisa was the culprit, but they said they had to investigate all angles. The husband is always a prime suspect when a wife is attacked. They had to rule Drake out.

That was the reality of things.

"Drake is going to meet with this editor at the Herald Magazine tonight to talk about a story they're going to run in the weekend edition."

"Oh, dear," Elaine said. "They're notorious about getting everything wrong."

I sighed heavily. "I know. I remember a few of their stories on cheating husbands and huge divorce settlements of the rich and famous."

"I'm sorry about all this. You have enough to think about, Kate. Don't worry about your father. He's fine. We knew he might have to start using a wheelchair to get around. He's excited about getting the latest model with all the bells and whistles. I've had to clear out a path from the kitchen to his office and to our bedroom so he can zoom around with no obstacles. He's *fine*, Kate. Really."

"If you say so," I said, unconvinced. "Maybe I'll come by tomorrow for a visit."

"Let me check his calendar and let you know when he's free. He has a lot of meetings about the new Congressman. Plus, there's some of his old golfing buddies in town..."

The way she let her voice trail off seemed that she was overwhelmed with my father's busy schedule, which was impressive considering his health.

"Are you okay?" I asked, worried about her.

"I'm fine. I thought your father wanted to slow things down after the stroke, but he seems determined to make up for lost time or something. I'll tell him you'd like to come by and he'll call or text you. He has a new iPad and has been using it all the time."

"Okay," I said and sighed. "Hopefully, Sophie and I can come by soon and visit."

"Bye, sweetie," she said softly.

"Bye," I replied. "Tell my dad I love him."

"I will," she replied and ended the call.

On my part, I sat staring at the cell in my hand while Sophie slept. Learning that my father had to use a motorized wheelchair to get around was not good news. Until I found out, I saw my father as still quite mobile, walking with a cane around the house and when he went places, only using a wheelchair when he went to the hospital for tests or treatments. The thought he needed a wheelchair permanently made my sense of gloom deepen.

I should have been ecstatic with my circumstances. I had a beautiful healthy baby and loving handsome husband who was devoted to me, but something prevented me from being able to enjoy anything. I felt as if at any time, the world would come crashing down and I'd be alone. Or dead.

I made sure Sophie was sleeping and was safe in the middle of the bed, with battlements made of pillows and receiving blankets rolled up surrounding her. She was still unable to do much of anything besides kick and punch and had yet to roll over so she wasn't going anywhere, but I had terrible images of her falling off the bed that I couldn't quite get out of my mind.

I walked to the living room and stared out at the dark sky. The streetlights had all blinked on and there was still foot traffic on the streets. Now and then came the blare of a horn.

I went to the drawer and pulled out the menu from *Quance* and sat thinking about what to order but my mind kept wandering to Drake and his visit to the Herald's office for his meeting with the editor.

What story would they run? How would it affect Drake? His career and his public persona?

Until the accident, it had been spotless – he was the brilliant young neurosurgeon who was a pioneer in robotic techniques, the billionaire son of a wealthy trauma surgeon turned medical implements manufacturer. Philanthropist and volunteer for Doctors Without Borders.

It would be horrible for him if his reputation was damaged because of what Lisa Monroe did. I could only imagine the fallout. I chewed a nail while

I looked at the menu from *Quance* and considered. Maybe he could convince the editor not to run the story, but I had little hope. Something as juicy as a Doctor Dominant spanking his submissives would be too good not to run.

I picked up my cell phone to order but before I could dial, the phone rang and I looked at the caller ID. Detective McDonald from the NYPD major crimes squad.

Oh, *great*. Something else to worry about.

"Hello?"

"Hello, Mrs. Morgan? This is Detective McDonald calling. I wanted to arrange a time for us to come and speak with you, if that's all right."

"You want to come to my home?" I said in surprise.

"Yes," he said, his voice emotionless. "We'd like to swing by tonight if possible. Will you and Dr. Morgan both be home in an hour?"

I checked my watch and realized that they would arrive before Drake could get home.

"Tonight's not a good night," I said. "Dr. Morgan is out at the moment. Maybe tomorrow?"

There was a pause on the line. "Oh, that's fine. We can come by and speak with you. We want to speak to you both at some point."

I frowned. "You've already taken a statement from me," I said, unable to hide the impatience in my voice. "I have a newborn, and she's a premie, in case you forgot."

"Is she not well?" McDonald said, and I could hear in his voice that he knew I was stalling.

"No, she's fine. It's just that I'm tired a lot as you can imagine. I'd rather Drake be here when we talk."

"Tonight's the best time for us. We'll see you in about thirty minutes."

Then he ended the call.

I stared at my phone. Tonight was not going well – not at all. In addition to everything, now I had to speak to the police again. I stared at the menu from *Quance* and didn't feel hungry any longer.

I went back into the bedroom and laid on the bed beside Sophie, who was sleeping peacefully. Thank God she was healthy.

I lay facing her and watched her sleep. Why did the police want to come by again? Hadn't I spoken with them enough already? They had to know that Lisa was a nutcase who was acting alone…

On a whim, I texted Lara.

KATE: Hey, the police are coming over in about 30 mins. They want to interview me. Drake is out meeting with the editor of the Herald over a piece she plans on publishing this weekend. What should I do?

There was a pause of a few moments and then a response came.

LARA: I'll be right over.

I frowned, alarmed now that Lara wanted to be with me when the police came by.

KATE: *Should I be worried? Why do you want to come over?*

LARA: *No, you shouldn't be worried but they shouldn't be coming over and bothering you. You've given them a statement already. That should be enough. I suspect they want to see your apartment."*

KATE: *Check it out for dungeon equipment? *I texted sarcastically**

LARA: *Ha Ha. Something like that. Hold tight. I'll be right over.*

I got up after checking that Sophie was still okay, and went to the bathroom to brush my hair, my teeth and try to look somewhat presentable.

Then I sat and waited, passing the time while Sophie slept reading my news feed and Facebook posts from my family and friends. I was nervous about the interview and went over in my head what I knew about Lisa and Drake's past.

They had been involved in dungeon play several times. Each time, Drake was asked to take part by Lisa's then-Master Derek Richardson, a wealthy friend of Drake's in the BDSM community.

She liked to be dominated and spanked. Drake tied her up and fucked her. That was the end to it. Richardson liked to watch her be taken by other men, and at the time, Drake was in between submissives and was available.

He thought nothing of it.

Seeing Lisa in his class of residents during morning rounds was the biggest shock of his life. Drake had a bad feeling about her being in the group and because of their past relationship, he eventually spoke with the head of the Fellowship program but had been encouraged to stay. That everything would be okay.

It wasn't, of course. She pushed Drake. And pushed him, insisting that he be her 'friend' and that they spend time together. Drake confessed to me how she asked him to come up to her apartment and help her install a heavy flat screen television. How after he was finished, she tried to seduce him, even tried to kiss him but he fought her off. How he did everything he could to dissuade her from any thought that there could be a relationship other than casual colleagues between them.

She didn't get the picture.

She must have grown more and more obsessed with him and then, when things came to a head, after Drake had gone to Fred Parker with his concerns, she sought revenge.

Attacking me was her way of getting back at Drake. Did she really think that with me and my baby out of the way that Drake would be hers?

If so, she was seriously mentally disordered. Delusional.

I made a pot of tea and then stood at the window, waiting for Lara to come by.

* * *

In about fifteen minutes, she arrived and I buzzed her into the apartment. I heard her footsteps on the stairs and stood at the entry and ushered her in. Lara gave me a quick hug and then handed me her coat. She looked stunning, even on a weekday evening, dressed in a women's business suit and white silk blouse.

"I'm sorry you had to do this without Drake," Lara said as we sat in the living room and had a cup of tea. "I didn't want the police to have unfettered access to you so I thought I'd better come by."

"Will you be my lawyer?" I asked, wondering if I needed one.

"No, sweetie," she said and shook her head, reaching out to take my hand. "You don't need a lawyer, but you do need a friend who's knowledgeable about your rights and about what the police can and can't ask you."

I nodded and took a sip of my tea. "I'm sure they'll understand that Drake had nothing to do with what happened soon enough."

She shrugged. "Not necessarily. If Lisa can spin a good tale, and convince her lawyer and the jury that Drake was her secret lover and trying to get rid of you, things might get messy. Not that I think Drake would be charged, but there might be enough doubt to ruin his career and reputation. We don't want that."

"Of course not," I said and frowned at the thought, my sense of doom deepening. "Why couldn't they see right away that Lisa's delusional? To attack me and think she could get away with it after renting a car in her own name?" I shook my head. "She had to have lost touch with reality."

"You and I both know that, but stranger things have happened. I've seen cases where the one partner in crime wanted to pin a death on the co-conspirator and gotten off because he could convince everyone he was the innocent party. It has happened before so the detectives will be keeping all angles open until the evidence leads them to one conclusion or another. Until then, we have to be careful so that they don't make any wrong assumptions about Drake and his time in the BDSM community."

"He's so not what Lisa has painted him to be. Or Sunita."

Lara took a sip of her tea and nodded slowly. "That damn video... I wish I had advised Drake at the time to be careful of any recording devices. I thought I knew Sunita well. I was wrong."

"Why did she do it?" I asked, wondering about Sunita. "Why would she deliberately hurt Drake?"

Lara sighed. "She was a sick woman who wanted Drake to be her father figure. You have to admit he's one of the best looking Doms around."

I smiled. "He is. But still, to do something so mean and to lie about things..."

"You're pretty naïve and very sweet if you think that there aren't women out there who are a bit broken and want to hurt the man who rejected them in some way. It's common enough."

Lara took a sip of her tea. "So, what did Drake say about this meeting with Peterson?"

I shook my head because I didn't know much. "Just that she was offering him a chance to respond before they went to print."

"Poor Drake. It's not like he's done anything wrong."

"I know..." I sighed.

At that, the doorbell rang and I glanced at Lara.

"What are you going to tell them about why you're here?"

Lara stood and straightened her suit jacket. "I'm only a friend offering advice."

I nodded and went to the doorway. When I got there, I took in a deep breath and tried to calm myself. Then, I opened the door.

There stood the two detectives who had interviewed me in the hospital – Detectives McDonald and St. James.

We said hello and I invited them in. Lara stood a few feet away from the entrance.

"This is Lara, a friend who will be with me while you interview me. She's a lawyer."

St. James frowned and looked Lara over. "You don't need legal counsel now," he said and handed me his coat. "You're the victim. We want to ask a few more questions about what happened and what you know about Ms. Monroe."

"I'm not here to offer her legal advice," Lara said, her voice calm. "I'm here to sit with her and be moral support. You have to understand that dredging all that up is upsetting to her, all things considered, Detective."

Lara held St. James's eye for a long moment and then he relented and nodded his head.

"Shall we get started?" he said and I pointed to the couches in the living room. McDonald and St. James sat on one sofa and Lara and I sat across from them.

McDonald took out a small notepad and pencil and flipped through the pages. Finally, he sat back and regarded me with a piercing gaze, his blue eyes intense.

"So, as you may have heard, we've found Ms. Monroe's personal diary and have been reading it to see what she might have written about Dr. Morgan and you.

"And?" Lara said, her voice sounding impatient. "I'm sure you found that she imagined a relationship with Drake that didn't exist."

McDonald shrugged. "She wrote very highly about Dr. Morgan and claims he was willing to maintain the relationship they had before, when she was

Mr. Richardson's submissive partner," McDonald said to me, after turning pointedly in my direction.

"That's not true at all," I said. "They had no relationship. Drake never saw her again after the last time they were involved with Mr. Richardson until the day his fellowship at NYU started."

"Did you know about that relationship before the accident?" St. James asked, his eyebrows raised.

I nodded, but I didn't like the way he was looking at me – like I was a naïve little woman who couldn't see the truth.

"When Drake and I became serious about each other, he told me about his past relationships. Not any details, but he told me that he'd been with several submissives. He didn't mention names or anything. But when Lisa showed up in his class, he told me about what happened between them." I cringed a bit inwardly because he hadn't told me immediately. He didn't tell me right away. We were getting married, and then there was Christmas...

McDonald nodded and wrote something down in his book. "And when did he tell you?"

I swallowed. "After Christmas when she started to bother him."

He glanced up at me. "What did he tell you?"

"He told me that Lisa was nothing but a friend's submissive who he topped a couple of times, but that they never met outside of those instances," I said, feeling weird talking so openly about BDSM. It now seemed second nature to me but to be talking about it to police officers felt very strange. "She wanted more than the occasional experience with Dr. Morgan. She pushed for a threesome, but neither of them wanted it. Richardson was a voyeur. He liked to watch."

St. James leaned forward. "Did he ever tell you that he exchanged personal emails with Ms. Monroe?"

"What?" I asked and frowned. "Do you mean work related emails?"

"No, personal."

"No," I said, a surge of something in my gut at the news Drake had sent her emails. "He never said he emailed her. Mostly, they talked in the hallways at the hospital. Or in meetings. During rounds, that sort of thing. He never said he emailed her..." I glanced at Lara. "Did he tell you he emailed her?"

Lara shook her head. "Not that I'm aware of. Can we see the emails?" she asked St. James.

"We have a few we can show you," he said. "As you can see, they're of a personal rather than professional nature."

He handed me a sheet of paper from a file. I took it and glanced at it, my heart in my throat.

She's not a real sub, Lisa. She fights me at every turn. I can't be myself with her because

14

she might report me to my employer if she thinks I've crossed the line...

My heart beat faster. "This can't be from Drake," I said and handed the letter to Lara, who read it over and shook her head. I was certain that Lisa had written it, but it did make me feel sick for a moment.

Drake didn't feel that way at all. He always said I was a perfect submissive — for *him*.

"These are from an address with his name, but we're still investigating. We will be contacting Dr. Morgan for more information based on some new evidence."

"Dr. Morgan didn't write this," Lara said and handed the letter back to Detective St. James.

"You're so sure?" he replied, his eyebrows raised.

"I know him," she said. "I've known him for years. He doesn't whine."

I caught Detective McDonald's eye. "She probably wrote that herself. You should be able to tell by the IP. Even I know that."

"Here's more," St. James said and handed about a dozen sheets of paper dated over the past year. One seemed familiar, and then I realized that it contained text from Drake's letters to his submissives.

I've known every part of you – every naked inch, inside and out.

    I can't wait to bind you with my leather restraints and make you cry out my name as you come, again and again. Then, I will really kiss you, smothering your moans with my mouth...

Lisa had copied them verbatim and used them in her fake letters. I didn't know what to say about it. Should I let them know?

"I wanted you to see what your husband has been writing to Ms. Monroe."

"My husband didn't write those letters," I said plainly. "That's not his email address."

"That you know of. Many people have several email addresses. Are you sure you know them all?"

"Drake is a happily married man and isn't interested in being part of that lifestyle any longer," I said, although that wasn't exactly true. He was only interested in it as fun and games now, with me. Maybe we might have considered going to a dungeon party for fun, and because it excited us both, but now that we had Sophie? We had better and more important things to do.

"It's my understanding that people don't change their interest in kink all that much," Detective St. James said.

"Maybe not for most, but for Drake, he did. That was a part of his life before he met me. Now, he's monogamous and happy to be so. He wanted a family and children more than anything."

"Funny way to get a family, being part of BDSM..."

Detective St. James sat back and nodded. "Whatever, we are interested in whether there was an ongoing relationship with Ms. Monroe the way she claimed and that was why she decided to do her residency in Neurosurgery – at Dr. Morgan's suggestion and with his encouragement. According to her journal, Dr. Morgan and Ms. Monroe had plans to open up a practice together once they both finished their respective courses."

My jaw dropped open at that. "What?" I sat forward, my hands gripping the chair's arm rests. "That's ridiculous! Can't you see that she's totally delusional?"

He shrugged one shoulder. "It's in the diary and letters," he said. "Ms. Monroe is painting a picture of Dr. Morgan that is very different from the happily married family man that you claim he is. She's painting a picture of is a married man with a pregnant wife, maybe pregnant with a baby he had no interest in, with a mistress who was in his medical field, and who he wanted to be with instead. She's painting a picture of Dr. Morgan as controlling her mind and behavior, suggesting that they could be together if only you weren't in the picture."

My heart pounded in my chest. "Surely you can see that she's making all this up."

"It's not out of the realm of possibility," Detective St. James said doubtfully. "I've seen cases like this before, although not with such direct ties to the whole Bondage and Dominance side of the equation. That's a first. Usually, these guys don't join websites dedicated to BDSM and do it so overtly. They're usually your ordinary run of the mill sociopaths and sadists, who dupe women into being their servants and doing their bidding."

"Mrs. Morgan, we know that Dr. Morgan was involved in the BDSM community prior to meeting you. We know that he's what's considered a 'Dominant' and has a very strong personality and likes to be in control."

"He's also a neurosurgeon and being in control is essential to their success rate. One false move..." I said, angry at the suggestion that Drake was controlling me, manipulating me to say what he wanted me to say.

"Yes, I'm sure that's the case," Detective St. James said quickly. "But we also know that he likes to control the relationship he has with women."

Drake did like control. In the past, he used control to keep his relationships with women at arm's length. He didn't need to do that anymore – not with me. He tried to keep women at arm's length because he was afraid to get hurt again.

How could I tell that to Detective St. James? He was probably titillated by the whole BDSM connection and the fact that Drake was a Dominant. He probably thought Drake was a control freak who liked to hurt women.

"And how did you meet Dr. Morgan?" St. James asked, leaning forward again like he wanted to push me.

I glanced at Lara and she nodded so I turned back and swallowed before answering.

"We met at a fundraiser my father held for Doctors Without Borders," I said, remembering it with a sense of happiness. "My father knew Drake before I did, although my father used to talk about Drake a lot."

"Was your father aware of Dr. Morgan's... interests?" St. James asked, his voice sounding suggestive, like this was scandalous.

I frowned, not liking the way this was going. "I don't know for sure when my father knew, but Drake went to him to explain because one of my..." I hesitated, not wanting to mention Dawn's name. "A friend felt concerned that I was seeing Drake and wanted to tell my father that he was involved in BDSM. Drake went to my father because he wanted to be the one to break the news."

McDonald nodded. "Drake and your father were close?"

"My father was like a father to Drake. My father and his father were best friends from Vietnam. They fought together. Drake's father saved my father's life."

"So there's a history between your two families."

"Yes," I said. "Our fathers went way back. My father thinks the world of Drake."

"So, when you found out that Drake was going to be involved with a former submissive, you weren't worried that he'd have an affair with her, given their past relationship?"

I shook my head. "Not at all. She was nothing to him. Nothing but a past sexual partner. He had no interest in her as a person. He's in love with me. He loves me. He loves his life with me and our baby."

"That's what he told us. In fact, that's almost exactly what he told us. Almost word for word."

I frowned and turned to Lara. She raised her eyebrows. "I think Mrs. Morgan has answered enough questions along this line."

"I'm surprised at how closely her testimony mirrors Dr. Morgan's."

"It's not testimony," Lara said firmly. "It's her statement. This isn't a court of law."

"No, it isn't. We're gathering information. I was merely noting how similar her statement was to Dr. Morgan's."

"Maybe that's because it's the truth," I said, my heart rate increasing at the insinuation that I had rehearsed what I was going to say – or worse, that Drake had coached me. That we were getting our stories straight, like Dana suggested previously.

"Maybe," Detective St. James said, pursing his lips as if he doubted it was the truth. "Or maybe you're afraid of him and are telling us what he wants us to hear."

"No--." I said but he held up a hand.

"Well, that's all we have." McDonald glanced around the apartment. "This is a nice place you have here. Can I look around a bit? I love these old apartments."

Lara stood, her hands on her hips. "What – are you looking for a dungeon or something? I can guarantee you there is none."

"No," McDonald said. "My uncle has one of these old places and is thinking of renovating. I like the way you've joined the two apartments."

McDonald turned to me and smiled. "Really glad to see that you're doing well. You were lucky that there was a security detail so close with medical training or you might have died."

I nodded and handed him and St. James their coats.

"I know. Drake was concerned about my safety. He ordered the security detail a week or so before the accident. He was worried about Lisa."

"He had good reason to be worried."

With that, the two detectives said goodbye and left us alone. I turned to face Lara, who sat back down at her place on the sofa.

"Well?" I asked. "What do you think?"

Lara reached out and squeezed my arm. "There's no way Drake wrote those emails. He would never complain, Kate. If he was unhappy in any way, he'd act. He wouldn't whine. He'd fix things."

"I know," I said, squashing down the tiniest bit of doubt.

"They're fakes. If Drake never said anything about emailing Lisa, I'm sure he didn't. Certainly not anything personal, unless he was trying to convince her to leave him alone."

"Why did they come by again? Just to show me the emails Drake supposedly sent to Lisa? They didn't ask anything different than before."

She shrugged. "The detectives like to get a sense of how a victim is doing and whether they might be lying. I'm sure they were looking for consistency in your story. Plus, maybe they showed you about the emails to see if you'd confess your doubts about Drake."

She shrugged and raised her eyebrows as if helpless.

Of course, I felt a sick at the thought Drake was carrying on an email conversation with Lisa about anything personal. Why would he? If he did, it had to be to shut her up or stop her from pestering him. I knew Drake loved me... I knew he had no interest in Lisa...

I sighed. "I told them the same story already so I hope they have everything they need. I appreciate you coming by."

She shook her head and waved me off. "Don't mention it. I think I'll stay until Drake gets back so we can talk about what happened."

"Sounds good to me," I said. At that moment, I heard some rustling from the bedroom on the baby monitor and went in to find Sophia was awake and kicking. Seeing her pretty little face made me relax a bit. I picked her up and carried her into the living room.

Lara stood and came over right away and looked at Sophie.

"She's so beautiful, Kate. You must be very happy."

I nodded and forced a smile. "I am. I wish all this was over."

And then, I started to cry. Tears filled my eyes and I couldn't help myself. I was so confused. So happy to have survived, so happy that Sophia was healthy and thriving. And yet – I felt like crying all the time. Even thought I didn't really believe it, the idea that Drake had been secretly emailing Lisa all along made it worse.

"Oh, poor Kate," Lara said and put an arm around me, kissing my forehead. "I'm sure Drake isn't involved with Lisa. In fact, I know he isn't. These are fake emails that she's made, nothing more. I know he has absolutely no interest in her. *None.*"

"I know," I said and part of me fought with myself. I knew Drake had no interest in Lisa… "I seem to cry so easily now."

"It's the baby blues," she said and squeezed Sophie and me. "I've read about it. All new mothers get it for a few days or weeks."

"It's been months," I said tearfully. "I still cry at the drop of a hat."

"Does Drake know?" she asked and pushed hair from my face.

I shook my head. "I don't want to upset him," I said, wiping my eyes with the back of my hand. "I should be happy. Why can't I be happy?"

She sat me down and took Sophie from me. Then, Lara glanced at me.

"You have PTSD, sweets," she said, her face so solemn. "You better go to a psychiatrist or see a therapist. It's very common in victims of crime. You had a terrible time of it – almost dying, losing your uterus, being in a coma. Drake should be aware of this."

"I don't want to burden him," I said. "It's been hard on Drake having this happen – Lisa attacking me, him giving up his Fellowship, putting his career on hold."

"Sweetie," Lara said and made a face. "This happened to you as well. Drake is much stronger than you give him credit. You can rely on him. Believe me."

"He didn't sign up for all this," I said with a catch in my throat. "He had everything in his life arranged the way he wanted it. It was all going smoothly. Then I came along and now his whole life is different. He never wanted to get married, he didn't ever think he'd be a father…"

Lara sat closer to me and put her arm around my shoulder. I took Sophie back from her.

"Hun, believe me, he is *so* happy that all this happened. He was trying to keep busy so he didn't have to think about why his personal life was a mess and why his marriage failed. He said to me once that he was never happier than when he was with you. He finally felt that he had a real life and not a busy schedule. So, don't ever think he regrets meeting you and doesn't want all this. And don't for a moment believe he was secretly writing to Lisa."

I let her hug me and tried to accept what she said but it was hard.

"You have the baby blues, hun," she said and looked me in the eye, brushing my tears off my cheek. "I'm going to stay here until Drake gets back so I can talk to him, make sure he understands that you're not doing well. He's a doctor, sweets. He knows how to handle this. He almost went into psychiatry, if I recall correctly."

"No, please," I said and sat up straighter, putting Sophie on my shoulder. "I'll talk to him. I *promise*. You go home. I realize now that my hormones are probably out of whack and that's why I've been a bit sad."

She glanced at me with narrowed eyes. "I don't know," she said, her voice hesitant. "You have to promise me you'll talk to him."

"I promise," I said quickly. "I'll talk to him tonight. After I let him tell me what happened with the editor. Then, I'll ask him about the emails."

"Promise?" she said again. "I'll call him myself and will let him know if you don't."

I shook my head and waved my hand. "I promise."

She stood up and looked me over from head to toe. "You look back to normal, Kate, but your hormones aren't. You have to let Drake know for your own good."

"I will," I said and forced a smile. If Lara didn't believe me, she left anyway.

"And tell him to call me and talk to me about the Herald article. We need some kind of PR response, depending on what it says."

"I'll tell him as soon as he gets in."

I thanked her once more for coming over and closed the door, glad for her to be gone so I could prepare for Drake's return. I didn't want him to arrive home to find Lara there with me. I had to pull myself together so I could ask him about the emails to Lisa, listen to what he had to say, and then decide what to think. When he was ready, I'd tell him about my sadness, but there was so much other crap going on in our lives now, I didn't want to burden him with my own lack of happiness.

I put Sophia down in her swing and went to the kitchen, determined to call *Quance* and order some food for us. Drake would be hungry when he returned and I didn't want him to come home to no supper on the table. Besides, cleaning would help me push thoughts about Drake's email to Lisa out of my mind for at least a little while…

* * *

CHAPTER 3 : DRAKE

I checked in with the front desk clerk who doubled as a security guard. He had me sign a roster and then gave me a temporary ID card. I took the elevator up to the fifth floor and emerged out of the elevator into a posh room with a modular reception desk and a pretty young blond sitting behind it.

"You're working late," I said when I went to the desk.

"The press never sleeps," she said with a smile. "Are you Dr. Morgan?"

I nodded. "Yes. I'm here to see Ms. Peterson."

She looked me over and smiled brightly. "Please go into the waiting room. She's down at the news room for an editorial meeting but I'll let her know you're here."

I nodded and went to the small waiting room, taking a seat by a table upon which lay a dozen glossy magazines. I checked my cell to see what time it was and then scanned the headlines on my news app.

Within about five minutes, the elevator doors opened and off walked Janice Peterson herself – late thirties, long blond hair to her shoulders, dressed in a crisp white dress and jacket. The skirt of her dress was rumpled and she looked tired, but she smiled when she saw me.

"Dr. Morgan," she said, all professional. "Thanks for agreeing to meet with me."

She offered her hand and we shook, her grip firm. Then, she led me into a corner office, which had floor to ceiling windows on each side of the room, overlooking Manhattan. It was quite impressive. I didn't realize how high up in the food chain she must be.

She pointed to a chair across from her desk and I waited until she sat and then I followed suit.

"Well, you must be curious about why I called you here," she said, sitting back in her chair, eyeing me carefully.

"I admit I was. I assume you've dug up something about my past and want my reaction."

"Precisely. One of my reporters came to me with a story about you and well," she said and laughed a bit sardonically. "I felt a need to check it out myself and then I realized I needed to give you the chance to respond before we went to press."

"I appreciate that," I said, crossing my legs and sitting back, trying to relax while preparing myself for what I'd find in the article.

"Like I said in my email, I usually do this over the phone, but in your case, I wanted to talk to you in private. Here's the article," she said and searched through a pile of print documents on her desk. "You can look at it but I have to get that back."

She leaned over and handed me the four-paragraph article with a few red marks on it. I read it over. It described me as the husband of Katherine McDermott, daughter of the well-respected former Supreme Court of New York justice, Ethan McDermott. It said she was involved in a hit and run attempted murder near Central Park in June. The article covered the incident and that Kate had emergency surgery to deliver Sophia. It also mentioned that Kate had to have a hysterectomy and would never have another baby. I frowned when I read that, not wanting the whole world to know that. It was none of their goddamned business as far as I was concerned.

I kept reading and then came to the section that I was sure she called me down to discuss.

It described me as a Dominant in Manhattan's BDSM community, and said I had been involved for the past six years. According to sources, I was into bondage and dominance, often did demonstrations of rope technique, and had several mistresses over the years. The suggested headline was 'Manhattan's Real Mr. Grey'.

"I'm not him," I said and threw down the article. "If you and your reporter knew anything about BDSM, you'd never even consider that for a headline. I'm so far from him that anyone in the lifestyle would laugh you out of the room."

"I know that," she said. "My reporter asked around and people have said that you're a kitten compared to him. *But,*" she said and looked at me pointedly. "We also spoke to someone who thinks you have a mean streak in you. She showed us some photographs of her bruises and welts."

"Who?" I asked, my back stiffening. It had to be Sunita, of course. She was the only submissive I had ever tried using a flogger and cane on – at her insistence. It was during the time when Lara was trying to see if I had any sadism in me. She tried, but of course she never found any.

"Who is none of your business right now. Let's say she has incriminating photographs and video which suggest you are into pain, no matter what you claim."

I shook my head. "There isn't any sadism in me. Quite the opposite. I love pleasure, not pain. Administering a punishment, such as a spanking, is done solely to reinforce our roles and I didn't enjoy it. I didn't get off on pain – not in the least bit."

She raised her eyebrows at me. "I saw the pictures. I saw you with her in various poses. And the video is, well, pretty damning."

I sighed heavily, and regretted *again* that I had ever agreed to do that video.

"That was when I was learning and discovering who I was. I learned that I didn't like pain – giving or receiving. I made sure from then on to screen my partners very carefully so I didn't get anyone who expected pain or was into it."

She nodded. "So my reporter says, but we still want to include that woman's experience in our story, although we will protect her privacy. And of course, we won't be showing any of the graphic parts of the video on our website."

"What about my privacy?"

She shook her head and smiled. "I'm sorry, Dr. Morgan, but you don't have the luxury of privacy any longer. Especially now that your wife's case is in the news. You better prepare yourself. It's not going to be pleasant for you or your wife."

"Why did you ask me here if you're going to run the story anyway?"

She shrugged. "I wanted you to have a chance to tell your side of things. We'll present both sides – your story and her story and let our readers decide which one is more believable."

I exhaled and leaned back. "The truth is that this woman you interviewed – and I know who it has to be because there was only ever one woman who might talk about pain when speaking of me and who would have a video-- she's a very unhappy young woman. She had a bit of an obsession with me and so she might be vindictive. If she says I enjoyed administering a punishment, she's lying. That's why we ended our association in fact. She wanted it and I didn't."

"That's not what she said. She said you enjoyed it and she broke up with you because you weren't skilled enough. You actually hurt her."

I sighed at the prospect that Sunita had lied about me. Again. She must have been hoping to hurt me, hurt my career, my relationship even more than she had already.

"Have you done any background research on Sunita?"

"We have," she said and nodded, a pencil in her hand. "We don't blame victims."

"She wasn't a victim," I said a bit more forcefully than I wanted. "She did this voluntarily. She signed waivers—."

"That doesn't mean she isn't still a victim. She was abused as a child, you know. She grew up being abused. Someone like that can't consent. It would be like saying that it was okay for her ex-husband to beat her because she agreed to live in his house."

"It's not the same at all. Safe, sane and consensual—."

"No, no," she said and held out a hand, wagging her finger, interrupting me. "Don't try to tell me that people who do this are sane. Sorry. Not buying it."

What could I say to that? Of course, I knew that a small percentage of people who got into BDSM did so to work through trauma. Some people found BDSM attractive as a way to deal with their issues. Most people liked the excitement of trying new things.

"She was a consenting adult. Any psychiatrist could tell you that."

"Consent is a tricky concept, Doctor. Can you consent when you're mentally ill?"

I closed my eyes. It was a question I had often thought of and why I steered clear of anyone who seemed the least bit motivated by a need to work through childhood trauma.

"She wasn't mentally ill."

We stared at each other across her desk. Finally, I took in a deep breath.

"Look, I can't stop you from publishing that article or releasing that video. But you should know that Sunita had a history before she ever met me. She was looking for something. I was looking for something else. It didn't work out for us and I moved on although she was quite upset for a while. If she suggests that I'm a sadist in any way, she's lying. Plain and simple."

Peterson made a face, holding the pencil between her hands and playing with it. "That's what other people told us – people who know you both. I wanted to meet you and see what you had to say for yourself."

"What I have to say is this," I said and leaned forward. "Lisa Monroe is a very sick woman. She was stalking me, jealous of my happy marriage, and when she was expelled from the program at NYU, she attacked my wife, almost killing her in the process. We had a few brief encounters at private parties— ."

"Dungeon parties," she added, her eyebrows raised.

"Private parties," I said again, and when she and her partner indicated they were interested in a threesome, I turned them down. You can contact Derek Richardson if you want. He'll back up my story."

"*The* Derek Richardson?" she said, an expression of surprise on her face. I grimaced, realizing that I'd outed him as a BDSM aficionado, but he was so rich that I doubted it would affect his business.

I nodded. "Yes. I spoke with him about Lisa and he said he was concerned about her mental health. You should talk to him."

She wrote something down on a sheet of paper. "You seem to have surrounded yourself with troubled women, Dr. Morgan."

I said nothing in reply. What could I say? I had the bad luck to run into two women who had emotional issues.

"So are you going to run the article as it is?" I asked, impatient.

She shrugged. "I'll think about it. I'll talk to legal and see what they say but I can't promise anything. You must realize, Dr. Morgan, that your situation is public now. If I don't run this story, some other paper will. We have the exclusive interview with this woman. We'll run it. I have a responsibility to the shareholders." Then she shrugged as if she had no other choice.

"Can you include some of your other sources?" I asked. "Sources that support my side of the story, at least?"

"Of course," she said. "But you have to understand that people will tend to believe this woman over you and over your friends and acquaintances. But you have a very stellar career as a neurosurgeon and your volunteer work for Doctors Without Borders. That may have some bearing on how people perceive the story. You know what they say – the bigger they are, the harder they fall…"

I stood up, my fists clenched at my side as I tried to get a hold of my emotions.

"If you have nothing else, I have work to do."

She nodded and leaned back. "I'm sorry to have to give you this news. Considering your wife is still recovering and your baby is home from the hospital, I'm sure this is pretty upsetting."

I turned to go, frustrated that I couldn't do anything to stop her from running with the story.

"Good luck," she said when I got to the door. "You'll need it."

I didn't respond, slamming the door a bit too hard behind me.

I strode down the hallway, past the receptionist and to the elevator. I stood with my back to the room and tried to get control over myself but it was hard. I could see the headlines now, and knew that there would be significant fallout. Not to mention making me seem unsympathetic to the police, in whose eyes I would be a suspect no matter whether it was true or not.

I had to meet with Lara and go over things as soon as possible, so while I took the elevator down to the main floor lobby, I called her on my cell but there was no answer. I left a quick message and then took my car back to the

8th Avenue apartment, glad to be going home to Kate but more than a bit upset with what I knew would be appearing in the papers the next day.

~

WHEN I ARRIVED HOME, Kate was sitting with Sophia on the couch. Kate looked freshly dressed and washed, wearing a different outfit from what she wore when I left. It made me feel good to see her there, with Sophie on her knee.

"I'm so glad to be back," I said and bent down to kiss Sophie and then Kate. "Home to my two favorite girls."

"We're glad you're back," Kate said and forced a smile that even I could tell was fake.

"What's the matter?" I asked, alarmed at the paleness to her skin. She looked as if she didn't feel well. "You look a bit pale."

"I'm fine. Just a bit tired. If you want to take Sophie, I'll get our supper. *Quance* delivered. Ribs, salad and some Greek rice. How does that sound?"

"Fantastic." I bent down to take her out of Kate's arms. "Just what the Doctor ordered."

I carried Sophie to the kitchen where plates were set out on the granite island. We had a formal dining table but Kate and I preferred to sit at the island and look out the windows at the skyline. I brought Sophie's bouncer chair and placed it on the island across from me so we could watch her while we ate. Kate served our plates, doling out ribs, rice and salad, placing my plate in front of me. It looked delicious and I was hungry.

When Kate sat next to me, she sighed heavily before she took her knife and fork in hand.

I turned, surprised that she sounded so down despite the smile on her face.

"Kate, tell me the truth. Are you okay?" I asked, waiting for her response. "You look pale and you sound upset."

"I'm fine," she said and smiled at me once more, but the smile never reached her eyes. "The police called after you left and wanted to come by and speak to me."

"What?" I said, anger filling me. "Why didn't you call me right away?"

"I'm sorry," Kate said and shrugged. "You had enough on your plate going to see that editor about the article. I called Lara and she came over to be with me while they interviewed me."

I sighed in relief, although I was upset that Kate didn't call me right away. "You should have called me immediately. I would have called the police and told them to wait until I arrived back home."

She shook her head. "I think they wanted to look at our apartment and talk to me by myself. Lara was here and everything was fine. How was your meeting? What are we going to have to deal with tomorrow?"

I put down my knife and turned to Kate. I stroked her cheek and brushed a lock of hair off her shoulder.

"I'm sorry you had to talk to the police by yourself. We'll deal with tomorrow, tomorrow. Tell me what happened. You must have been upset."

"Lara was there," she said. "I'm fine. It's you I'm worried about. You had to deal with that woman at the *Herald*. What can you do? You should call Lara."

"I will. Look, don't worry about the article," I said. "There's nothing I can do to stop her and anyway, you already have enough on *your* plate. Besides, I've already been in contact with the hospital about the issue and Fred Parker was fine with it. I've already pulled back a bit from the Foundation. At least, my face and name won't be on any promotional materials."

"That's so unfair," Kate said and frowned. "You've kept it going since your father died. You're the one who gives it direction. It's your vision. Why should you be pushed out?"

I sighed. "Because big donors won't give money if they think their names will be associated with someone scandalous. Until this all washes over and clears up, my name is off all the materials and website."

She shook her head and seemed upset about it. It made me feel good to know how much she cared, but I didn't like to see her so upset. There was ample reason for it, so I merely noted it and tried to offer her as much comfort and support as I could.

After we finished eating, with a major interruption of Sophie grousing for a feed when Kate had nicely lit into her ribs, we tidied up and then Kate and I gave Sophie a bath, put her in her jammies, and she went down for the night.

By then, it was ten fifteen and Kate was yawning, hiding it behind a hand. She turned and smiled at me but it was clear that she was still not one-hundred percent happy. There was this look in her eyes...

"Come here," I said and sat down on the sofa, motioning to my lap. "Sit with me. I need some Katie time."

She complied and sat on my lap, her arms around my shoulders. Being that close reminded me of that night so very long ago when I went back to her tiny apartment in Harlem after dessert at The Russian Tea Room and seduced her. I hoped this position would remind her as well and maybe light a spark inside of her that would turn to passion, but I still wasn't going to push.

"Other than Detective Mutt and Jeff visiting, how was your evening?" I asked, stroking her cheek with the backs of my fingers. "Did you watch anything on television?"

She shook her head. "No," she said a bit hesitantly. "I pretty much spent time with Sophie."

I nodded. "Are you tired?"

She exhaled. "It seems like I'm always tired. I can't seem to catch up, even when I sleep during the day."

I nodded. "Until she sleeps through the night, you'll have broken sleep."

"I'm not complaining," she said quickly. "I'm always a bit exhausted. I don't even want to watch TV or read. Too tired for anything but looking after Sophie and sleeping."

"I know," I said and nuzzled my face into the crook of her neck, kissing her skin. Of course, she might have been too tired for anything but sleep, but my very healthy and normal male body couldn't help but react to her softness in my arms, the scent of her hair in my nose, the feel of her skin beneath my lips. "You can go to bed if you want. I have a few things to do before I can go to sleep, so I'll go to bed later. I'll get up with Sophie for her first feed. You can sleep."

"Thank you," she said and kissed me on the lips, chastely. "I'm sorry I'm not better company but I'm so—."

I put my fingers over her lips to stop her from saying it. "You don't have to apologize. I understand completely. You had a terrible shock. You take as much time as you need. Soon enough, Sophie will be sleeping through the night and you can, too. Things will be a lot different then."

She nodded and rose from the couch, off my lap. I pulled my cell out of my pocket and pointed to my messages.

"I'll answer a few messages and then I have to check over something for the Corporation. You go to bed."

She bent down and kissed me on the lips once more. "Drake, I'm sorry I'm not much of a wife for you. Until this happened, I thought we were happy. Weren't we?"

"What?" I said, frowning at the very notion that she doubted it. "Why would you even say that? Of course we were happy. We *are* really happy." I looked her in the eye. "What's this about? Tell me what's wrong." I pulled her back onto my lap. She slipped her arms around my neck, but glanced away, not meeting my eyes.

"Tell me," I said. "Is it something the detectives said? Something about the case?"

She nodded and still avoided my eyes. "They said they had some emails you sent to Lisa before the accident."

"What?" A shock of adrenaline went through me. "They said I was emailing Lisa? That's categorically untrue. I never emailed Lisa. Never."

She nodded, but I could tell she wasn't sure.

"You believe me, right?" I said, tilting her chin up and forcing her to look in my eyes.

"Of course," she said and once more, she plastered a smile on her face.

"They showed me three that came from an email with your name, but even Lara said they were obviously fake."

"What they hell? What did they say?"

She shrugged, not meeting my eyes. "One said you were sick of me fighting you all the time and that I wasn't a real submissive. That you couldn't do with me what you really wanted because you were afraid I'd report you to your supervisor and get you in trouble…"

"That's ridiculous," I said, a shock going through me that Lisa would stoop so low and that the emails might make Kate doubt me. "They're fakes. I never emailed Lisa. Nothing professional and certainly never anything personal so I don't know where they got that idea."

"They had emails…"

I took her face in my hands, needing her to understand. To know that they weren't real.

"Kate, you have to believe me. I would have told you if I ever emailed her for any reason. And you are a perfect sub for me. I loved you from the start. Everything about you."

I frowned, trying to think of how Lisa would get email from me. Then it hit me. I had sent several emails to the group of new residents in neuro-surgery about rounds, but Lisa would only be cc'd on the email. Like every other resident in the program. Nothing was addressed to her directly. Still… She could have taken the email and done something to it. I didn't think it was possible to edit an email you received from someone else, but I wasn't all that technically savvy. For all I knew, she could have done something with them. Edited the emails to make it look like I sent them to her alone. Faked them.

"There were a couple of group emails I sent to the program about lectures I'd be giving on robotic surgery in pediatric patients. But nothing was ever personal and nothing was addressed only to Lisa."

Finally, Kate met my eyes on her own. "Do you think she was trying to set you up?"

I shrugged. "I wouldn't put anything past her. At this point, I think she's capable of anything. She thought she could force me into a relationship with her. When she couldn't, she figured she could take you out of the picture…"

Kate brushed her fingers through my hair. "She probably thought she'd console you on the loss of your wife and unborn baby and you'd fall into her arms…"

"She's delusional if she thought that. More likely she was trying to hurt me because I rejected her."

Kate sighed and laid her head against my shoulder. "I'm so sorry all this happened. I feel like I'm not being a good wife for you. No sex for months…"

"Shh," I said and shook my head. "Not another word about it. You go to bed if you're tired. I'll come to bed when I'm finished."

"Are you sure?" she asked, meeting my eyes.

"Yes," I said and kissed her softly on the lips. "You go. You're tired. I'll be up soon."

Then she left the living room and took the stairs to the second floor where our bedroom and Sophie's room were located. There was also a guest room, two bathrooms and my office, now that we had both floors renovated.

On my part, I quickly tidied up the main floor, tucking the *New York Times* into its place by the fireplace, then folded the throw blanket on the sofa. While I tidied up, I thought about the news that Lisa had some fake emails from me and wondered what they said. She could have written anything.

I turned off the lights and climbed the stairs to the second floor and went to my office, which was off Sophie's room. I was careful to be quiet and sat down at my desk, clicking on my iMac so I could check over my email once before I headed to bed.

I searched my email for anything from Derek Richardson, wondering if I should contact him and see what he knew about Lisa and what he thought she was capable of. I hadn't spoken to him since before the attack.

I found his cell number and called, but there was no answer and the phone went right to voicemail – a pre-recorded message by the automated system. Instead of leaving a message, I sent him an email.

TO: Richardson, Derek (Richardson Securities Inc.)
    FROM: Morgan, Drake, MD.
    RE: Lisa

Hey Derek. When you get this, please give me a call. I'm wondering what you think of everything that's happened since the attack on my wife, Kate. The police asked me about my relationship with her and you, so be prepared to get a call or visit. Did you have any idea that Lisa was this unstable? Did she do anything during your time together, did you ever hear anything about her background that might make you concerned? Thanks for any help you can provide.
    Cheers,
    Drake.

I SENT OFF THE EMAIL, and put it out of my mind. The police would eventually find out that Lisa was mentally unbalanced. Still, I felt uneasy about the case.

Then, I remembered that Dave had promised to send me a report on performance of our new program to provide food and medical care for pregnant women in the Sudan so I could read it over and offer feedback.

I found his email, downloaded the report and printed it off, glad that I spent the extra money to get a top-of-the-line printer that was quiet enough so it didn't wake up Sophie. I sat at my desk and read the report over, trying to focus on the numbers, trying to analyze the data and think of a response, but my body still ached from the feel of Kate sitting on my lap, my dick still semi-erect and seemingly not going to cooperate and deflate so I could focus on more important matters.

During the months since the accident, while Kate recovered, I'd consoled myself with solitary bouts of masturbation to get through the week. Being celibate had never been a real problem before because I used to resort to my book featuring photos of my former submissives when I needed something to help me get off. Now, I felt that would be cheating on Kate.

I didn't use that book anymore. Instead, I brought up a few photos I had taken of Kate while she was restrained on our bed, a blindfold on, her hands and feet tied to the bed posts, her body naked and on full display for my eyes only.

I didn't need kink anymore, but we had engaged in some bondage and dominance on occasion, when we both felt a need. Now, I'd be ecstatic if she would be willing to let me fuck her or even if she would watch while I masturbated. Even the feel of her eyes on my dick would be good, but I wanted to let her decide when our sexual relationship would start up once more.

So it was that I took my iPad mini and went into the extra bathroom on the second floor and decided to beat off to pictures of Kate, bound and blind-folded. I slipped off my belt and let my slacks fall to my ankles, opened my shirt and stood at the sink, the iPad and picture of Kate tilted so I could see while I masturbated.

That was how Kate found me, erection in hand, leaning against the wall for support while my hand flew over my cock.

The door opened and I was so close to the edge that I didn't notice until I heard Kate's gasp. I caught sight of her face as she left and ran off. I stopped immediately and tried to pull up my slacks, but outside the bathroom door, I tripped in my haste to catch up to her, falling into the hallway.

"Fuck," I said a bit too loudly as I crumpled to the ground, sliding down the wall until I was semi-reclining, toppled over to the side.

Kate stopped at the end of the hallway and then, Sophie cried out. Kate stood there for a few seconds, then she turned to me. I scrambled up, pulling up my slacks properly, and went to her.

"Kate," I said, breathless, my face hot. "I'm so sorry you had to see that."

Sophie cried out more loudly now. Kate seemed torn and turned to the door to Sophie's bedroom, then back to me, her hand on the doorknob while I tried to fasten my belt. Her face was expressionless, and then, it changed.

She laughed out loud.

Hearing her, I did as well and the two of us laughed uncontrollably for a few moments, Sophie crying even more vigorously in her room. Then, Kate's laughter changed, and now, instead of laughing, she started to cry.

I went to her and pulled her into my arms. "Katie," I said softly, rocking her in my arms. I knew that sometimes, when people laughed hard, they often began to cry. The line between tears and laughter was fine and it was easy to slip from one to the other.

"I'm okay," she said and wiped her eyes. "You looked so funny lying there on the ground with your slacks around your ankles."

"I know," I said and smiled, when I saw her smile through her tears. "I'm a total idiot. I didn't want you to get the wrong idea."

She shook her head. "Believe me, there was no way I could get the wrong idea about what you were doing."

I pulled away and looked in her eyes. "What idea *did* you get?"

She sighed. "I saw a horny husband who has a wife he hasn't had sex with for months trying to get some relief."

Then she began to cry again, and Sophie screamed out loud this time. Kate pulled out of my arms and I let her, following her into Sophie's room. Kate went right over to the crib and lifted a crying Sophie into her arms. Then she began to rock back and forth, patting Sophie on the back, trying to calm her, all the while still crying herself.

She slipped Sophie's pacifier back into her mouth and soon, Sophie's eyes were closed. I took Sophie from her and put her back into the crib, tucking a blanket around her, making sure the sleep apnea monitor sock was on properly. Now, Sophie sucked away on her pacifier and closed her eyes.

"Kate, I'm so *sorry*," I said, taking her hand and pulling her with me downstairs into the living room. I felt totally useless and guilty for upsetting her and waking Sophie in the process so I wanted to make it all right again and quickly.

"Come here," I said and sat down in the middle of the sofa, the way I did just an hour ago. "Sit on my lap."

I patted my lap and nodded to her, not saying anything else. She eyed my lap dubiously and then complied, sitting so that her legs straddled my hips. By now, my erection had deflated to half-mast and was no longer much of an issue between us. She nestled in, her hands on my shoulders, but she avoided my eyes.

"It was holding you in my arms earlier that did it. I needed to take care of some man plumbing issues. You know," I said, trying to get her to laugh again. "Build-up of excess fluids. Need to let off pressure to keep the system running efficiently..."

I lifted her chin and looked at her face, but there were still tears in her eyes.

"I understand," she said softly, tears still brimming and spilling out onto her cheeks. "You deserve to have a wife who wants to make love with you. I'm the one who's sorry that I've let you down."

"Don't say that," I said and searched her eyes. "You haven't let me down. There's no way you could let me down."

"It's just that," she said and shook her head quickly. "I don't have any excuse. I didn't push a baby out, so I'm not healing or anything."

"Shh," I said and put my finger over her lips. "You had a huge abdominal incision and internal injuries. That alone takes more than six weeks to recover from. Some people take six months."

I pushed hair from her face and held her chin so she had to look in my eyes, finally. Really look in them.

"You almost died, Kate," I said, my voice breaking. "You almost died." Then, tears filled my own eyes as the reality of her near-death experience struck me hard. "I almost lost you and Sophie. I know that you're not ready yet. I can wait. I waited all my life for you. I can wait a few weeks more," I said. "Months might be hard, but I'd wait if that's what you need."

"Months?" she said with a look of horror on her face. "I was thinking maybe days. I'm still so tired. And worried about Sophia. The sleep apnea… I'm always afraid she's going to stop breathing."

"She's fine," I said, trying to reassure her. "We have the monitor. It's there for our comfort only. She hasn't had any bouts of sleep apnea since the NICU."

"I can't stop thinking about it," Kate said. "I have a hard time sleeping because of it. Sex is the last thing I think about after a whole day of everything else. In fact, I don't even think about it."

"I know," I said, nodding. "That's why I haven't made any real advances. I know you'll show me that you're ready."

She raised one shoulder like she felt awkward. "Isn't that going against our usual relationship? You're the one who decides?"

I shook my head and took hold of her chin. "That was when we first met and I was still trying to keep some kind of control over my emotions. Now, I don't feel that need. At least, not as often. I can respond to you when you come to me in need. Believe me, I can respond. Happily. You come to me when you need me and I'll be there, ready and waiting." I smiled at her and wiped the tears off her cheeks. Finally, she offered a faint smile.

"Okay," she said softly. "If you say so. I'll let you know." Then she played with my collar and smiled to herself. "Should we have a code word?" she said and looked in my eyes. I could see a tiny hint of tease in them.

"Code word?" I said and frowned, pretending not to understand.

"Yes, code word. You know. I could say something like, I feel like relaxing tonight. Something subtle."

"You don't have to be subtle with me, Kate. You could say, 'Now, Drake,' and I'd be ready. Any time, any place." I grinned at her and she finally cracked a huge smile and leaned forward to kiss me.

"I love you," she said softly when she pulled back. "Thank you for understanding."

"I love you," I said back. "More than anything. I can wait."

She sighed and laid her head on my shoulder and I pulled her tightly against my body. We remained like that for a moment and of course, the feel of her softness against me aroused me once more but I did my best to quash the desire, imagining a slimy pit of snakes at the bottom of a well, my childhood fear, to ward off an inconvenient erection.

"Did you want me to watch you?" she said, her voice almost a whisper.

"I pulled back and looked in her eyes. "You want to watch me beat off?" I grinned.

"If you want me to," she said. "If it would get you off better than some nameless tart on the internet."

"Nameless tart on the internet? Did you think I was looking at porn?" I said in mock affront. "I'll have you know I was watching the highest quality sex goddess around."

She frowned.

I picked Kate up as I stood and carried her upstairs to the bathroom where I'd dropped my iPad in my haste to zip up. I opened it and showed her the pictures of herself, bound and blindfolded, I had been masturbating to only moments earlier.

"There," I said and showed her. "That's my goddess, the woman of my dreams, fulfiller of my fantasies."

She took my iPad and examined the first image of her on the bed, her thighs spread as I fucked her. Then she flipped through a few more images, all of her in various poses, with or without my dick inside of her – her mouth, her pussy, her hand, between her breasts.

"You were using these to jerk off?" she said, a smile on her lips that she was trying hard to hide.

"I'll have you know that I don't jerk off. I beat off," I said with a laugh. "Jerk sounds so... so... unsophisticated."

She laughed and turned to me, putting down the iPad. Then, she wrapped her arms around me and I pulled her into my arms for an embrace.

"You are *very* sophisticated," she said and kissed me. "Beat off does sound so much better."

We stood like that for a few moments, our foreheads pressed together.

"Is everything okay now?" I asked, not wanting to let things drop if she still felt guilty or upset about finding me masturbating. "You're feeling better about the whole fake email thing?"

"Everything's fine," she said softly. "Everything will be fine."

I nodded and buried my face in the crook of her neck, inhaling the scent of her hair, the trace of her perfume, and a definite baby-momma smell.

"Let's go to bed," I said and led her into our bedroom. "I'm tired and the dragon is out of fire."

So we did. She crept in beside me once I was naked except for my boxer briefs, and we spooned, her back pressed against my body, my arm around her waist. Sleep was a long time coming for me, for I was trying to figure out what Lisa had done to make it look like I wrote her personal emails. Damn... She was a nutcase. A very dangerous nutcase, but still insane if she thought any of this was going to win me over.

I tried to blank my mind of thoughts about Lisa and the case, but it was hard. In addition to thoughts about Lisa and the police, I still had a bit of blue balls, a sweet ache in my body that spoke of unmet need, but I had Kate.

That was everything.

∼

CHAPTER 4 : KATE

The night went as usual, with Drake getting up in the middle of the night to feed Sophie one of the bottles of expressed breastmilk that was stored in the freezer. I stayed in bed, although I could have given Sophie a feed because my breasts were getting quite hard and full of milk. She'd want another feed in a few hours and I'd be more than ready by then.

When I woke several hours later to the sound of Sophie making noises on the baby monitor, not quite upset but starting to work up to a cry, I left Drake sleeping and slipped out of the bed. I took a quick pee before I went to get her.

Inside her bedroom, the early morning sunlight was peeking through the blinds and she looked like a little angel in her crib, her eyes wide open, her arms flailing around when she saw me. I smiled and picked her up, then sat on the glider chair beside her crib and proceeded to feed her. She ate hungrily from one breast and then the other, stopping only for a brief time, during which she cried lustily as if the worst thing in the world had happened when I pulled her off the nipple for a burp.

When she was finished, she was ready for a change, and then I laid her back into her crib, pacifier in her mouth, and she went back to sleep. She was usually sleepy in the early morning, and today was no different.

I yawned and went back to our bedroom, only to find the bed empty and Drake gone. I checked in the bathroom, but he wasn't there as well. Then I remembered the Herald magazine's online edition. Maybe Drake was checking it out.

I also remembered the whole email business and of course, my day went from great to bad. I didn't want to believe he wrote her any email, even innocuous email that she could twist to her own devices. I wanted to trust Drake.

So I did. I put the email issue out of my mind. I thought about my own email program and was sure I couldn't just go in and change them. They had to be forgeries of some kind.

I went downstairs after I finished washing up a bit, brushing my hair and teeth, and found Drake sitting on the sofa, his laptop open, a browser with the latest edition of the *Herald* open.

He was reading, leaning close, his eyes moving over the screen.

"How bad is it?" I asked and laid my hand on his shoulder, squeezing softly to offer him some comfort.

"Bad enough," he said, his voice low. He kept reading, so I went into the kitchen where Drake had the coffee brewing and squeezed myself a glass of fresh orange juice. I opened a cupboard and found some bread and popped two slices into the toaster, planning on having toast and eggs for breakfast.

"Would you like some scrambled eggs?" I asked Drake.

There was a pause. Finally, he responded. "Maybe some Hemlock would be better."

I frowned at his reference to Socrates' choice of poison. "Is the article that bad?"

I brought in a cup of coffee for Drake and placed it on the coffee table. I tried to read the article over his shoulder, but the text was small. All I could make out was a line about him being a renowned neurosurgeon who was one of only a very few performing specialized robotic surgery for movement disorders.

"What did they say? Did they mention Sunita?"

Drake flipped through a few screens to another page with a pic of the back of Sunita's thighs, which had long welts on them. I had to admit I felt a little sick to see those welts. Had Drake done that to her? It made my throat choke.

"Did you do that?" I said, my voice barely audible, my throat dry.

"I did," he said, sighing heavily. "She liked being caned. She wanted bruises and welts. I tried, but it did nothing for me. *Nothing.*" He turned to me, his blue eyes wide. "It went against something in me as a doctor. First, do no harm. That was the last time we were together. Lara had been working me up to it, and finally, when we had a scene using a cane and flogger, I said no more."

"I'm so *sorry*," I said and stroked his back. "All of the nuance of what happened would probably be lost to the casual reader. They don't know about the whole training of a Dominant, learning your limits, your preferences. To them, it's just violence."

Drake nodded, and closed the screen. He turned to me and pulled me down onto his lap.

"Now, with the fake emails the police have, it's going to look really incriminating. I wonder if the police will release the contents of her diary before the trial or if it'll only come out during the trial." Drake sighed. "I'll have to ask Lara what the whole procedure is."

I craned my neck and read the article. "What's it say?"

"It's all bullshit. The reporter is a campaigner against BDSM," he said, his voice low. "She claims that Dominants are woman abusers who can get away with it because they hook up with damaged women. She's been on a campaign ever since *Fifty* came out."

I put my arms around his shoulders and shook my head sadly. "I know. There are a few puritans out there who can't understand the difference between abuse and consensual SM."

Drake pushed his face into my neck and I heard him take in a deep breath. We sat silent for a few moments, the two of us in each other's arms.

"Well," he said and pulled back, looking in my eyes. "Nothing to be done about it. I'll have to wait for the fallout." He stroked my hair, his expression thoughtful. "I've already pulled back a bit from the Foundation, and I've spoken to Fred Parker at the hospital, but who can say what else will happen? Who among my employees or funders will be offended?"

I shrugged. "You're a neurosurgeon. The article even says that you're one of the best in the world at what you do. That won't change because of this article."

He sighed but I could tell he wasn't convinced. "I hope not. What can change is that patients won't want me as their surgeon. Donors won't want their donation associated with my name."

The timer in the kitchen went off so I jumped up and went to the stove to finish getting breakfast ready. When the eggs were finished cooking, I buttered the toast and brought two plates to the island so Drake and I could eat our breakfast.

"Breakfast is ready," I said, and went into the living room where he sat still hunched over the laptop, his face dark. He glanced up and forced a smile, but I saw him inhale heavily and knew that the whole business was a heavy weight on his shoulders. Finally, reluctantly, he stood up and closed the laptop, putting on a brave face and joining me at the kitchen island.

He sat beside me and leaned over, kissing my cheek while I placed a napkin beside his plate. "At least I have you and Sophie. I don't know what I'd do without you."

"If you didn't have us, none of this would have happened," I said, for although I couldn't imagine not having met Drake and not having Sophia, I knew it was because of us that he was in this predicament now.

"If I didn't have you and Sophie, I'd be an empty shell of a man running fast between one part of my life to another to ignore how lonely I was."

I met his eyes and felt mine well up with tears.

"Come here," he said and pulled me onto his lap, our breakfasts forgotten. "What's with the tears? We're together. The three of us are a family and we'll always have each other."

I nodded and thought about my talk with Lara, but I didn't want to admit how sad I had been in the last couple of weeks. I'd hidden my sadness, my tears, wanting Drake to feel happy with his life considering how he had to give up so much for us. There was no need for both of us to be unhappy. Drake needed me to be positive, supportive, happy, so I pretended that I was.

Finally, I tried to move over to my stool, but he prevented me.

"Wait," he said and adjusted me on his lap. "Let me feed you, mommy."

"What?" I said and made a face, smiling.

"I'm serious," he said. "All you do, all you've done since Sophie was born is feed her, change her, bathe her, hold her. You need someone to give you some TLC. Let me feed you. You know I love doing it."

I laughed finally, smiling at him through my tears, which seemed to have stopped. "You love doing it as a prelude to sex. I'm afraid Sophie's going to wake up soon and that'll be it for the rest of the day for me."

I made a pouty face, feeling bad that I'd mentioned sex – or our lack of a sex life.

"Shh," he said and put his finger over my lips. "I want to feed you because I want to look after you. You have to realize that it brings out these very Dom feelings in me, being able to look after you."

I finally nodded and waited while he forked some egg and held it up to my mouth. I accepted it and chewed while he lifted the corner of toast and I took a bite. I washed it all down with a mouthful of coffee, which I held myself.

Drake fed me the entire plate, using the fork to feed himself as well, and we talked in soft voices about the rest of the day, what groceries we needed to order from the organic grocer down the street, who delivered, and what meals we'd like to make for the week.

Finally, when we were finished eating, we tidied up quickly and then Sophie started grousing again on the baby monitor so I went into her room and watched her in the dimness. She was feeding every two or three hours and so I didn't want to get her up too quickly. She settled down and so I crept out of the room and went to have a shower while Drake was busy in his office, reading over the article and speaking on the phone to someone.

It felt good to stand in the hot water and let it roll over me. I washed myself and then came out of the shower, just as Drake came in.

"My turn," he said and stripped off his boxers, stepping in the shower and turning it on.

40

While I finished drying off, I watched him in the mirror as he washed. Even through the steam, I could see him – his delicious body, all man, and all mine. I admired his physique, knowing every inch of his body so well after these past two years with him. Still, seeing his semi-erect cock did nothing for me and that made me feel bad. I'd never been so sexless in my life – especially around him. I knew it was the result of hormonal changes in my body due to the pregnancy and nursing, but it felt strange not to want him the way I did even before Sophia was born. As big as I had been while I was pregnant, I had wanted Drake – sometimes desperately in need of his cock inside of me.

Now, I only felt tired when I saw him naked.

I bit my bottom lip and left the bathroom, quickly dressing in a pair of yoga pants and one of my breastfeeding bras and a loose top so I could easily pull out a breast to feed Sophie when she needed me. I stood at my dresser and brushed my hair, studying myself in the mirror. I looked the same, although there were dark circles under my eyes that no amount of sleep seemed to be able to erase.

I knew I should have spoken to Drake about my sadness, being tired all the time and this dark oppressive cloud hanging over my head, but I felt that if I brought it up, I'd start crying and would never stop. So I didn't.

Drake finished his shower so I went downstairs to the living room and had a second cup of coffee – decaf so I didn't upset Sophie. I wanted her to sleep as much as possible, because then I could as well. In fact, despite having at least six hours of sleep, I was ready to lie down and sleep more.

I plopped down on the sofa and picked up my iPad, thinking I might read some news headlines, but instead, I yawned. I scrolled through the news feed and then I saw it – the *Herald* article on Drake. I couldn't resist reading it although I knew it would make me sad or mad – one or the other. Mad felt better so I read it.

The article did a brief recap of the story – I was pregnant and was struck by a car rented by a previous sexual partner of my husband, Drake Morgan, MD, renowned neurosurgeon. Then, the article talked about how Drake was known as 'Master D' in BDSM circles, and had an online presence, recently deleted, as well as letters that directed his 'submissives' how to act around him and what to expect.

Then, the interview with a 'former submissive' of Drake's – who went by the name 'Sunny' but whom I knew was Sunita. Described as a colleague of Drake's who was in the lifestyle and who became involved with Drake as his submissive, the article claimed that Drake got sexual pleasure when he whipped and caned her (that was a clear lie), demanding that she was to be on her knees at all times (that I thought might be true).

"He enjoyed it," the woman who calls herself 'Sunny' said to this reporter. "He insisted

that I crawl on the ground to him, and kiss his feet. Then he caned me until he drew blood. He liked it."

The article mentioned a temporary restraining order Dr. Morgan's former wife took out on him during their divorce. When asked about the restraining order, Dr. Morgan's former wife refused comment.

This reporter wonders whether his former wife is still afraid of Dr. Morgan...

That made my face hot with anger. It was pure gossip and untrue. Maureen wasn't afraid of Drake. She was upset at him, had found someone new, and didn't care about Drake anymore.

The reporter went on to wonder what Dr. Morgan's patients might think of his sexual interests, and noted that he had already taken a year leave of absence from his position as a staff neurosurgeon at New York Presbyterian.

Perhaps trouble is brewing for Dr. Dominant at his place of employment?

I was so angry by then that I almost threw the iPad across the room. In fact, I did plop it down on the coffee table a bit too hard and was afraid that I'd cracked the screen. My heart rate was increased and I was on the verge of tears of anger when Drake walked into the living room and saw me.

"What's the matter?" he asked, his brow furrowed.

"I read the *Herald* article," I said, my voice wavering with emotion. "I can't believe they can get away with this. Can't you sue for defamation or libel?"

He shrugged. "I'll speak with Lara. I'm sure I need proof that the article has hurt my reputation, and it's too soon. There's a lot these gossip rags can say, using 'fair comment' as justification. Lara will probably do some sleuthing and let me know."

"I'm so sorry this happened to you," I said, my eyes brimming. "Sunita was so long ago. Why can't she let things be?"

He shook his head and flopped down beside me, his wet hair hanging in his eyes.

"She's trying to get right with God, or something. She's joined this crusade against BDSM and I guess I'm the bad guy."

"That's so wrong," I said, my fists clenched. I took in a deep breath and tried to relax, but it was hard. I turned to Drake and searched his face. "Has anyone at work seen it? What about at NYU?"

He shook his head. "Too soon to know what the fallout will be. I sent an email to Fred to give him a head's-up about it but haven't heard back yet."

He put his arm around my shoulder and pulled me closer. I snuggled into his arms and we sat in silence for a few moments. He kissed the top of my head and it was done totally out of affection, not to signify that we were in scene, but it made me think back to the last time we had done a scene. It seemed like so long ago – before I started to show. Once I was pregnant with a big belly, I didn't feel like being tied up and blindfolded. I couldn't explain it, but it didn't feel right somehow.

Now, I wasn't sure I ever wanted to do a scene again. All I'd be able to think about was Drake with Sunita, him with a cane in his hand, striking her on the backs of her thighs. I pushed that out of my mind. BDSM – at least the BD and D/s part of it, was part of our relationship and probably would be for a long time. I had enjoyed that part of our relationship. It was how we came together. It was how I came to understand my own sexual needs and desires for the first time.

I was so confused about how I felt. Part of me felt sad and angry at the same time. Part of me felt dread about what was coming. There was only a very small part of me that felt any happiness and that was only fleeting.

I should have spoken to Drake about my unhappiness, but he had enough on his plate now that the article had come out and his past in BDSM was public knowledge.

So I didn't.

～

CHAPTER 5 : DRAKE

I didn't like to leave Kate alone for long but I had an appointment with Dave Mills about the foundation. After Kate fed Sophie and we both held her for a while, Kate put her down for a mid-morning nap.

I kissed Kate goodbye and left the apartment and walked down the street to the parking garage.

On my way, I called Lara.

"Drake," she said when she answered. "Just the man I wanted to speak with. How are things? Is Kate okay? How about Sophia?"

"We're all fine. I wanted to talk to you about the emails I supposedly sent to Lisa. What do you know? What do you think?" I stopped at the streetlights and waited for the crosswalk. "I never emailed her personally," I said, anger like a coiled snake in my gut. "I only ever emailed the group."

"I know, I know," Lara said and I heard the frustration in her voice. "I said they were obviously faked. I told them you never whined, and the emails were from a Dom whining about a sub. What a joke... They were sent from a private email address if I remember correctly."

"Private email?" I replied, frowning as I entered the garage. "I don't use any private email account. I have my personal email through my cell provider and I have my business email through the hospital. I had a separate email for the Fellowship at NYU."

"This was a Yahoo account," Lara said.

"I don't have a Yahoo account."

"Apparently, the police believe you do. She must have created a fake account for you and then written letters to herself using it."

"What a fucking bitch," I said, totally in awe that she could be so demented. "She created a fake account for me and then used it? How did she manage to confirm it?"

"That's a mystery, but the police have forensic people checking the email out. I'm sure they'll realize it's fake and discount it. Until they do, I must admit it looks pretty damning. St. James said there were others with some pretty incriminating content."

"Oh, crap." I rubbed my forehead. "Who the hell knows what she wrote? She could have written anything. No wonder the police are suspicious about me."

"That's not your only problem," Lara said. "The *Herald* article is pretty nasty."

I arrived at my car and opened the door, sliding into the driver's seat. "I know. I guess the reporter who was doing research on the accident found out who I am and talked to a few staff members at NYP. She found Sunita and has the video Sunita took."

"Yeah, I knew that video was a bad idea back in the day," Lara said, her voice falling. "I read the article. You better come down and meet me at my office."

"How soon do you want me there?"

"Like, right now."

"I'll have to rearrange a meeting but it should be no problem. I'll be ten minutes," I said and closed my eyes. "Fifteen if the traffic is heavy."

"The traffic is always heavy, Drake. See you when you get here."

I ended the call and drove off.

I FOUND a parking spot a few blocks away from Lara's office, taking the rest of the distance on foot. I arrived at Lara's building and after checking in with the security desk, I took the elevator to her floor.

Her receptionist greeted me and ushered me into Lara's office in the corner of the law office.

"Hey, Drake," Lara said and stood up from behind her desk. "Close the door and come on in."

I closed the door behind me and turned to face Lara, who came around her desk and held out her arms. "Give me a hug. I haven't seen you for a while."

"Kate told me to give you a hug from her," I said and embraced Lara, patting her on the back with warm affection. We held the embrace for a minute and then parted. She led me to a small seating area with two over-stuffed sofas facing each other.

"Have a seat. Can I get you a drink?"

"It's a bit early," I said with a laugh.

"Not when you have this in front of you. But I mean coffee, silly."

I shook my head. "No, I already had a cup. But thanks."

"Soo..." she said when I sat across from her. "What do you think?"

"What do I think?" I said and shrugged, although I felt sick. "What do you think? You're the lawyer."

"It's bad," she said, her voice level. "Those fake emails. The paper has the video that Sunita took of one of your sessions."

I sighed heavily. "I'd be suspicious of me."

"Did Kate know about that video?"

"Apparently, yes," I said. "Sunita contacted her early on when we first started to see each other. She wanted Kate to see it, but Kate declined."

"She didn't see it?"

"No," I said. "She thought it was none of her business. At that point, she knew she had to either trust her gut or end things with me. She said she couldn't even think of ending things so she said no."

"Thank God for that. I knew right away that you didn't have it in you to be a strict Dom or Master. You weren't into pain at all. No sexual response to it."

I sighed and rubbed my forehead. "It's these emails that have me worried," I said and stared into the distance. "How do we prove I didn't create the email account and write those emails?"

"I've been talking to our IT guy. He said they can check when the account was created and when the email messages were sent. I'm sure with a little digging, the police will realize Lisa did it all herself. Maybe she sent them all from the same IP. That would be a dead giveaway."

I shrugged and ran my fingers through my hair, which was badly in need of a cut. "Until then, can we get access to the emails?"

"I suspect the police may want to ask you directly about them, so don't be surprised about a call asking for a meeting. I was shocked that they talked to Kate about them first. Maybe they were hoping to jar her into confessing something incriminating. Turn against you or something."

I nodded as I thought about how difficult that must have been for Kate to hear. "Poor Kate," I said. "How was she?"

"She was a bit startled," she said and leaned forward, her arms resting on her knees, her eyes expectant. "I was able to calm her down after. So, tell me what this bitch at the *Herald* said to you."

I leaned back and loosened my tie, thinking about Peterson. "She called Sunita a victim and a mentally ill person who couldn't give consent so anything I said about 'safe, sane and consensual' went out the window."

Lara shook her head. "Some people will never get it. They don't want to get it because it threatens their little fantasies about humans and our sexuality."

I nodded. Of course, Lara was preaching to the choir.

"What can I do about the article, if anything?"

She shrugged. "Nothing. Best to let it go. If you're asked about it, have a very simple statement prepared. You tried it and didn't like it. You're not that kind of Dominant. You don't enjoy pain. End of story. From a PR perspective, that's the most you can do. Hope it blows over."

"If it doesn't?"

"It will, believe me. I've dealt with these cases before. It might be a bit rocky for a while, but your services are in demand. I'm sure once this blows over, they will be again. People have short memories."

I wasn't so optimistic. "What if it doesn't blow over?"

She leaned back and shook her head. "Worst case scenario? You leave Manhattan. Start up your practice somewhere else. Somewhere more sympathetic to sexual freedom. Maybe Key West. Or California. I hear San Francisco is really progressive."

"Manhattan is our home. Kate's parents live here. The foundation is here. The headquarters for the corporation. Mersey…"

"Both of you are young and can start a new life somewhere else. I doubt it will come to that, but if it does, move to San Francisco. They have a great hospital there. The scenery is fantastic."

I said nothing for a while, thinking of having to move away. I knew Kate would be upset at the thought of leaving her father, and rightfully so. His health wasn't all that good.

"I hope it doesn't come to that. So, there's nothing I can do to get that article pulled?"

Lara shook her head and gave me a hard glance. "Nope. It's entirely factual, aside from a few titillating bits of speculation."

I sighed. "Should I put out a response?"

"No," she said. "If you're contacted, give the canned response, like I suggested. If you want, I can write something up for you. In this case, less is more. Keep it simple. Keep it consistent. It'll blow over. If it doesn't, we'll deal with it."

I nodded. "Okay."

Then Lara turned to me and held my eye. "So, what did Kate tell you?"

I shrugged. "Just that you were there to help her while the police visited. Thanks, by the way."

"No problem," Lara said. "What else did she tell you?"

I frowned. "Other than telling her about the email, they asked a few questions about what she knew about Lisa being in the NYU residency and when she knew it. The same questions they asked before. She thought they were trying to see if her story was consistent. Maybe check out our place. See if there was a hidden dungeon."

"That's about it. Did Kate tell you anything else?"

I frowned at the tone of Lara's voice. It was suggestive – of what I didn't know.

"About what?"

"How she's doing."

I leaned back and considered. "How she's doing?" I thought for a moment. "She's doing as well as can be expected, given she was almost murdered by a jealous ex-sex-partner of mine whose face I never actually saw without a mask on. That she had an emergency C-section, lost her ability to have more children, and has a preemie to look after. Why do you ask?"

"Did she tell you that she's sad and depressed all the time? That she cries when she's alone?"

A surge of adrenaline went through me. "What?" I said, my body tensing. "She told you that?"

Lara nodded. "She cried on my shoulder. Said that she felt sad all the time. That she was always tired. That she didn't want to tell you because you had enough going on and she didn't want to burden you with it. I made her promise to tell you. I told her that if she didn't, I'd be talking to you myself."

I closed my eyes and rubbed my forehead. "Oh, God," I said, my throat choking with emotion. I looked back at Lara. "I knew she was having problems sleeping. She's very emotional, but she's never cried in front of me..." Then I remembered how she'd gone from laughter to tears in a few seconds flat when I fell outside the bathroom. I shook my head, knocking myself on the temple with my fist.

"Dammit all," I said. "She did cry last night. We had a laughing fit and she went from hysterical laughter to tears. I asked her how she was, but she never said anything."

Lara sighed. "She's probably thinking about the emails and the article and figured that you had enough to worry about. At least now you know."

I looked in Lara's eyes. "Thank you for telling me. Seriously, I've been watching her for signs of postpartum depression but it's hard for me to know what's normal for a new mother versus what's serious. I'll have to speak with her, maybe get her some extra help and counseling. I've been there almost all the time to help with Sophie, but there's some things she must do – like nurse Sophie. I get up in the middle of the night to give her a bottle of expressed milk so Kate can sleep. I bathe her every other day, so Kate gets a break. I change her..."

"Drake, it's not your fault. It's post-traumatic stress disorder, if anything. She almost died. Her baby could have died. That's a lot for someone to take in. If it had been a regular accident and not an attempted murder, it would be hard, but it's that, too. She has to worry about the trial, about the publicity, about the repercussions for you in terms of your career. No wonder she's depressed and tired all the time."

I nodded. "I'll hire a nurse to come over and let Kate sleep in every morning. She can do things for Sophie so I can spend more time with Kate. Right now, Kate feels protective towards Sophie. She practically watches her breathe, even though Sophie only had a brief period when her breathing was being monitored and we have an apnea monitor. Sophie's doing well, considering."

"Will it stress Kate to have someone else look after Sophie?"

"I'll see," I said. "The least I can do is get a housekeeper to come in and clean the place, maybe make us some meals so we can only think about Sophie and ourselves. I'm tired, but that's fine. Nothing happened to me physically."

Lara shook her head. "Drake, you almost lost your wife and baby. You're facing damage to your professional reputation because of the publicity surrounding the trial. You are *not* fine. You're a new parent, too. Don't deny your own needs. You have to be in top health, mentally and physically, to be there for Kate and Sophie."

I nodded, shifting position on the sofa. "You're right. I guess I'm so used to stress that I don't notice it. I've always been so busy with such a tight schedule, it's second nature."

"You need to slow down. Hire the housekeeper. Better yet, find a nanny who's willing to do housework and make meals as well as tend to Sophie when needed."

I shrugged. "I'm not sure Kate will want a nanny this early in the game."

"Give her the option," Lara said. "Better yet, hire someone and have her come over to start taking care of things. Don't tell Kate that the woman is also a nanny. Tell her she's a housekeeper and will cook meals. Hire a middle-aged woman with experience. Pay her well."

"Maybe you're right," I said, then checked my watch. I had to meet Dave in fifteen minutes, but luckily, the foundation was down the street. I turned to Lara. "So, you'll write up a canned response to any press inquiries for me?"

She nodded. "You should memorize it. In fact, you should carry a copy around in your pocket, have a copy on your cell and put a sheet beside the phone. That way, if anyone calls, you and Kate will know exactly what to say about the whole business."

"What about 'no comment'?"

She shook her head. "No," she said and stood up when I did. "That's only for people who are guilty. The public and the press will expect you to explain. You need short talking points that are easy to memorize and will not invite more questions. I'll send you something later today. Until then, screen your calls. Don't answer from any numbers you don't recognize. Don't return any calls from the press until you've got my text. Okay?"

She came over to me and put a hand on my shoulder, smiling. I nodded, and exhaled heavily, feeling a weight off my shoulders that Lara was going to help.

"Thanks, Lara. For this and for going to the apartment and being with Kate while the police were there. You're a true friend."

We embraced briefly and I must admit I was thankful to have her at that moment, for everything almost overwhelmed me.

"Everything will work out fine," she said and let go of me. "You'll see. This will all blow over, and if it doesn't, we'll find a way to move forward. You and Kate love each other. You two have bright futures for yourselves and with each other. You have beautiful Sophia. Remember that."

"I will," I said and smiled at her.

I waved at her as she sat back down behind her huge mahogany desk and left the office.

～

INSTEAD OF TAKING MY CAR, I walked the five blocks to the foundation's offices and went inside, taking the elevator to the main offices.

As I exited the elevator, I noticed the discussion among the staff fall silent and felt their eyes on me. I frowned. Had they already read the article? I glanced at the receptionist, who quickly averted her eyes.

Then, I went to Dave's corner office, stopping briefly to say hello to Dave's admin person, Brenda, to make sure Dave was in. She smiled briefly and nodded when I asked if Dave was ready for me.

Dave was seated at his desk and on the phone. When he saw me, he held up one finger and I nodded. I took a seat across from his desk and unbuttoned my suit jacket.

Finally, he said goodbye to whomever he was speaking and put down the receiver.

"There you are," he said and stood, extending his hand across the desk. I shook it and sat back down. "Thanks for coming in."

"Why so formal?" I said, frowning. "You don't usually shake my hand."

He shrugged and looked a bit sheepish. "I just got off the phone with an irate donor and I guess I was still in formal mode."

"What's wrong? No," I said and held out my hand. "Let me guess. The donor read the *Herald* article and doesn't want to be associated with me anymore."

He chuckled. "No, actually. It was some Florida resort owner who doesn't like that we're providing birth control education, including information about

51

access to Planned Parenthood, in some of the poorer parts of the South. It's part of our Mother-Baby program."

"We're usually focused on international aid," I said and tilted my head, interested in learning more. "I don't remember any projects in the US."

Dave sighed. "We did some research on poverty in the US and in some of the poorer areas of the South, there are third-world conditions for many small towns and rural communities. I did a bit of groundwork to identify the need. They met our criteria for aid, so I did a pilot project in Mississippi and Florida. I can provide you with the project data if you want."

I nodded, trusting Dave to pick good projects. "If you think these projects fulfill the foundation's mandate, I trust your judgement."

"Thanks," he said. "So, back to the matter at hand..." He searched around on his desk and found the *Herald* article, which he had printed off. "It's only a matter of time before we start getting flack. I overheard some discussion about it around the staff water cooler today, so you should know it's out there. I want to develop a response to it so we don't lose many donors. Not that I'm expecting it, but just to be prepared."

I sighed and folded my hands in my lap, wishing all of it would go away.

"What about you?" I said, wondering how to broach the subject. "Do you have any questions? I realize this must be a shock to you as well."

Dave shrugged but shook his head. "None of my business, frankly. I think what goes on in a person's bedroom is their own and their partner's business. As long as it's adults and they consent, I have nothing to say."

He finally met my eyes, and I didn't see any judgement in them.

"But first," he said and leaned back in his chair. "Before we get into any business, how is Kate? How's Sophia?"

I shifted position, a gnawing sense of gloom coming over me when I thought about what Lara told me. "Kate's having problems. PTSD, I think. The accident, the surgery, Sophie being premature, the usual new parent fatigue. She's struggling."

"Sorry to hear that," Dave said, his expression genuinely concerned. "I know it's hard in normal circumstances when you have a new baby. People always talk about how tired they are, how much sleep they're missing, the whole physical adjustment. Add to that the accident, and Sophie being premature..."

I nodded. "Yes, it's all adding up to more than Kate can handle. I'm going to hire a housekeeper-nanny to help out so Kate and I can both get more sleep and so we can spend our time with Sophie and not cleaning or cooking."

Dave watched me, his eyes narrowed. "How are you doing? This has got to be a shock to you as well."

I took in a deep breath. I didn't want to bring up the email issue. If it came out later in the press, I would discuss it but until that time, I didn't want to have one more thing out there that could blow up in my face. Even though Lara seemed to think the cops would discover the account was fake, if word got out there were emails…

"Yeah, I'm pretty exhausted. Running on adrenaline at times. I'm doing a lot better than Kate. I'm used to the stress."

He shook his head. "Don't think you're invincible. You're human, too, Drake. You probably have PTSD as well."

"Nah, I'm fine," I said, waving him off. "I'm tired. Nothing that a little sleep won't cure."

"My uncle's wife, Karen, is a retired nurse who was a doula. She might be willing to help you out if you need it. She loves babies."

"Talk to her and see if she's available," I said, genuinely interested. Dave's aunt would be a great choice if she was willing. From what Dave told me, she almost raised Dave after his mother became ill when he was a child."

"I will," Dave said.

We spent the next hour going over foundation business – a report on projects that were on-going, starting up and finishing, and I was glad that Dave was still his old self with me. I had only a few close friends, and I didn't want to lose Dave.

Finally, when we were through, Dave turned to me, his expression curious.

"What *are* you going to say in response to the article?"

"Lara's working on some text for me," I said.

"Your lawyer friend from college?"

I nodded. "Yes," I said. "She's going to develop talking points for me and Kate so we stick to the script."

"That's a good idea. You want to respond, but not too much. You want to talk about it being in your past and that now you have a loving wife and child and are focused on your family and on your future. Something like that. This woman who tried to kill Kate? She's a nutcase. Kate's the innocent victim in all this."

I nodded.

"And you, of course," Dave added quickly. "You did nothing to bring this on."

I shrugged. "I'm the one who was involved with her in the past. I obviously didn't handle things well enough when I learned she was a student in my Fellowship program."

"It's not your fault, Drake. That's clear. I know you."

"Our donors don't know me. For all they know, I was having an affair with a student doctor and asked her to kill my wife so we could be together."

"That's what she's telling police?"

I nodded. "Yep. She told them that I wanted Kate out of the way so we could be together." I wasn't going to say anything about the emails, but I felt

Dave needed to know everything so he could be prepared. "She even faked some emails from me. Created a fake account and sent herself emails and responded to herself."

"That's crazy. You cheating on Kate is the biggest lie in the world," Dave said with a sardonic laugh. "You're crazy about Kate. I told the police detectives that."

I frowned. "They talked to you, too?"

He nodded. "Yeah, they came by last week because they learned we're friends, besides the fact that you're my boss. I told them that there was no way in hell that you would harm a hair on Kate's head. That you were deeply in love with her and were so happy about the baby. That you took a year off so you could spend it with Kate and the baby. That you were a humanitarian and saved the life of your son from another marriage. I was adamant that there was no way you would ever become involved with that woman."

"Thank you for that," I said and shook my head. "I can't believe that all of this is happening to us. Lisa went off the deep end and I didn't see it coming fast enough."

"Were you concerned?"

"Yes," I said and remembered back to the week before the attack. "I went to my supervisor the week before and told him I had to withdraw from the program because of Lisa. That she was acting inappropriately and I didn't want to jeopardize my position. They decided to expel her instead. That must have driven her over the edge."

Dave grimaced. "You think so?"

I nodded, feeling guilty for it. "So this might actually be my fault. If I hadn't insisted that I'd quit because of her, Kate might have still been able to have more children."

"Nah," Dave said, shaking his head firmly. "With someone like her, she probably would have done it anyway and Kate might have died. You can't know the future, and you can't know what might have happened if you didn't go to the head of your program. Don't think that way. Deal with reality."

I sighed heavily, wishing all of this would go away so that Kate and I could focus on what mattered – Sophia and each other. Sadly, that would not be the case.

Just then, the phone rang and Dave picked up the receiver.

"Hello, Dave Mills speaking," he said and then covered the receiver with a hand. "It's Michael from the Board."

Then he listened and took out his pen and began to write on his desk pad.

"Do you think that's necessary?" Dave listened some more and then he frowned. "Well, I have him here right now, if you want to speak to him."

Dave glanced up at me and I could see he was getting upset, his face flushing.

"I don't think--."

I held out my hand. "Tell me," I said, bracing myself for the worst.

"Just a minute, Michael." Dave put his hand over the receiver again. "Michael says they had an informal meeting of the rest of the Board and they want you out. Vote was 9-1 in favor."

I sighed. "Who was the lone holdout?"

"Michael. He's sorry, but there was nothing he could do."

I nodded and loosened my tie, which felt like a noose around my neck suddenly.

"All right," Dave said on the phone. "I'll make the arrangements. I want to voice my disapproval of this. You can tell the Board that I think they're being short-sighted and that this will all blow over."

Obviously frustrated, Dave continued to listen to Michael's instructions.

"Okay, I'll tell him. Goodbye."

Dave hung up the receiver and leaned back in his chair.

"I take it you get the gist of my conversation with Michael?"

I nodded. "Let me guess. They want me off the board or they'll withdraw from it."

"More or less," Dave said. "Just until all of this does blow over. They don't want to leave the board, but they want you off. They think it's best if you take yourself off for the interim. Don't attend any Board meetings or events."

"It's my foundation," I said, but that sounded whiny. I understood completely how my name would negatively affect the willingness of donors to hand over checks. Most organizations and corporations made donations in part as a good tax write off and in part as publicity. It looked good on corporate promotional material to list the various charities that benefitted from your organization's donations. It raised the brand identity and social proof.

If the foundation developed a bad name over my involvement in this case and the information about my past in the BDSM community, it would prevent donors from feeling free to give it money. It didn't matter how good the projects were or how beneficial to people in third world countries -- or as I later found out – in the poorer areas in the US. It only mattered how being a donor looked on corporate materials and for the bottom line.

"I knew this was coming." I said and rubbed my forehead. "I expected that they'd want to take my name off promotional materials, but I didn't think they'd want me to completely recuse myself from any involvement in the Foundation. Do I have to temporarily turn over the director position to someone else?"

Dave moved some papers around on his desk. "You leave it to Michael to check into it for you. Michael wants to meet with you later this week, when you're available, and he'll have everything ready. He's upset and thinks this isn't necessary, but he's willing to go along with the majority. You could let them all go and appoint a new board, but then that would be a scandal in and of itself. What you want to do is make a move, do it fast, do it quietly, and then have talking points ready if anyone asks."

"That's sound like a good idea. A quick surgical removal of the founder should clear things up."

"I know this stings, but it's only temporary."

I stood, buttoning up my jacket, my face still hot from a mixture of anger and embarrassment. "I better go. I don't want to leave Kate alone for too long."

Dave stood behind his desk and extended his hand once again. We shook and he held my eye.

"Give Kate a big hug for me and tell her I hope she's doing well. Maybe we can all go out for dinner some night when things have quieted down."

I nodded. "We'll see. There's a lot going on with her family right now. Ethan isn't doing well and so I doubt she'll feel like going out and leaving Sophie any time soon. But maybe when this all clears up."

"Sounds good," Dave said and walked me to the door to his office. He opened it for me and watched while I left the room and made my way to the elevator. I ran the same gauntlet of staff as I approached the elevators and turned, noticing that several of them glanced quickly away. Would that be how it was from now on? I'd walk into a room and people would stop talking, staring at me as if I were a sexual deviant and attempted-murderer?

I said a quick goodbye to the front receptionist and left the building, her red cheeks not lost on me. She probably read the article and thought I was a deviant, too.

I had thought I'd be there to oversee the business of the Foundation, but instead, I was there to remove myself from any public participation. I started the foundation as a tribute to my father, to carry on his work. I was immensely proud of it and it gave me a way to keep connected to my dad in a way we weren't when he was alive. I enjoyed my time there, feeling like I'd done something beyond myself when I did Foundation business.

Sadly, for the time being at least, that wasn't going to be the case.

$\sim$

CHAPTER 6 : KATE

Drake and I hunkered down in the apartment for the next week, watching the television and reading the gossip columns. Luckily, the news about the case died down as things were slow and the police were still investigating.

I was still feeling down, and one afternoon while Drake was out shopping before a late meeting, I found myself crying about the whole case as I remembered the way St. James had looked at me, like I was a poor little woman whose husband wanted to kill me.

"Poor Sophie, has a mother who's been interviewed by the cops and a dad who's a person of interest." I sat and wiped tears away from my eyes. Just then, Drake walked in the apartment, two bags in hand, with some celery sticking out the top of one and a fresh baguette out of the other.

He saw me and immediately placed the bags on the dining room table, a look of concern on his face.

"Katie," he whispered and knelt where I sat on the couch. "What's the matter?"

He took my hands and then sat beside me, his jacket still on. He wiped tears off my cheeks and of course I felt like a baby, crying like that.

"Oh, nothing," I said and tried to control my emotions. "It just upset me, that all this is happening. And I hate him," I said, remembering the expression on Detective St. James's face. So self-satisfied. "That Detective St. James."

"Oh, sweetie," he said and pulled me into his arms. I let him, burying my face in his jacket, which smelled of the outdoors, still a bit cool. "I know how upsetting this has all been for you. We'll get through it."

We sat like that for a few moments and finally, I felt somewhat better. I picked Sophie up out of her chair, wanting to feel her warm little body in my arms. I put Sophie up on my shoulder and she seemed content to sit with me and look at the big painting behind the sofa. It had bright colors and dark lines, and seemed especially interesting to her.

"Why is Lisa doing this?" I asked, frustrated that we couldn't get her out of our lives no matter what. "She must be nuts."

"She's definitely off the deep end if she's suggesting I asked her to run you down. You know that, right?"

I frowned at Drake. "Of course I do," I said, feeling bad that he even had to say it out loud. "I know you love me. I know you tried to quit when you learned Lisa was in your class."

Of course, that made me cry again and I wiped my eyes, not wanting Drake to see how close to tears I always seemed to be.

"Kate," he said and took Sophie from me. He placed her in her swing again and turned on the little mobile that hung above her head. She was happy to sit there and watch the little stuffed toys bounce around. Then he came to me and pulled me into his arms.

"I'm hiring Dave's aunt, Karen Mills, to come in and help us. You need to have some sleep and you need to stop worrying so much about everything. I'm fine. Sophie's healthy. You're healthy. This trial will be over soon enough. They'll try Lisa for attempted murder, probably find her not guilty by reason of temporary insanity and lock her up in a psychiatric hospital. Then, we'll be able to spend time with Sophie, maybe take a nice holiday with her and get away from it all. How does that sound?"

I leaned into his arms and buried my face in his shoulder. "It sounds wonderful. I'd love to go somewhere warm, but is Sophie old enough?"

"We'll go in March. Sophie will be seven months old and will have all her first shots."

I nodded and closed my eyes, thinking about escaping the whole business of the trial for a nice white-sand beach.

"Maybe we could go back to the Bahamas."

"We could. Or maybe we could go to Africa. Visit my dad's grave like we've been planning.

I glanced in his eyes. "Is it safe to take a baby to Africa? What about malaria and all those other tropical diseases?"

He nodded. "We should probably wait until she's a year old for that. We could always go down to Key West or Pensacola."

"Sounds wonderful," I said and tried to brighten up before Drake left the apartment for his meeting.

~

WHEN HE ARRIVED BACK HOME, he came in the living room and found Sophie and me on the sofa, after having a nap.

"There you are," he said and kissed me, then stroked Sophie's cheek. "Are you okay?"

I nodded and took in a deep breath, not wanting to upset him.

"I'm fine," I said, trying to keep my voice light. "How are you? How was your meeting?"

"Meeting was fine," he said. "I got a call a few minutes ago and have been invited down to the precinct for a little chat tomorrow. I've already talked to Lara. She'll come with me."

"Oh, Drake, you too?" I said, and pulled Sophie off for a burp. Drake reached out and took Sophie from my arms. "My God, haven't they interviewed you enough either?"

He shrugged and put a receiving blanked on his shoulder than held Sophie up for a burp, patting her back. I followed him downstairs to the sofa.

We sat down together and finally, after she'd given a small burp, Drake handed her back to me. When I finally had her latched on the other breast and feeding nicely, I looked into Drake's eyes. He was watching me with an expression of such warmth and affection that it made my breath catch in my throat.

How could they be so wrong about Drake?

It upset me so much to think of the police putting Drake through the wringer over the lies that Lisa told them.

"We'll get through this," he said and stroked my cheek. "We have each other. The three of us against the world."

I smiled, but after reading about men falsely accused and wrongly imprisoned, I knew we had to be on our toes.

CHAPTER 7 : DRAKE

I met with Lara an hour before my scheduled meeting with Detectives McDonald and St. James. She was waiting at her office, and greeted me with a hug and peck on the cheek. The expression on her face was somber, and I knew she wasn't feeling all that comfortable with the fact that the detectives were interested in me as a possible suspect.

I unbuttoned my jacket and sat down across from her, bracing myself for what was to come.

"So," I said, wanting to get right to it with no small talk. "What do you think? Why are they interviewing me yet again? Don't they know from talking with Lisa that we have no relationship – that it's all in her head?"

"You'd think so." Lara shrugged and opened a file. Inside were hand-written notes on a yellow notepad. She read over the notes for a moment.

"I spoke to one of my contacts in the major crimes unit and he said she claims you saw each other at a benefit concert that was sponsored by Doctors Without Borders."

"That's news to me," I said. "If she was there, she never came up to me or spoke to me."

"She claims you snuck off together and had sex in a broom closet in the concert hall."

"*What?*" I said, a shock of adrenaline coursing through me. "Believe me, I'd remember if I had sex with her in a broom closet at Carnegie Hall…" I shook my head and ran a hand through my hair. "Seriously? She's making shit up. What else did she claim?"

Lara flipped through a few pages. "She claims you met her for dinner several times over the past years. She has dates from when you were working on staff at New York Presbyterian. Seems that she has a half-dozen dates, all of which match up with time you were between surgeries."

"None of it's true," I said and frowned. "I never once saw her between the time at Derek's dungeon, which I can barely even remember, frankly, and the day she turned up in my Fellowship course. Not one time. It's all lies."

Lara shrugged. "I believe you, Drake. I know your sex life and submissives probably better than you do, because I arranged most of them. I have a list of them," she said and handed me a sheet of paper. It was a spreadsheet, neatly done with columns and names and dates.

"Holy crap," I said. "You sure are thorough."

"Do you have anyone to add?"

I checked over the list. There were seventeen names.

"There might have been a few more. One-off's during dungeon scenes. I wouldn't even be able to tell you their real names. A lot of that was private and anonymous."

She nodded and took the sheet back. "I'm prepared to turn this over to the police as evidence that I was your, shall we say, facilitator. That you turned to me for help finding partners. That I would have known that you were seeing Lisa. In fact, this list might be helpful, if we can get a list of dates Lisa claims you two were together and compare them with your known dates you were with submissives."

I rubbed my temple, grimacing at the fact that things had come to this. "I hate the fact that my sex life will be evidence and that any jury and judge, and any interested parties, can look and see how active I was."

"Yes, it sucks," she said and looked at me squarely. "And you had better brace yourself. If the police think they have enough evidence, they could arrest you or at least, make you suffer a lot of questioning. These so-called emails from you to Lisa have me worried. They should have written them off by now, with their forensic team. I don't know why they haven't. Hopefully, we'll find out more today."

I sat in mute silence for a moment. "Do you think they could arrest me? None of what she says is true."

"They don't know that. All they know is that she's making these statements and giving dates, times, and making allegations. Plus, they have the letters... The husband is always the first suspect in any murder or attempted murder. *Always.*"

"But it's not true," I said, frustration overwhelming me. "Can't they see that she's certifiable? She's nuts at best, a sociopath at worst. None of it happened and she's fabricating this story to cover her ass or get me in trouble as some kind of revenge."

"I know that," Lara said. "The police might suspect that, but if they can't rule you out somehow, then they'll have to act. It depends on the DA and how she wishes to proceed."

The DA. I hadn't thought about her. "What kind of DA is she?"

Lara shrugged and raised her eyebrows. "She's new. She's hoping to be a hotshot and she wants to make a name for herself, according to a few of my friends inside the DA's office. I have no idea whether she's for us or against us, in terms of her attitude towards BDSM. That'll count for a lot. If she's a religious type, she might be out to prove something to her constituents."

"Great," I said. "I already had to deal with the editor, who has a reporter with her sights set on hurting the kinky crowd. Will I have to deal with a DA out to prove herself?"

"That's the way the system works," Lara said. "But don't worry too much. There is no real evidence. There isn't. I know this is all a lie she's concocted. Sooner or later, the police will figure it out as well. The most important thing is to be as open and transparent as possible with them. Cooperate. When they realize she's suffering from some kind of erotomania delusion about you, they'll back off and focus back on her alone."

I sighed and rubbed my chin, the grizzle in serious need of a trim. I'd let myself go a bit lately, what with the late nights with Sophie and the general sleeplessness.

"What are they going to ask me today?"

She tilted her head to the side. "Everything they've already asked you when you were in the hospital. They'll be looking for consistency. If you tell a slightly different story each time or if your story is consistent. If you change your statement in any way. That's why it's important to be absolutely truthful and fully disclose everything."

"How can I prove I didn't fuck her in the damn broom closet at Carnegie Hall?"

"Who were you with?" Lara asked.

"One time, I was with one of the donors to the foundation. We'd gone out for dinner and then to hear a concert. I can give you his name. Steve Benson. He's from California and was in for the week so we got together. I've been there a few times in the past five years. I'll have to think about it."

She nodded. "You make sure you write down every time you were at Carnegie and who you were with. We should be able to refute her claim."

Finally, it was time to go, so we stood and I buttoned my jacket.

"I'm not feeling all that confident about this," I said.

"Don't worry too much," Lara replied, coming around her desk, squeezing my shoulder to give me courage. "We have the truth on our side. They must have a psych consult, and they must see she's nuts. Until then, we should be careful, that's all."

~

WE DROVE to the precinct house and my driver dropped us off in front. We walked up the stairs to the main desk. They knew Lara there and the desk clerk smiled at her and took her name, then motioned to the waiting area while we waited for the detectives to come for us.

I waited for Lara to sit before I did and then I tried to calm myself, even though I knew I had nothing to hide. What I feared was that the detectives would be so prejudiced against BDSM practitioners that they'd see guilt where there was none. They might be more sympathetic to the so-called victim of a sadist than looking for the truth.

I hoped I was imagining things, and that my sense of how it could go was wrong.

Finally, a couple of minutes later, Detective McDonald came around the corner and nodded at the two of us.

"Come right this way," he said to Lara and then tilted his head towards me.

He was joined by Detective St. James as he led us down a couple of hallways to an interview room in the interior of the building. It was small, with no windows. There was a lone table in the room with two chairs on one side and two on the other. Lara and I went behind the table and took our seats. McDonald and St. James sat down across from us.

"First of all, thank you for agreeing to come down and speak with us further, Dr. Morgan," he said and flipped open a file. "We want to ask you a few questions, clarify what happened the day your wife was attacked."

"No problem," I said, although there was a big problem, as far as I was concerned. "I'm at your disposal." I held my hands out, and then folded them, trying to relax and not look as frustrated as I felt.

"First, I want to show you these," he said and flipped open a file. Inside was a stack of papers that looked like the printout of emails. "Can you identify the email address and contents?"

I glanced at the first three. They were from a Yahoo account. DMorganMD and were dated during the past two years. I read a few over. Intensely romantic and using a lot of terminology from the lifestyle – limits, submission, punishment, obedience. One demanded that she did certain things to prove her willingness to follow orders.

I want you on your knees, Lisa, blindfolded, waiting for me when I come to you. Naked. Wet. I'm going to push your boundaries tonight. Every single one. As soon as I can get away from her, I'll be there and I want you ready for me. Every hole in your body open and ready for me. In every way...

These were all things a Dom might do as part of training a sub, but they were completely fabricated. I hated that they had shown the fake emails to Kate. That was the very last thing she needed, given her delicate mental state.

Then I found one email that contained texts from one of my letters written as guidelines for my new subs.

> *Your naked skin is sensitive now, exposed to the ambient temperature change. The silk of your pillow is cool against your calves as you sit waiting. A cool breeze wafts in from your open window, and your nipples pucker. You think of my mouth on them, my tongue wet and warm, and a stab of lust flows through you.*
>
> *My key clicks in the lock, the door creaking open, my footsteps loud on the hardwood floor, the thunk thunk as I remove my boots.*
>
> *I open the refrigerator and remove the bottle of vodka you keep just for me, pour the liquid in a shot glass, and then my lips smack in satisfaction. It's my favorite Russian vodka infused with anise, called Anisovaya. I have only one shot, for I must keep my mind clear so I am in total control of everything – you, the scene, and most of all, myself.*
>
> *Then, the zhrrr of a zipper and the swish of fabric sounds so loud. Your body tenses for a moment as you anticipate my next move.*

My pulse increased. She'd copied the letters and included them in emails from me. Like she wished I had written them for her.

Did she do this to incriminate me? Or did she write these emails and create this fake account because she wished it were true?

Either way, she was insane.

"These aren't my emails. I never wrote these," I said and threw the letters onto the table.

"They're from an account with your name, signed with your name. We found them at her apartment."

"I didn't write them. I mean, I wrote some of this, but she copied it from material I posted on a private website. I'm sure if you do some forensic work, you'll see."

"We're doing it as we speak," St. James said, a note of gloating in his voice. "We'll know what IP address was used to send those, so if you sent them from work or from home, we'll know."

"I didn't send them. You won't find anything."

St. James shrugged. "We want to ask you to go over your relationship with Ms. Monroe. When did you meet her, how did you meet, what was your relationship with her."

I sighed and then re-told the same chronicle of events I told them in the hospital. He watched me as I recounted the whole sordid story.

Then, McDonald turned to me.

"Dr. Morgan, we'd like to know where you were on the following dates. They're in the past few years, so I'll ask that you try to account for your whereabouts and get back to us as soon as possible."

He handed me a sheet of paper with a list of type-written dates on it. There were fifteen in total, ranging back five years. I looked it over and folded it up, tucking it into my jacket pocket.

"I'll check my calendar at work and my personal calendar."

"Thank you," McDonald said and stood. He extended his hand and I realized it was time for us to leave. "I appreciate your cooperation."

Both Lara and I stood and I offered my hand. "Tell me, Detective," I said, trying to keep my voice light. "Am I still a suspect?"

He stood, his hands on his hips, and tilted his head to the side.

"I can't comment on that now," he said, his voice patient. "But you get that list back to us as soon as possible so we can conclude our investigation and make sure Mrs. Morgan gets the justice she deserves, okay?"

He looked me in the eye, and I thought I saw sympathy, as if he didn't believe I was guilty.

"Thank you," I said and Lara and I left.

"Stay in Manhattan, Dr. Morgan." St. James said crisply. "Once we get your response to that list, and corroborate it, we may need to speak with you again."

"Don't worry," I said and waved him off. "We're not going anywhere anytime soon."

Lara turned to me, a look on her face that was hard to describe. A mixture of frustration and disbelief.

"What's that look?" I said, following Lara out of the precinct. We stood on the sidewalk and she turned to me.

"Total disbelief that Lisa was that crazy to create a fake account and send herself letters from you."

"I know," I said. "Who would have thought?"

The limo driver opened our door and the two of us slid inside. Lara glanced at me, her expression one of concern.

"Let me see that list," she said after she finished buckling her seatbelt. "We'll stop by my office and I'll get my assistant to copy it and check it out against known concerts and dungeon parties."

"You may want to add on Doctors Without Borders events as well. I'll check *Mersey's* schedule, to see when we played."

"And afterwards," Lara said and tucked the paper into her bag. "We're going out to get drunk."

"You think so?" I said, not sure if I wanted to leave Kate alone for so long with Sophia. "I probably should go home to be with Kate."

"Kate can wait," Lara said. "You need at least one drink after that."

I nodded, feeling like a shot of vodka or three might do me good.

As we drove off, I still had a bad feeling about my situation and seeing those letters hadn't dissipated it.

∼

CHAPTER 8 : KATE

Drake arrived home much later than I expected. "How did it go?" I asked, carrying Sophie with me to the door to greet him. Sophie was a bit fussy, and had been hard to pacify.

Drake removed his jacket, an expression of concern on his face.

"Well enough, but it's hard to say."

I leaned up to kiss him, and could smell the vodka even before our lips met.

"Hmm, vodka," I said with a smile. "Looks like someone needed a drink."

"I did," Drake said and fumbled with his shoes, leaning against the closet door like he was a bit dizzy. "Lara wouldn't take no for an answer. You know what she's like."

"I do," I said, trying to keep a grin off my face, but Drake a bit tipsy was always amusing. "She's a dominatrix for a reason."

He nodded and when he was finished, he tucked his shoes into the closet, and closed the door.

He turned to me and reached for Sophie, but I pulled her away slightly.

"Maybe you shouldn't," I said. "Drinking and parenting don't mix well."

"Aww," he said and leaned closer, peering at Sophie, who was sucking intently on her pacifier. "I'm sorry, lil girl, but Daddy is a bit tipsy. Don't want to drop you or fall with you in my arms." He pouted and shook his head when he met my eyes. "I'm sorry. You probably hoped I could take over when I got back. I didn't think…"

"It's okay," I said and squeezed his arm. "She just fed so it's time for her to have some swing time and maybe a nap."

"Good," Drake said and plopped down onto the sofa, his feet up on the coffee table. He watched while I put Sophie into her swing and turned on the timer for 20 minutes. I hoped that would give me time to relax, put my feet up and listen to what Drake had to say.

Once she was set, I watched to see if she would fuss, but she seemed content to stare at the tiny mobile that hung from the swing and suck on her pacifier. If she settled, she'd sleep for a while.

I sat down beside Drake, my own feet on the coffee table, glad to finally rest myself.

"So, tell me what happened," I said and turned so I could watch Drake's face. He looked haggard, his eyes dark under a frown.

"The same things they asked me at the hospital. This time, McDonald showed me the letters and gave me a list of dates to check. I imagine they're the dates that Lisa has claimed we were together plotting your death."

"Oh, God, Drake," I said, a surge of adrenaline going through my body. "What a crazy bitch she is. Doesn't she think the police can check those emails to see if you sent them? Doesn't she think you'll check and can prove you weren't together?"

Drake shrugged. "She claims we were together secretly at functions. That we snuck off to meet in broom closets and basements. It'll take time to do the forensic work on her computers to see where those emails originated."

"She's lying, so I'm sure they'll find out soon enough. You can prove you were with other people on those dates."

"I hope so, but I did often get up to leave the concert to take a call from the hospital or go to the washroom, for Christ's sake. How can I prove I took a piss and that I didn't meet with Lisa instead? Unless they have video footage of me standing at a urinal, I don't know how I can prove anything."

"The hospital will have records. Your cell will have records. You weren't with her," I said adamantly. "There's no way she can prove you were."

"It's all about reasonable doubt," Drake said, his voice tired. "If she can make them doubt my statements, they could arrest me. I've read about cases where innocent people are convicted. It's not necessarily a given that I'll be safe."

I sighed and leaned my head back, closing my eyes. I was tired, and had a bad night of sleep, even though Drake got up with Sophie to give her a bottle of expressed milk. My sleep was plagued with weird dreams, and I felt exhausted even though I napped during the day when Sophie did.

Besides that, my nipples still hurt like hell when I fed Sophie and at times, tears would run down my cheeks from the short intense pain. Elaine suggested I quit nursing but there was no way in hell I was going to give up. The midwife told me that it sometimes takes eight weeks before everything was good. It had been more than eight weeks since I started nursing Sophie.

I kept holding out for the day when it would be easy.

"Come here," Drake said, his voice low. "I need you."

I turned my head and saw him looking at me, an expression of desperation in his eyes. I knew what he meant, but I wasn't ready yet. He told me he'd wait and let me signal to him when the time was right for us to resume our sex life, but that wasn't now. Especially not today, when I felt so crappy.

But he looked so forlorn, leaning back, his head against the back of the sofa, his body limp. His expression tugged at my heart, but my body didn't respond to the idea of us being sexual yet.

"I'm sorry," I said and shook my head. "I can't." Then, my eyes filled with tears and I glanced away, unable to stand the look of rejection on his face.

"No, no," he said and reached out to me. "I mean, just for a hug. I need to feel your warmth. I promise, no sex, okay?"

"I'm so sorry," I said and covered my face with my hands, crying in earnest now. "I don't know what's wrong with me. I'm so tired all the time. All I want to do is sleep."

I felt his arms go around me, pulling me against his body and onto his lap and I didn't fight.

"Shh," he said, his voice soft and warm. "Katie, *Katie...*" He kissed my forehead and my cheeks and tilted my head up so that I had to look at him. I finally met his eyes and there was complete sympathy for me. "You're still getting over a major trauma. I don't expect anything from you except getting better. I'll do anything I can to help you. I told you I'd never push and I meant it. All I want is to hold you and for us to comfort each other."

I wiped my eyes and nodded. Then, I leaned my head on his shoulder and sighed, giving in to him. His body felt so damn good against mine, so warm and firm and he smelled so good, his cologne bringing back so many good memories of our life together. I wanted to be lovers again, but at that moment, I was still so tired and felt so worn out, I couldn't imagine doing anything sexual.

"One of these days," I said and slipped my arms around him. "We'll get back on track as a couple."

"Whenever you're ready," he whispered, his face tucked into my neck, his lips beside my ear. "I'll leave it up to you. Just sit with me for a while..."

So I did. We sat together like that, me straddling his hips, my arms around him, my head on shoulder. He said nothing and did nothing, and I said nothing and did nothing. It was nice to sit like that and feel connected physically to him the way we once were.

So much had happened so quickly in our lives. My pregnancy had been difficult, with me being nauseated for so long. Then, the problem with Lisa, and how Drake felt he had to pull out of the program because of her. Then the attack and my surgery, Sophia's premature birth. Now, the investigation and the way Drake had been publicly outed as a member of the BDSM community. How it affected his Foundation…

We both needed a vacation.

"I wish we could run away, the three of us," I said, thinking of a trip to the Bahamas. "We could stay at the hotel where we stayed before."

"We will," Drake said. "As soon as this is over. As soon as Detective McDonald gives me the all clear to leave the state, we'll fly there for a couple of weeks. You, me, Sophie and the sun and surf. It will be wonderful."

I pulled up and looked in Drake's eyes, smiling at him. He was such a sweet sweet man, underneath the Dom and highly skilled surgeon persona.

I was so incredibly lucky to have him.

At that moment, I was filled with so much love for him and for Sophie that I felt as if my heart would burst.

I leaned down and kissed him, my hands on either side of his face.

"I love you, Drake Morgan," I said in a soft voice.

"I love you, Katherine Morgan," he replied.

When I kissed him again, he pulled me more tightly against him and I thought he might have misunderstood the kiss as a signal that I wanted to make love, but he didn't make another move or do anything but hold me.

I sighed and closed my eyes, my head against his shoulder – his strong firm shoulder – once more.

~

WE HAD a quiet week for the rest of the week, and I started feeling a little bit better once Dave Mills's aunt Karen came by. A tall strong woman with silver hair and piercing blue eyes, she was formidable looking, but also had this kind expression in her eyes. She reminded me of one of those stolid women you might see working in the fields, pulling a tractor in good old Soviet Russia. A permanent smile on her face and a light green nursing uniform on, she felt good. It felt like she knew what to do and how to do it.

She had so much experience that I felt comfortable letting her take Sophie from me.

We had a nice meeting, she met Sophie and then described what she would do for us – take Sophie for a while each day, cook a meal for us and do some light housework. I liked her a lot and she held Sophie with a sense of comfort that made me relax.

The first afternoon Karen came to work for us, she entered the apartment, checked out our home as if looking for work to do, took Sophie from my arms, checked her out from head to toe, and then smiled at me.

"Go and sleep," she said and waved at me. "You look like you need a bath and then a nap. I'll change her, feed her a bottle of breastmilk, and keep her occupied while I fix supper. As for you," she said and turned to Drake. "Go out and do something manly. Go work out at your club. Play a game of – what was it? Racquetball, Dave said? Call him and get out of the house. The two of you need to get a bit of normalcy back into your daily life."

Drake glanced at me and chuckled. "What? No bath and nap for me?"

Karen shook her head and plopped Sophie's pacifier into her mouth. "No. You didn't merely go through a pregnancy and major life-saving surgery. You need to get back into your regular routine as much as possible. Go. Dave will be glad for a break from work. You're his boss, so it's entirely up to you."

Karen smiled at Drake and fully expected that Drake would comply.

He looked at me again to see my response.

"Go," I said and nodded. "She's right. We need to find a new normal."

He shrugged his shoulders. "Who am I to argue?" He kissed my cheek, then stroked Sophie's cheek before leaving to go to his office . "I'll call Dave and order him to meet me at the club for a game of racquetball."

Karen turned to me. "You go and run a nice warm bath with lots of lavender scented Epsom salts. You'll find them in the bag I brought. It's over by the door."

I went to the re-usable cloth bag by the door and sure enough, inside were several objects I didn't recognize but thought they might be part of a massage therapy kit, and a glass container with a scoop attached. The label had been hand-drawn and said *Lavender Epsom Salts. ½ cup to 1 cup added to running water.*

I took the container and went upstairs to the bathroom, following her orders, glad that someone else could take over for a while. On my way to the bathroom, I passed Drake, who was pulling on his sweats by our bed.

"Are you okay with this?" he said softly, stopping to kiss me.

"Yes," I said. "She seems like she knows what she's doing."

"Good," he said and finished dressing. "I'll be back in a couple of hours."

Then, I went and ran my bath, pouring in the Epsom salts and enjoying the scent of lavender that filled the room. For the next half hour, I luxuriated in the warm bath, letting my mind drift off while I did absolutely nothing. I heard the stereo turned on and some soft music drift into the bathroom through the heat register. It sounded like something classical, soothing. I could practically see the candles lined up along the mantle and her giving Sophie a massage with baby lotion.

My eyes blinked open. I still couldn't relax completely. There was a part of my mind that seemed on hyper-alert, listening for Sophie's lightest sound or cry.

I got out of the bath and wrapped my bath robe around me, then ventured down to the main floor. There I found Karen working away in the kitchen. She had Sophie in her chair on the island, watching her work.

I smelled garlic and onion sautéing in a pan on the stove.

"What are you cooking?" I asked, moving closer.

"Beef Burgundy." She pointed to a shank of beef and some aromatic herbs. "I brought the ingredients, based on what you indicated you liked for meals. It cooks for hours in the oven, until the meat is fall off the bone tender. It should be ready for seven o'clock. I'll fix some noodles and sautéed vegetables to go with it."

"Sounds yummy," I said with a yawn. "Sophie seems happy."

"She had a bottle and seems content to watch her mobile. She'll probably go down for a nap soon, I would think. You should, too."

I sighed. "You seem so in control of everything."

Karen laughed. "I had five children of my own and worked as a pediatric nurse for fifteen years before I became a doula. Now, besides being a doula, I freelance as a lactation and nursing consultant. I love babies. Now, go to bed. I'll wake you in 30 minutes."

"Okay, if you insist," I said, smiling.

"I insist. Everything's fine. Look at her," she said and gestured to Sophie while she chopped some carrots. "Her eyes are heavy. I'll put her in her crib soon, on her side. You go nap."

"I will," I said and took one last look at Sophie before doing exactly what Karen said.

My bed never felt quit as good as it did at that moment and I slept within moments of my head hitting the pillow, the blankets warm around me.

I WOKE to the scent of delicious and very aromatic Beef Burgundy, wafting up from the kitchen on the main floor of the apartment. My bed was warm and comfortable, and I almost snuggled down into it for a longer nap, but I checked my watch and saw I'd already been asleep for almost an hour.

I jumped out of bed and quickly brushed my hair, adjusted my clothes, and went to see how Sophie was doing. I went to her bassinet, which we kept in the back bedroom, and saw that she was still asleep, so I smiled and went into Drake's office to use my computer and check my mail.

I sat at the desk and opened my laptop, to find I had several new messages, from various junk mail providers, all of which I deleted.

There was nothing from my father, which made me frown, and so I decided to call the house. There was again no answer.

I left a message and then sat for a moment, my cell in my hand, and wondered where they were that they couldn't answer the home phone. So, I tried my father's cell and got the same response – no answer and then his voicemail. I left a new message there.

*Hey, daddy. I hope you're okay. I tried to call you at home but there was no answer so
I'm assuming you and Elaine are out. Please call me back when you get this message and
let me know everything's okay. I love you, Kate.*

Then I tried Elaine's cell, thinking that she should be able to answer. On
the third ring, just when I thought I'd be sent to voicemail, she finally
answered.

"Hello," she said, her voice a bit brusque.

"Hey," I said, glad to hear her voice. "I've been trying to call you but you
were out. How is everything?"

When I heard her sigh, I knew things were not good. "Your father's in the
ER here at NYP. He's being examined right now, and so I'm out here in the
waiting room."

I frowned, a jolt of adrenaline coursing through me. "Why didn't you call
me right away? What happened?"

She paused on the other end. "I'm sorry, Kate, but he asked me not to. He
didn't want to worry you over nothing."

"Nothing? Why would he be in the ER if it were nothing? What
happened?"

"He fell," she said, her voice wavering. "I wasn't strong enough to get him
up. That's all, dear. It scared us both, because usually, I can get him up. I'm
strong enough. But he was unresponsive for a couple of minutes and I
thought he was unconscious."

"Did he have a stroke?" I asked, fearing the worst.

"Maybe," she replied, the fatigue clear in her voice. "The doctors are examining him now and he's going for a CT with contrast to see if there's been a
new bleed. It could be a balance problem – you know, he doesn't have the
strength in his left side anymore and sometimes, he stumbles a bit."

"I'll be right down," I said and took in a deep breath. "We have a new nanny
working for us. She can keep Sophie until Drake gets home from his fitness
club."

"You don't have to come down, Kate. I'm sure there's nothing you can do
until they get the results back from the CT scan. Why don't you wait?"

"I want to be there with my dad," I said insistently. "I can't sit around here
and wait. I'll go nuts."

"You have your new baby and you're still recovering."

"I'm fine and Sophie's fine. I'll be there in thirty minutes."

I hung up, hoping that it was merely a minor loss of balance and not a
stroke. I went right to the kitchen where Karen was busy tidying up the
counter, putting things away from her preparations for our dinner.

"What's the matter," she said when she saw me. "You're white as a ghost."

"I just found out that my father is in NYP ER and is having a CT scan. He fell at home and his wife thinks he was unconscious for a few minutes. He had a stroke last year and so it could be another."

She wiped her hands on her apron. "Do you want to go and be with him?"

I nodded, and of course, my eyes filled with tears. "Yes. Can you stay with Sophie until Drake gets back?"

"Of course, dear," she replied, a look of sympathy on her face. "You sure you don't want to wait for Drake to get back?"

I shook my head and struggled to speak for a moment as emotion overwhelmed me. "No," I managed to say. "I want to go right away."

"Okay," she said and came over to me, putting her arm around my shoulder and squeezing. "You go right ahead. Sophia's having a good sleep. When she wakes up, I can give her another bottle. She'll be fine until Drake gets back. He said he'd be here around six, so that's only in another hour."

"Thank you," I said and at that moment, I felt such affection for her for understanding my need to go right away to be with my father. "I appreciate it."

"No problem," she said. "You go. I've got this handled."

I nodded and left the kitchen, taking my cell out and calling for the limo service to take me to NYP. Then, I took the stairs to the second floor so I could quickly wash my face and brush my teeth, make myself a little more presentable.

By the time I got down to the street, after pulling on my fall jacket and shoes, the limo was already waiting for me, the driver standing beside the back passenger door.

He opened it for me and I got in. While the driver got inside, I took out my cell and sent Drake a text.

KATE: *My father is in NYP ER. He fell at home and Elaine couldn't get him up so she called an ambulance. She thinks he lost consciousness for a few minutes. I'm on my way there now. Karen's staying with Sophie. Please text me when you get this.*

We drove off to NYP and I wondered what I'd find when I got there.

THE ER WAS busy as I walked inside, stopping at the reception area where they triaged patients to find out where my father was being kept. The nurse behind the desk glanced at me and asked who I was.

"I'm his daughter, Katherine McDermott Morgan," I said. "His wife might have said I was coming."

The nurse glanced at the screen and told me what room he was in and then buzzed me into the back area where the ER bays were located. She gave me directions, and I walked past a dozen tiny cubicles filled with patients, family members and banks of telemetry so the staff could monitor the patient's vital signs. My heart rate increased as I glanced down the long hallway to a larger room where my father was housed. It was empty, except for Elaine, who sat there waiting for me. When she saw me, she stood and opened her arms.

"They had to take him to surgery," she said and squeezed me.

What felt like a lead weight fell on me and I gasped. "Did he have a stroke?"

She nodded and pulled back, brushing my hair from my cheek. "Yes, sweetie. He had another stroke while they were doing the procedure. They had to rush him into the OR to try to stop the bleeding."

We hugged again and then sat on two chairs side by side, our arms still around each other.

A nurse popped her head into the cubicle. "He's been assigned a room in the ICU, if you want to go and wait. There's also a patient room in the surgical wing you can go to and wait for his surgeon to come out." She handed us a small pamphlet that had the layout of the hospital with a bright pink X where the surgical patient waiting room was located.

"Thank you," Elaine said. "We'll go there now. Thanks for letting me wait for my daughter."

The nurse smiled. "We need the room now so it was good timing."

Elaine and I stood, she gathered her bag and jacket and together, we took the long hallways to the bank of elevators that would take us to the surgical floor, where the OR suites were housed. Once there, we sat in the large patient room, which was bright and airy, with windows to an interior courtyard. There were big comfortable couches and tables, as well as a small kitchenette with a coffee maker, hot water for tea and a small bar fridge filled with juice and sodas.

Elaine fixed herself a cup of tea and I took a juice, not wanting to test the decaffeinated tea in case it was really old.

We sat on a sofa side by side and my cell dinged. Drake must have received my text after his game.

DRAKE: *Sorry I didn't get this until now. How is Dad?*

KATE: *He's undergoing surgery for a bleed on his brain. I'm in the patient waiting area outside the OR theatres. We're waiting to hear from his surgeon, Dr. Franks.*

DRAKE: *Franks is first-rate, so Dad is in good hands. I'll be there as soon as I can. Karen will stay the evening so we can wait together and see how he's doing.*

KATE: *Please tell her thanks so much. I don't know what we'd do without her...*

DRAKE: *I will. I'll be there in 30 minutes. I love you.*

KATE: *Are you going home first or are you coming right over?*

DRAKE: *I checked my messages and saw that you'd texted me. I called Karen as soon as I learned. I called over to NYP to see how Dad was. I'll fill you in when I get there.*

KATE: Okay. I'm so scared...

DRAKE: Hold on. I'll be there soon.

I put my cell away and turned to Elaine, who was sitting with her eyes closed, her face ashen.

"Drake says Dr. Franks is fantastic."

Elaine opened her eyes and glanced at me. "Yes," she said in a tired voice. "The nurses in the ER told me Dr. Franks was the on-call neurosurgeon and that he was top in his field, especially in this area. We're lucky."

I nodded and tears welled up in my eyes once more. I covered them, not wanting to break down, and tried to breathe deeply to control my emotions. I glanced around the room. There were five other people in the room in two clusters, so there must be three surgeries going on at the moment. I sipped my juice and leaned back, taking in a deep cleansing breath to calm myself. I closed my eyes, and repeated the deep breathing exercise I had used before to regain calm and it seemed to do the trick.

"How are you, dear?" Elaine said softly.

"Fine," I said and turned my head to look at her. She looked better as well, like the tea was calming her. It gave us both something to do.

"You said he'd been stumbling a lot lately," I said and turned to her, feeling guilty that I hadn't been around much or checked more often to see how he was doing. "But I thought it was him getting used to the after effects of his stroke."

"We didn't want to alarm you, dear," she said and took my hand in hers. "He wasn't feeling well but thought it was a cold. I guess he had something going on and when he fell earlier, I thought it was another example of him having trouble with his left side. I knew as soon as I bent down to help him that it wasn't just another fall."

"What happened?" I asked, my gut in a knot about it.

"His eyes were closed, but I thought maybe he was in pain," she said, and squeezed my hand once more. "I asked him how he was, and he didn't reply. I tried to shake him, to get his attention but nothing. That was when I knew he wasn't grimacing in pain. He was unconscious. He's heavy, and I couldn't get him up on my own, so I called 9-1-1 right away. Luckily, my training came in handy and I was able to get him in a better position, checked his airway, and waited. I rushed to the door to unlock it and I called down to the concierge to let them know that I'd called 9-1-1. The firemen were the first to arrive."

I thought about how afraid Elaine must have been, waiting for help to arrive. It brought me back to my own accident – or should I say, attack.

"You must have been frantic," I said and shook my head.

"It seemed to take forever for them to arrive but finally, they came in and took over. Your father was breathing fine, but he was unconscious. When they began to work on him, assessing him, he regained consciousness, but I could see him already changing. His face had that strange mask-like look and the side of his face drooped. I knew it was a stroke."

"What did they tell you about his prognosis?"

She closed her eyes. "It's hard to say," she said and then glanced at me. "The bleed was big. They'll do what they can, but Dr. Franks told me to prepare myself. That's why I answered your call. Your dad asked me not to call you until I knew how he was going to be. He didn't want to stress you needlessly."

"He was able to talk though? That's good, right?"

She nodded. "Yes, but then he stopped being able to say anything. He only nodded or shook his head."

"He was just going to die and have you tell me later?"

"No," she said and squeezed my hand again. "He wanted for me to wait until after the procedure. He said there was no use having you disrupt your entire life until you had to. He was concerned about you."

"And you went along with him? You should have called me last week. You should have called me as soon as you were finished calling 9-1-1. What about Heath? Have you called him?"

She shook her head. "He's in Haiti for the month. Your father didn't want to cause any problems until we knew more."

Tears filled my eyes once more despite my anger at my father for trying to protect us, and at Elaine for doing as he asked.

"I would have come down right away and spoken to him," I said, wiping my eyes with my free hand. "I could have told him I love him in case he doesn't make it through surgery. Heath would fly back right away..."

"He knows, dear," she said and smiled sadly. "He knows you love him. He knows that Drake loves him, too. Having you two together has been one of his greatest joys. Seriously, he was so worried about you before you met Drake. He was afraid you were losing your way, and would never do what you wanted. When you met Drake, you blossomed. You became who you were meant to be. That made him so happy."

I sat and cried for a few moments, silently, tears sliding off my cheeks. I wanted to be able to speak to my father before he went into surgery, to hold his hand, and to tell him how I felt and how lucky I was to have had him as a father. All those years, I was so wrong about him and how he felt towards me. I always felt like he didn't approve of what I wanted to do and I had to do what he wanted or he wouldn't love me. Instead, he was always encouraging me no matter what I said.

In about half an hour, after Elaine and I caught up on how my father had been during the previous week, the door to the waiting room opened and in walked Drake. I was so glad to see him, dressed in his camel coat, a plaid scarf around his neck, his hair still a bit damp at the edges. He had a cloth bag in hand.

He came right over and I stood so we could embrace. His arms went around me and he pulled me close, his face pressed into my neck. I heard him inhale deeply and knew he was smelling my perfume. Then he kissed me and hugged me again.

"How are you?" he asked when he pulled away.

"I'm okay," I said. "He's still in surgery."

Drake nodded, his expression solemn. "He'll be a few hours. I stopped by the apartment to check on Sophie and brought this," he said and held out the bag. I took it and peered inside. It was my breast pump and container for breast milk. "You'll probably have to expel soon."

I nodded. "Thanks," I said and took the bag from him. "I probably will. I had a nap and Karen fed Sophie a bottle so I'll be more than in need of expressing." I set the bag beside me.

He turned to Elaine. "How are you doing?" he asked and held his arms open for her. She stood and stepped into his embrace for a brief hug and peck on the cheek.

"I'm fine," she said with a tired smile. "I've spoken with his doctor and know that if he makes it through surgery, it will depend on how the mend works."

"He had a bleed and they'll have to go in and repair the vein. It may take some time for him to regain function. We won't know for a while."

Drake took off his coat and scarf, hung them on the coat rack, and then returned to where we were sitting. He glanced at the two of us. "If you're okay, I'll go and talk to the nurses, then be back with any news."

I nodded and he squeezed my hand, kissing my cheek before he turned to leave us.

"I'm glad you called," Elaine said when he left and we were alone. "I was feeling bad not calling you, but I have to respect your father's wishes. It's better that you're here. How is Sophie?"

"She's doing great," I said and smiled softly. "She's gaining weight and sleeping longer."

"Good," Elaine said. "I'm also glad that you got a nanny-slash-housekeeper. New mothers need far more help than they get. I learned that when I worked for a while on the maternity ward. I'd never want to have a baby and be completely alone. I volunteered for a while with single moms who were receiving aid. They do so much. There's so much stress."

"I'm so lucky I have Drake at home with me. I don't have to worry when I need a break. He's always there. Plus, now we have Karen Mills. She's cooking dinner and did some tidying, plus she took Sophie so I could nap. I feel bad leaving her with Sophie the first day on the job."

"I'm sure she understands, considering what happened with your father."

I sat back and took in a deep breath, calming down somewhat now that Drake was here. He'd go and find out what happened to my father and report back what he could find out. Elaine was good because she was a nurse and knew medicine, but she hadn't been practicing for several years. It was good to have Drake there.

I hated to think of leaving Elaine alone at the hospital, however Drake or I would have to go back to the apartment, either to feed Sophie or to take back the bottles of breastmilk. Karen couldn't be expected to stay for the entire evening.

Elaine and I sat together and talked about my father for about fifteen minutes. Finally, Drake returned.

He sat beside me and put his arm around my shoulders. He glanced between Elaine and I and his face seemed a bit more relaxed than when he arrived.

"I popped in and watched surgery for a while on my screens," he said. "Things are going according to plan. That's all I know. We'll have to wait to see how he does. He should make it through surgery. They didn't seem overly concerned."

"That's good," I said and closed my eyes, trying hard not to start crying again. I covered my eyes with a hand, and Drake pulled me into his arms, not saying anything. The feel of his arms around me was comforting, and I was able to get control over my emotions once more. When I pulled back, he caught my eyes and his expression was so tender and compassionate. How could anyone ever think he was a sadist? If they knew him, they'd know he could never hurt anyone on purpose or get any pleasure out of it.

"I'm okay," I said. I inhaled deeply, trying to be strong. I had to face whatever happened. I couldn't be a mess. I had Sophie and Drake and Elaine to think about.

"I spoke with Karen and she said she'd be happy to stay until midnight, if that's necessary. I told her that I'd call her and let her know, depending on how Ethan is."

I nodded and sat back, sitting between Elaine and Drake, watching the clock and waiting for news of my father.

It was going to be a very long day.

CHAPTER 9 : DRAKE

As a neurosurgeon, I knew that Ethan was in considerable peril, given the new bleed and how weak he already was. But as a neurosurgeon, I also knew that the brain was much more resilient than we previously understood.

If Ethan got through surgery well and didn't have any complications, he would probably survive. It would be a long slow recovery, and he might lose even more function, or recover less than he previously had, but he would likely survive.

I hoped.

Kate was struggling to keep from breaking down. I could see it on her face, which was haggard already from disrupted sleep due to nursing. Now, she was even more ashen and her eyes had a haunted look that suggested she thought Ethan was going to die.

There was nothing I could say to her to alleviate that fear for even I had no idea whether he would survive. His chances were about 50-50, but I wasn't going to tell her that. If he survived surgery, they were still about even, so it was truly touch and go as far as Ethan surviving was concerned.

We sat in the waiting room for surgical patients, hoping for news of Ethan's condition. The longer we waited, the less concerned I was. If he died, he would have probably died quickly, and if he survived, the surgery would take a while. So every passing quarter of an hour gave me hope.

Finally, Dr. Franks came to the door and waved at us. The three of us stood and went to the hallway, standing in the empty corridor with Dr. Franks He had pulled down his mask and was smiling. That was a good sign.

"Mrs. McDermott, Dr. Morgan, Mrs. Morgan," he began. "We're finished with Ethan's surgery and he's done remarkably well, considering the extent of the bleed. We were able to repair the rupture in his vein and will be treating him with medications to keep him asleep for a while to let him heal. He'll slowly regain consciousness over the next few hours, so he's not conscious at the moment. You can go in and see him in ICU. He'll be there once he's stable. They'll take him to recovery for a while to make sure everything is stable and then bring him to ICU."

I extended my hand and we shook. "Thank you. I appreciate it."

"Yes, thank you," Elaine said and she shook Dr. Frank's hand as well. On her part, Kate smiled at him but seemed unable to speak. Of course, her eyes filled with tears and she covered them with a hand.

"Thank you," she managed to whisper. I caught Franks' eyes and he nodded knowingly, understanding that Kate was overcome.

"I'll be stopping by to check on Ethan later, so we can talk further if you have any questions."

We said another thank you and then went back into the waiting room. I hugged Kate, and she stood in my arms and let me embrace her.

"He survived the surgery," I said in a soft voice. "Now, we have to get through the first twenty-four hours."

Kate nodded, her face pressed against my shoulder. "I want to stay here," she said and then she pulled away. "Can you go home and give Sophie another bottle?"

"I could bring her here for a feed, if you want."

Kate shook her head. "I don't want her in a hospital with all the infections."

"I'm sure Karen will stay until midnight. She'll give Sophie a bottle when she's hungry."

Kate looked up at me with huge haunted eyes. "I don't like both of us to be away from her for so long."

"I'll pop over for a while and check on her, if you want."

She nodded and closed her eyes, leaning her head against my chest. I could tell she was exhausted and so scared. She was right to be. Ethan was in a precarious position and could go either way in the next twenty-four hours. I didn't want to leave the hospital, just in case. While he had an excellent surgical team looking after him, and would have an equally great team in the ICU, it was still dangerous. He could die.

I didn't want to even consider it. Usually, as a neurosurgeon, I had to take an objective look at my patients and realize that for some, there was only so much I could do. I'd looked over Ethan's CT results and his stats, and knew that his condition was critical.

No matter how good his surgeon, there was still a huge risk that he'd hemorrhage and not recover or would have irreversible brain damage that would kill him or leave him a vegetable. I knew his surgeon's work well, and he was top rate, but even top-rated neurosurgeons lost patients. All the time. It was the nature of the beast.

I held onto Kate firmly, closed my eyes, and said a silent prayer for Ethan, who had been my second father even before I married his daughter. I felt a weight of sadness in my gut over the situation. Nothing could comfort someone who was possibly losing their father. Nothing.

I knew that only too well when my own father died. No matter how distant we had been at times over politics and how I felt he could never show or tell me how much he cared for me, I knew from Ethan that he did very much. He never had a father and didn't know how to be one. I hoped to escape that fate.

No, that was wrong. I *would* escape that fate. I'd be the father to Sophie – and Liam, if I had the chance – that my father had never been to me. I'd give them more than financial security, which my own father seemed to think was all he needed to provide. I'd be their rock the way Ethan was for Kate and Heath. I'd be there, strong, sure, for their entire lives, if I had my way. And I intended to have my way.

"I'll wait until I can see Ethan in the ICU and then I'll run by the apartment and give Sophie a bottle," I said and kissed Kate's cheek. Her eyes were red, her nose a bit swollen. She forced a smile I knew she didn't feel and then glanced away quickly, as if she'd start to weep again if we looked at each other too deeply.

I led Kate back to the small seating area we had claimed in the patient waiting room and once we were back over at our little alcove, we sat for a moment, while Elaine collected her things. It was time to move to the ICU waiting room instead.

For the next half hour, I kept a vigil with Kate and Elaine in the ICU waiting room, stopping every few moments to ask the nurses when we could see Ethan.

"He'll be up in a few minutes," the nurse said to me with a sympathetic smile. "They wanted to make sure he was stable before they brought him here. He should arrive soon, but we can't predict. Every patient is unique."

"Is there a problem? Dr. Franks said surgery went well."

She checked her screen and called over to the surgical suite where Ethan had been. She spoke in a quiet voice and nodded, listening to the other person on the line.

"Thank you." Then she turned to me. "They had some problems with his blood pressure and had to treat him in the OR suite. He should be up as soon as his vitals stabilize."

"Thank you," I said and sighed, running my hand through my hair. "Please let us know if anything happens."

"We will, Dr. Morgan."

I went back to where Elaine and Kate sat, their eyes blank. "He should be here as soon as everything's stable. Sometimes, patients stay in recovery for as long as their surgery took to finish."

"There's something wrong," Kate said, her face pale. "Dr. Franks said he'd be up soon."

I shrugged, trying hard not to impart any of the anxiety I felt about Ethan. "Sometimes it takes longer," I said. "They were making sure his vitals are all stable before they transport him. He's in post-surgical recovery. Once everything is good, they'll move him here."

She nodded, but I could see the doubt in her eyes. "Maybe you could go and see Sophie now," she said. "While we wait for daddy to come here."

I nodded. "You don't want me to stay with you until he does?"

She shook her head. "No," she said. "I don't want Sophie to be away from either of us too long. She doesn't know Karen. She might be upset."

"I'll go," I said and stroked Kate's cheek, wishing I could allay her fears – about Ethan and about Sophie – but I knew I couldn't. I hoped that she and Elaine would take comfort in each other's company for the next hour while I was away checking on Sophie.

"You could call Karen and ask her how Sophie's doing," I said, preferring to stay and be with Kate in case something happened to Ethan in the next hour. "I could stay with you."

Kate was adamant. "No, please," she said. "Go and make sure Sophie is okay. I can barely stand to be away from her this long. Come right back after she's fed and happy."

I stood and bent down to kiss Elaine on the cheek. "You okay?" I asked, searching her face. "You two will be all right while I'm gone?"

"Go," she said and pasted on a smile for me. "Take care of Sophie for us. We'll be fine." She reached over and took Kate's hand and squeezed.

Then I bent down and kissed Kate on the cheek, which was still damp from her tears.

I turned to go, wishing I could stay, afraid that by the time I got back, Ethan could be gone.

ON MY WAY HOME, I got a call from Mark Dupuis, the Deputy Chair of the Board of Directors for the corporation.

"Hey, Mark," I said, frowning, wondering what he'd be calling about. "What can I do for you?"

I heard him take in a breath, like he was preparing himself for a difficult conversation. "Drake, I hate to do this to you, and I hate to be the bearer of bad news, but can you come down and meet with the Board? They've called an emergency meeting to discuss the, well, shall we say, negative publicity around the corporation."

"What?" I said and frowned, checking my watch for the time. "What negative publicity?" Then of course, I remembered. "No, forget that. I know what negative publicity." I sighed heavily and tried to figure out the proper response. "Look, normally, I'd be right there to meet with them, talk about strategy, but I have an emergency on my hands right now. I have to go to my place and feed my daughter— "

"This is a bit more important than that, Drake. I hate to say it, but this is pretty serious."

"No, I mean, my father-in-law is in New York Presbyterian. He's had a stroke and came out of the OR. He's not doing well and now is not a good time for me to be coming down for a session with the Board. Please ask them to reschedule."

"Oh, I'm sorry," Mark said quickly. "I understand. I'm sure the Board will understand but I'm also sure they want to ask you to resign from the board completely and let them manage things while this court case is ongoing."

"For Christ's sake," I said and pulled over, unable to concentrate. When I was stopped completely, I closed my eyes. "All right," I said. "You can tell them I'll withdraw for a year. Tell them to appoint whomever they decided as acting Chairman. I want to be kept up to date with any decisions they make, but I understand the necessity of this."

"Thanks, Drake. I regret having to do this, but I think it's for the best. We've had people calling from the papers asking about your role in the corporation and we've had to continually reply with 'no comment'."

"Tell the Board that I respect their need to appoint someone temporarily to take my place."

"I will, and Drake? I hope everything works out for you. For your dad and for the case."

"Me, too," I said and ended the call. Then, I wondered what he meant by the case. Did he think I was maybe guilty? For a moment, anger filled me that Lisa would do this to me.

I did nothing to her. I never led her on or made any promises. She had to have lost touch with reality. That was the only explanation for her behavior.

Why?

Did she imagine that by ruining my life and reputation that hers would be better? That she'd get off lighter when it came to sentencing? Thing is, if she insisted that I was involved and if they believed her, it would be harder on her than if she pled not-guilty by reason of insanity. Sure, she'd go to some psych hospital – maybe for years – but at least she'd get off lighter than if she was found guilty of attempted murder and conspiracy to commit murder, and spend decades in jail, or whatever the penalty ended up being.

Then, my cell rang again. It was Lara.

"Now what?" I said, my bad mood getting the better of me with my one best female friend, aside from Kate.

"You haven't read the *Herald*?"

"No," I said, angry. I finally reached the front of the apartment building, where a spot miraculously appeared as if the parking gods were feeling bad for me and opened a spot for me. "I've been at the hospital. Ethan had another stroke. He just got out of surgery and I'm going home to feed Sophia because Kate doesn't want to leave the hospital."

"Oh, Drake," she said, her voice full of sympathy. "I'm so sorry... and I hate to be the bearer of bad news..."

"You're the second person who's said that to me today. What nastiness did the venerable reporters at *The Herald* have to say about me? Let me guess – *Doctor Dom Does Dirty Deeds...*"

"No, more like *Spanking Surgeon and Submissive Sweetheart*," she said sardonically. "There's a photo of you with Lisa at a dungeon party. Or at least, it looks like you. You always wore a white shirt and black leather pants, as well as a black mask. Your shirt is open to display a nice six-pack and she's bending over in front of you."

"Oh, *God*," I said and rubbed my eyes. "We're not actually having sex, are we?"

"No, you're fully dressed, but she's bending over, and you have your hands on her hips."

"I remember that there were a few photos being taken. Derek liked to have a record of all the men she was partnered with. He'd use them later when he punished her."

"Yeah, I remember. Well, looks like Lisa turned some photos over to the press. *The Herald*, that venerable institution, decided to publish one."

"No wonder the Board at the corporation wanted to kick me off."

I heard her sigh on the other end of the line. "Oh, crap, Drake. That's too bad."

"Tell me about it. So, I'm off the Foundation and Corporation boards, I'm on a leave of absence from my Fellowship program and I'm on a leave from NYP. My father-in-law is in danger of dying and my wife has a touch of post-partum depression. What else can fuck up in my life?"

"I'm glad you and Kate finally talked about her depression.

I frowned. "Yes," I said. "I could tell that she's under stress, tired and finding it hard but I didn't recognize it as depression until you said something."

"Did she tell you she cries all the time and is afraid that Sophie will stop breathing?"

"No, she won't talk about it," I said and frowned, adrenaline flowing through me that I had misjudged Kate's mental health so much. "I knew she was tired and she does cry easily, but that's to be expected after major trauma like she had."

"Well, she needs help," Lara said. "She needs medication or some counseling to deal with everything."

I sighed heavily and sat there with my eyes closed for a moment. "Thanks for calling. I'll make sure she gets help. We have a nanny-slash-housekeeper coming in several days a week now to help. Maybe that will do. I hope..." I said and realized that if Ethan died, it would be another blow to an already delicate Kate.

"I hope that Ethan survives," Lara said softly, as if she had read my mind.

"Exactly. If he dies, and there's a fifty-fifty chance that he will based on his stats, I don't know what Kate will do."

"She's on the edge, Drake. Watch out for her."

"I will," I said and took in a deep breath. "I gotta go. I have to feed Sophie and get back to the hospital."

"Okay," she said, her voice soft. "You go and look after that beautiful baby of yours. I'll keep track of the media and let you know if anything needs attention or a response. I can be your spokesperson, if you want. Give anyone my number and I'll take care of things for you."

"Thanks," I said, feeling so tired at that moment that I felt like I could collapse in bed and sleep for hours. "I will."

I ended the call, turned off the car, and went upstairs to the apartment.

KAREN WAS WALKING AROUND with Sophie on her shoulder, moving between the stove where dinner was cooking and the counter where Sophie's bottle of breastmilk was warming in a container of hot water.

"Drake," she said with a smile. "How is everything? How is Justice McDermott?"

"He's still alive," I said and threw my coat and scarf on the back of the sofa. I went to her and took Sophie from her arms. I kissed Sophie's cool plump cheek and smiled at her. In return, she gave me a huge smile. I glanced over at Karen. "He's very sick."

She made a face. "What are his chances?"

"Fifty-fifty," I said and removed the bottle from the warm water, testing it on my wrist to see how warm it was. It was perfect so I went to the living room and sat on the sofa. I lowered Sophie into my arms and held the bottle for her. She took the nipple hungrily and sucked away, her little hand reaching up to touch the bottle. I thought that she would usually be touching Kate's breast, and felt bad that she was being bottle fed instead of being with her mother, but I was glad to be able to feed her.

"You received a few calls that went to your answering machine," Karen said, her voice soft. "I couldn't help but overhear them. Detective McDonald called as did a woman called Lara. And a Mr. Dupuis from the Board."

I nodded and met her gaze. "You know about the court case."

"Hard not to, since it's all over the papers," she said and wiped the counter.

"It's not true," I said and watched Sophia drink her milk. "She's out of touch with reality."

"I know," she said and came to stand beside the sofa, watching me feed Sophie. "Dave told me as much. Said this woman was probably suffering from erotomania."

"Something like that," I said, not wanting to talk about Lisa. "We had a brief relationship in a previous life. She imagined the rest."

"She sounds crazy," Karen said. "Delusional. Maybe bi-polar and having a manic phase, concocting fantasies about things. I've seen it before, sadly."

I nodded and pulled the bottle out of Sophie's mouth so I could burp her. I put her onto my shoulder and she did not like it one bit, arching her back and screaming at the top of her lungs. I caught Karen's eye and we both smiled.

"She loves her bottle," she said. "You're lucky you can go from breast to bottle like that with no nipple confusion. I didn't have that kind of luck, and my daughter stopped nursing completely."

Just then, Sophie let out a good solid burp and so I laid her back down again and popped the bottle back into her eager mouth. She sucked away happily once more, the redness to her face fading, her eyes heavy. She'd sleep soon.

Karen went back to the stove and continued to stir the very delicious smelling dish she was cooking. My stomach rumbled but I wanted to get back to Kate as soon as I could.

When Sophie was finished with her bottle, she gave a little squeak when the bottle came out of her mouth but I managed to slip her pacifier back into her mouth and she closed her eyes and sucked away happily. I stood and walked around with her on my shoulder, knowing that she'd soon fall asleep.

At that moment, I felt so happy, with my beautiful baby in my arms. If only Ethan was well and Kate wasn't so exhausted with new motherhood, and if only Lisa was in jail and the court case over, and if only the publicity surrounding the case was gone, I might consider myself the luckiest man in the world.

I was a lucky man, but there was going to be a lot of hell to get through in the next few hours, days and weeks.

I had to be strong for Kate.

CHAPTER 10 : KATE

The hour that Drake was away was hell.

Elaine and I sat in the waiting room, hoping to hear word that my father was on his way to ICU, but there was still no word of his transfer. I was beginning to panic even more than I had been. While Drake had said that sometimes, surgical patients have to wait in post-surgical recovery for as long as they were in surgery, most of the time they came out as soon as their vitals stabilized.

By my count, my father had already been in recovery for as long as he had been in surgery.

I went to the nursing station. "Is there any news?"

The young nurse with dark hair and a kind face gave me a sad smile. "I'm sorry Mrs. Morgan, but he's still up there. We have his ICU room ready, but he still needs more time. I promise as soon as I get any word, I'll let you know right away."

I nodded. "Thank you, and I'm sorry to keep bothering you."

"Don't mention it," she said and smiled.

I turned back to the waiting room just as Drake walked down the hall from the elevators.

He came right over to me and kissed me. "Is he here yet?"

I shook my head. "No, and there's no news."

Drake removed his coat and scarf, kissed Elaine on the cheek and then gave me a hug. "Sophie had a bottle and went down without any fuss," he said, then pulled back. "Let me go and check on things."

He left, taking the hallway to the surgical suites so he could check on my father.

"Thank God Drake's here," Elaine said, her voice soft.

"Yes," I said and sat beside her, taking her hand and squeezing. "Thank God."

We sat and waited, watching the small screen in the waiting room, which was set to a local news channel. The volume was turned down and so we watched the news feed along the bottom.

It was then I saw the headline.

Local doctor caught in murder plot mystery

"Oh, my God," I said and watched in horror as an image of Drake appeared on the television screen.

"What?" Elaine asked. I pointed wordlessly at the television. Elaine watched as well, and I saw her face fall when she read the headline. "Oh, God, those bastards."

The photo had been taken of him leaving the hospital, and he looked devastatingly handsome in his white lab coat and scrubs, his dark hair a little long. It was taken earlier in the year, since Drake hadn't been working or doing his class since the accident.

We couldn't hear what the reporter was saying but there was a new photo of Lisa, taken from court where she appeared to be charged and her bail set. She looked disheveled in her prison orange, her face ashen. Then, a photo of me, taken when I had been with Kurt outside the Doctors Without Borders event so long ago.

"Why are they doing this?" Elaine asked, shaking her head. "Drake had nothing to do with the attack."

I shrugged, although I didn't feel at all relaxed about it. "It's because of Drake's past before he met me. Anything to sell a newspaper or get more viewers, I guess."

"Couldn't Drake sue them for defamation or something? They shouldn't be allowed to run his name down in public like this."

I sighed. "Until the police put the whole story she's telling to bed, there'll probably be speculation."

"They should come out and say he had nothing to do with it," Elaine said angrily. "The woman's clearly delusional."

"I know that and you know that, and Drake knows that. Until the police do, they're going to keep this rumor alive."

I watched as the news story changed to something else and felt a sinking sensation. This was going to harm Drake – maybe permanently. People always remember the lie but usually are uninterested in learning the truth.

That's what decades of politicians had realized, using it to their advantage. The media was using it to sell copy or ad time. It sickened me, and made me feel totally helpless at the same time.

Drake arrived back about fifteen minutes later. His face was unreadable. He sat down beside me and glanced between Elaine and me.

"He's had a complication and they'll be keeping him in recovery for a little while longer. His blood pressure – they're having difficulty stabilizing it."

"But he's okay," I said, panic rising in me. "They'll give him some medication to fix it, right?"

"They're doing what they can, but it's touch and go," Drake said and looked at Elaine. "He's had another stroke. This time, it's what's called a brain stem stroke. Part of the brain that controls certain vital functions has been affected."

"What do you mean?" she replied, her face pale.

"The part of his brain that controls blood pressure. That's why they're having trouble stabilizing it. They have to go back in and treat it."

"He's going back in for more surgery?"

Drake nodded. "They'll use medication to break up the clot, but that could lead to more bleeding. I hate to tell you this, but it could go either way at this point. The damage to his brain… it may be too much."

"When can we go see him?" I asked, hoping beyond hope that I could go and hold his hand. "When will he be out of surgery? Maybe if he hears us, he'll fight."

"He's back in the OR. When he comes out, he'll be back in recovery until he stabilizes. He'll be sedated so he won't be able to hear you," Drake said, his eyes filled with sympathy. "They have to keep him sedated to give his brain time to recover from the trauma."

"Is he going to die?" I asked finally, barely able to speak because my throat was so dry. "Tell me the truth."

Drake looked at me with such an expression of pain and sadness that I knew he was trying to prepare us.

"Things are not going as well as I'd hoped and now with this new complication," he said and squeezed my hand. "He's not responding the way he should. The damage was to a part of his brain that controls blood pressure and other vital functions. If the blood flow doesn't improve, he might not survive."

"Oh, God," I said and covered my eyes, tears spilling over once more. I fought my tears, wanting to be strong, but the realization struck that my father was probably dying.

I felt Elaine's arm go around my shoulder, and sat there being consoled by the two of them. Drake held my hand, kissed it briefly, and Elaine squeezed my shoulder with affection. She seemed so calm. She'd seen a lot as a nurse and so was prepared.

"When will we know?" I looked in Drake's eyes. "How long?"

He shook his head. "It's hard to say. The next hour or two will be important. If he survives this second surgery, he'll start out at zero again. His chances improve with each passing hour. It depends on whether they can stabilize him. If not, they'll have to intubate him again."

"He didn't want to be kept alive with any heroic measures," Elaine said, her voice shaky. "He signed an advanced directive. The doctors know."

"What do you mean?" I said, horrified. "He wants to live. I'm sure of it."

"Not if it means he'll be a vegetable," Elaine said. "If the brain stem is involved, he could be locked in."

"Locked in?" I asked, frowning. I thought I knew what that meant. He would be aware of everything but unable to communicate with us.

"Locked in means he can't communicate at all," Drake said. "He can't move anything except his eyes. Sometimes, not even those."

"Ethan was clear," Elaine said softly. "If he had another stroke and it damaged his brain enough that he'd be even worse off, he wanted the doctors to not use any heroic measures. No tracheotomy. That kind of thing."

"He never said anything to me," I protested.

"He didn't want to upset you, but he knew he was at risk of another bleed so he signed an advanced directive after his first stroke."

I sat and let myself cry for a few moments, unable to deal with things any longer. Drake pulled me into his arms and held me, letting me cry on his shoulder.

Elaine wiped her own eyes as she prepared for the worst.

WE SPENT the next hour like that, the three of us silent, watching the news. I hoped that the story about Drake didn't come back on, but if it did, we missed it and I heaved a sigh of relief. I didn't want that whole mess to come and plague us while we were in the hospital.

Finally, after about ninety minutes, Dr. Franks came to where we sat and pulled up a chair. His face was calm as he removed his cap. He didn't look sad.

"Just thought I'd update you about how Ethan is doing."

I met his eyes, and didn't see anything bad in them so my hopes rose.

"Ethan has come out of surgery and is now back in recovery. We had to perform what's called an embolectomy. We threaded a thin catheter into his brain to remove the clot and restore blood flow to his brain stem. He seems to have survived the procedure pretty well so far. The next couple of hours will be key. We're going to keep him sedated, but you can go in and see him now if you want. His vital signs have stabilized enough that we're moving him to ICU. He should be in his room within thirty minutes. You can go in one at a time and then he needs to be kept quiet for the next twenty-four hours. I'd advise you to go home, get some rest. It's going to be a long night."

"Thank God," I said and covered my face, my relief so strong that I felt a bit faint.

"He'll have a long period of recovery but if he survives the next few hours, I have hope that he'll do well. The stroke was caused by a small clot from the earlier surgery."

I nodded and Drake stood when the surgeon did, and the two colleagues shook hands.

"Thanks," Drake said. "I appreciate everything you're doing for my father."

"No problem," Dr. Franks said and smiled before leaving us alone in the small alcove.

"Shall we go get some tea or a bite to eat?" Drake asked.

I nodded and checked my watch. My stomach rumbled, telling me that it was time to eat something.

"I'll stay here," Elaine said. "Bring me back a tea and sandwich, will you? Turkey or ham. Whatever they have that looks decent."

"We will." We stood and walked down the hallway, taking a maze of stairs and passages to get to the cafeteria where several dozen staff and visitors sat, chatting and eating their meals.

Once we had chosen our drinks and food, we carried them on trays to a table where we sat and ate, saying little because we were both so exhausted. While we were sitting there, I noticed several of the nursing staff glancing over our way, no doubt because they knew who Drake was.

I wondered if they were merely remembering him from the time he was on staff or whether it was recent news coverage. I glanced at one of the television screens that hung in the corner of the room and saw that the channel was turned to a news station.

Had they seen the news cast with the photo of Drake?

I felt a lump in my throat. Should I tell Drake? Or should I let him eat his meal in peace? He had enough on his plate without having to confront the nasty rumors that were going to be circulating that he'd conspired with Lisa to kill me.

How could anyone who knew Drake believe that he would do such a thing? It was impossible...

"People are looking at us," Drake said, catching my eye over his forkful of pasta salad.

"I know," I said with a sigh. I hated having to tell him about it, but apparently, I had no choice. "There was a news report on the case. They had a photo of you..."

He put down his fork and I heard him exhale heavily. "On television?"

I pushed food around on my plate, suddenly not hungry any more. "Yes," I said. "On the local news."

"What did they say?"

"Only that you were 'embroiled' in an attempted murder case from a hit and run earlier in the year. They said your ex-girlfriend and 'submissive' sex partner in a kinky relationship had driven the car and it wasn't clear yet if you were a suspect. They showed a picture of you leaving the hospital in your scrubs and then one of Lisa in an orange jump suit. That was all I caught."

"She isn't my ex-girlfriend so they got that wrong. I expected as much." Drake put down his fork and looked at me intensely. "You know there's no truth to it, right?"

"*Drake*," I said, surprised that he'd even have to say it. I reached out and took his hand in mine. "Of course not. I *know* you despised having to continue dealing with her. You told me everything. That's what I told the police. They should be laughing Lisa out of the interrogation room instead of keeping you on their radar. Why would you even say that? Do you think I would even suspect it for a moment?"

He shook his head and glanced around the room, as if looking to see if anyone could overhear. "The police always look at the husband first, or boyfriend or ex. They're the most likely culprit when a woman is murdered or if there's an attempted murder. It's almost never a woman or disgruntled ex-girlfriend. Plus, there's those letters..."

"Those letters are fakes," I said and squeezed his hand. "Besides, I know you. They don't know you and they don't know me. They don't know our relationship. The police must follow procedure. Once they do, I know they'll write you off as a suspect."

He pulled my hand up to his lips and kissed my knuckles. "I love you, Kate."

I smiled at him, the tenderness in his voice making my throat tighten. "I love you, Drake. We'll get through this."

"We will," he said, "but we may have to start new lives somewhere else, if my reputation is harmed enough."

"Don't say that," I said. "Anyone who knows you knows that you're a stellar person and highly skilled neurosurgeon. A great humanitarian. Look at your foundation. Look at all the time you spent in Africa. All the money you raised and donated... How could they think you're a murderer? Why would they treat you like one?"

He looked down at his plate and moved his food around some more. "People can turn on you in an instant. I found that out with Maureen."

He glanced up and we locked eyes. "I'll never turn on you nor will your true friends," I said softly, emotion making my voice hoarse.

His eyes moved over my face. "How is it that I'm so lucky to have met and won you? How?" He kissed my knuckles once more and smiled at me.

He glanced around and I did as well, catching a few people quickly look away. They'd been watching us, and I felt glad that they saw us being affectionate with each other. That would show them what our relationship was really like.

"I hate that they're all watching us like vultures. Let's take our food and go back to the waiting room. I'll take the trays out."

I nodded and collected up the plastic containers with our sandwiches and Drake's pasta salad. I had a cardboard carrier for our tea and coffee and Drake carried the trays to the dishwashing station and left them on the line.

"Let's go," he said when he came back to me, his arm around my shoulder. He leaned down and kissed me. Just then, I caught someone with their cell phone held up, taking a picture – or video – of us. When I turned and stared at the woman, she hastily put the cell away.

"What was she doing?" Drake said, his voice affronted. "Was she taking a video?"

"Or photos," I said. He started to go towards her but I grabbed his arm. "Don't," I said softly. "Don't make it worse. It's good they got a picture of us kissing."

Drake glared at the woman but then he must have thought better of it and turned back, pulling me against him one last time.

WHEN WE ARRIVED BACK at the waiting area, Elaine smiled and took the tea and sandwich.

"You look upset," she said to Drake, who sat on the other side of me, his arm over the back of my chair.

"Some people recognized Drake in the cafeteria," I said and made a face, raising my eyebrows, hoping to signal to Elaine we shouldn't talk too much about it. "They took a video or picture of us kissing."

"I can't believe it," she said, her mouth open. "People have no respect for privacy anymore. Not with all these cell phones and Snap Chats and the like. It's none of their business."

"The news has made it their business, I guess," Drake said and pointed up at the screen on the wall.

I glanced at it and saw that the very same news report was being repeated. It was short and only featured a scandalous headline, and a picture side by side of Drake and Lisa. I was glad we couldn't hear what she said.

"Goddammit," Drake said, his voice choked. "I'm going to call Detective

McDonald and ask that he clear my name publicly so all this speculation will stop."

Elaine held out her hand. "Don't Drake," she said, shaking her head quickly. "That would make things worse. Believe me. The police will either charge you or they'll clear you as a suspect soon. Until then, anything you do will only delay things. Keep a low profile."

Drake's fists clenched and I could see a muscle twitch in his jaw. I rarely saw him angry about anything, so it was hard to watch him feel so much negative emotion. Usually, he was so positive about everything.

I felt frustrated myself. I knew there was no way Drake had been involved. Why couldn't the police figure it out?

Lisa must be spinning a pretty convincing story for them to keep Drake on the suspect list – if he was even on it. It was those damn letters. Still, someone at the police department must have spoken to the news reporter about the case for them to know the details. I felt like calling up Detective McDonald myself and speaking with him, to find out what they thought.

"Lara will take care of this," Drake said, his voice low. He turned to me. "She knows the procedures. She'll talk to the Assistant DA and find out what the hell's going on."

I nodded. "Thank God for Lara."

For the next hour and a half, we sat in the alcove and watched the news. The report came back on again and luckily, Drake had a magazine in hand and didn't see the feed, but it was pretty much a repeat of the previous news story. I decided to go to the desk and ask if we could change the channel.

The nurse looked up at me, smiling sweetly. "Sure," she said. "Let me get the remote. We don't want the volume up so we don't bother any patients or other family members. There's a more comfortable lounge down the hall if you want. You can close the doors and turn up the volume."

I shook my head. "We want to stay close to where my father will be, so we'll be fine here. I want to change the channel."

I took the remote and changed the channel, flipping through the selections until I came to the National Geographic Channel, which had a show on birds in the Amazon. It would be a peaceful alternative to the local news and its endless repeat.

Finally, the nurse came over to us to tell us my father had been brought to his ICU room from post-surgical recovery and we could go in and see him as soon as he was settled.

"He's breathing on his own and his blood pressure has stabilized," she said, glancing between Drake and me, and then to Elaine. "He'll probably be sleepy and may go in and out, so don't expect too much at first, but he should wake up over the next hour or two. You can go in one at a time, and please, no longer than five minutes each at first." She smiled at us.

Drake nodded. "Don't worry," he said. "We'll go easy on him."

When she left, the three of us looked at each other.

"You should go first," I said to Elaine.

She shook her head. "No, dear," she said softly. "You go first. He's your father."

"Thank you," I said and took in a deep breath, steeling myself for what I'd see when I went into his room. I turned to Drake, who was looking at me intensely.

"He might be pretty pale and he'll have a bandage on his head from the surgery," Drake said. "He may not be able to speak at first, so don't be upset if he's quiet or doesn't seem to be able to talk. It'll take a few hours for him to get over the anesthetic."

"Okay," I said doubtfully, my gut tight at the thought he'd been so close to death. "I'll go in. Can I give him anything to drink or ice chips?"

"He may have problems swallowing at first because of the airway during surgery. If you have any questions, ask the nurse. If you're concerned about anything, use the call button, but they'll be watching him very closely for the first few hours."

I took in a deep breath and walked down the hall to the room where my father was being kept. It was narrow, with a large window, and had banks of telemetry surrounding him. There was a quiet beep-beep-beep from one machine and he was receiving oxygen through a thin plastic tube with a cannula that threaded around his nose. At least he didn't need a mask.

His eyes were closed, his bed was raised slightly, and one arm had a blood pressure cuff on it. A thick white bandage circled his head. He looked so fragile and so unlike the father of my memories, strong and firm, in charge of everything.

I went to the side of the bed and took his hand in mine.

"Hi, Daddy," I said and leaned over, kissing him on the cheek. "It's me, Kate."

I squeezed his hand and he squeezed back, but his eyes remained closed and I wondered if he was still too sedated to speak.

"Drake and Elaine and I are here," I said, tears starting in my eyes once more. "We have a new doula – nurse named Karen who's looking after Sophie for us. We've been waiting for you to come out of surgery. The surgeon told us that everything went well, and now all you have to do is recover and regain your strength."

I wiped the tears from my cheeks, and stood there, watching him, surrounded by machines and the sound of oxygen. If that was all I could do, I was happy. I checked the clock on the wall, and saw that I'd already been there for three minutes.

"We're only allowed to stay for five minutes at a time, so I have to go, but I wanted you to know," I said and then had to stop, my throat constricting. "I wanted you to know that I love you," I said, tears spilling down my cheeks once more. "You've been a wonderful father."

That was all I could say, as I started to cry in earnest at that, squeezing his hand and wanting him to know how I felt.

His face changed slightly, almost like a smile and his lips moved. I couldn't hear what he was trying to say, so I leaned closer, my ear next to him.

"I love you," I think I heard him say. Then, "Be happy."

I leaned down and kissed his cheek once more. "I'll try," I said. "I am happy."

Of course, that made me think of how unhappy I'd been for the past weeks after the attack and after I came out of the hospital. How anxious I'd been, how tired and how afraid I was of every little thing going wrong. Now, here I was in the ICU with my father, who could have died. Who still could die...

I realized at that moment how lucky I was. How much love I had – from my father, from Drake, and now, from Sophie. My heart filled up with so much emotion at that moment that I sobbed out loud. My father squeezed my hand once more and I tried to hold it in, not wanting to lose control in front of him. Finally, I checked the clock once more and realized I had overstayed my five minutes.

"I have to go," I said and squeezed his hand once more. "I'll be back later."

I leaned down and kissed his cheek once more and let go of his hand, wiping my eyes on the sleeves of my sweater, trying to get hold over my emotions.

I left the room and was met by Drake, who pulled me immediately into his arms.

"Oh, Katie," he whispered in my ear, kissing my cheek and neck. Elaine touched my arm and went past us into the room. Drake led me back to the small alcove and we stood in each other's arms while I recovered my composure.

"I spoke with the nurse," Drake said and pulled back, wiping my cheeks with the backs of his fingers. "She said your father is doing quite well, all things considered. We can go home and they'll call us if anything happens in the night."

"I don't want to leave," I said and looked into Drake's eyes.

"Sophie needs you," Drake said softly. "Your father is in the very best of hands."

I rested my head on Drake's shoulder and closed my eyes, not wanting to leave my father, but realizing that I had to go back home to my baby, who needed me as well. My father knew I loved him. Sophie needed to know that I did as well.

"Okay," I said. "After your visit."

Then we sat down and waited for Elaine to come out. When she did, Drake left the two of us in the alcove and went in to see my father for himself. Elaine was very composed when she returned from seeing my father. She sat beside me and took my hand.

"He's doing quite well," she said and smiled. "You should go home and feed that baby of yours. How are your breasts?"

I smiled and slipped a hand up to feel one. "Rock hard," I said. "I forgot to express."

"Sophie will be hungry and will drain you," Elaine said. "You two go. I'll be fine here. I'll check out the lounge. The nurse said there's a recliner chair there I can sleep in if I want. When he's a little more stable, they'll move it into your father's room so I can sleep with him."

"That's good," I said and smiled, feeling a little better that my father wouldn't be alone for the whole night. Even though he'd spend most of it sleeping off his anesthetic, I didn't like the idea of him being all alone with those tubes and wires and machines surrounding him. Drake returned and I could see the tears in his eyes, despite the fact he smiled when he saw us.

"He's doing well," Drake said and sat beside me. He took my hand and smiled. "He told me to go home, so we better follow his orders."

"Did he actually say that to you?" I asked, surprised.

"Yes," Drake said with a soft laugh. "I squeezed his hand and told him to get better because he was my only father. He said, 'Go home.'"

I smiled and nodded. "We should go. Elaine will be able to take the reclining chair into his room later."

Drake squeezed my hand. "Sophie needs to be fed from her momma," he said and stood. "I'll get our coats and talk to the nurses before we go." He left us in the alcove and I stood up and hugged Elaine.

"Call us if anything happens," I said, my fatigue catching up with me finally. "We can be here in fifteen minutes."

"I will. You go home to that baby and sleep."

We kissed and I went to the nursing station where Drake was standing with our coats in hand. The nurses smiled at me and then the two of us left the ward, on our way home to our baby.

~

CHAPTER 11 : DRAKE

ater, when I saw Kate in the slider feeding Sophie, Sophie's little hand on Kate's breast and nursing happily, I finally felt that all was right with my little world.

Finally.

I'd been on edge all day due to Ethan's surgery and near-death experience. The news reports about the attempted murder case didn't help, especially the suggestion that I had been involved with Lisa and had encouraged her to try to kill Kate so the two of us could be together.

I'd wanted to punch someone, and I was not prone to fits of violence.

Now, with Ethan stable, and with Kate seemingly willing to leave him at the hospital in the care of the staff, and now with her feeding Sophie with such a look of contentment in her eyes, I felt I could relax.

My life was truly blessed to have the two of them – and Ethan – in my life.

I went to the kitchen and thanked Karen for staying to reheat our supper before she left for the night.

"You don't know how much of a Godsend you've been to us," I said and walked her out of the apartment, handing her the bag she brought with her. "I know that Kate felt completely secure with you caring for Sophie so that was a big load off her shoulders."

"I hope everything works out for your father-in-law," Karen said and squeezed my arm. "I'll be over tomorrow so you both can go up and see him. Sophie's a very easy baby, considering all she's been through."

"She is."

We said our goodbyes and I went back to Sophie's bedroom to watch while Kate deftly slipped Sophie's pacifier back into her mouth and laid her down in her crib. She'd fallen asleep on the breast, as she did almost all the time at night, and was now sleeping on her side, her little fists clenched and by her face, her back arched, sucking away on her pacifier.

Kate turned to me and smiled. We tiptoed out of the room and I closed the door softly behind me after taking one last glance at my sleeping baby girl. She was so beautiful, so precious – even more so since we almost lost her and Kate. Had I not hired the security staff, and had the man not been there to administer first aid, Kate or Sophie – or both – could have died.

Kate laid a hand on my shoulder and leaned up to kiss me on the cheek. I smiled and then kissed her back, lightly, on the cheek.

"I'm going to have a shower," she said and held a hand over her yawn. "It's been a rough day and I need to go to bed now."

"Sure," I said and nodded, rubbing her shoulder with affection. "You go right ahead. I'm going to check my mail. I'll be up later."

She left me in the hallway, on her way to our master suite and the bathroom. I went to my office and sat at my desk and opened my email, checking to see what messages I'd received and whether there was any news from Lara.

Sure enough, there was an email from her. I opened it, a knot of anxiety in my gut.

To: Morgan, Drake MD
Reply-To: MistressLara
Re: The Case
Drake:

Hope things are better re: Ethan. I'm sure this is just one more thing that you don't need to think about, so I'm doing it for you. I've done some sleuthing and spoke with GaryM, whom you will remember from our days at Yonkers. He is a close friend of Derek Richardson, who apparently moved to Singapore to start a new business. I tried to reach out to Derek, but he's not involved in the local community and I have no contact info. GaryM recalls that Lisa was causing problems back in the day when you topped her a couple of times. In fact, she kept pushing to have you involved in their regular play, but Derek refused. He could see she was not truly submitting and was trying to force the issue so they broke up, quietly. Derek felt bad but still wanted to warn others. Word got around to male Dominants in his network that she was not safe and so she had some difficulty finding experienced partners. The reason you weren't informed was that you were already known as a soft Dom and would not be a match for someone like Lisa.

Apparently, she did some switching after she and Derek broke up, trained a while with JohnG, (the guy who liked breath play – remember with the silly dyed blonde tips?) and then she subbed to a newcomer to the community, MasterMikeFromJersey. I can't find any contact info on him right now and he seems to have left the community. No trace of him and no way to find out who he is so I can interview him to see how Lisa was with him. I expect the detectives involved in the case (McDonald?) will be in touch again soon to get your alibi for those days. Will send you whatever I find out. Don't be too worried. Most of the time, the cops are on the right track in a case like this and can see Lisa for what she is – a fucked-up woman who was obsessed and couldn't take no for an answer. Later…

I responded immediately.

To: MistressLara
    Reply to: Morgan, Drake MD
    Re: Re: The Case

Lara – thanks for all the work you're doing on my behalf. I truly appreciate it. Ethan is stable now, so we're at home and Kate will be going to sleep. I'll be up for a while trying to get a few details of my exit from public life settled. If you want to call, I'll be up for a while. Too hyped up to sleep. Cheers, Drake.

I SENT off the email and waited, wondering if she was up and would call, or whether she had already signed off for the night. Sure enough, my phone rang and I checked the display to see it was Lara.

I answered. "Hey," I said, glad to her hear voice. "Thanks for calling."

"No problem, Drake. You know I feel responsible for you. I feel responsible for this whole mess, since it was me who hooked you up with Lisa and Derek in the first place."

"Don't feel that way," I said and rubbed my temples. "I wanted to get some exposure, and you know everyone who is anyone in the community."

"I didn't know Lisa well enough," she said, her voice sounding tired. "I know Derek and he's pretty solid."

I frowned, wondering why I hadn't heard of him leaving New York. "When did he leave for Singapore? I don't remember hearing about him moving."

"I have no idea," Lara said. I heard her flipping through some papers. "Sometime in the past few months. Since the accident, I think."

"Yeah," I said, remembering the text I got from him when I first realized Lisa was in the fellowship program. "I got a text from him last year after I started my fellowship at NYU. He didn't mention anything about it. I emailed him for some info on Lisa but I haven't heard back yet."

"He's a pretty free spirit," Lara said. "From what I heard, he put the mansion on the market, and there was a feature article on it in the New York Times real estate section, if I recall correctly. Once it sold, he left for Singapore. Haven't heard from him since. I called the Ritz but there's no record of him there so I'm not sure he stayed. Maybe went somewhere else in Malaysia. His former partner said he always wanted to relocate there and focus his business in the Asian market."

"It sure would help to know what he thought about Lisa's stability," I said, leaning back in my chair and exhaling slowly. "I'm going to try to write out a list of all the functions I've gone to in the last three years. I have pretty much everything in my planner, so I'll have something to work on to counter Lisa's claims that we were seeing each other secretly."

"That's a good idea," Lara said and I could hear hesitation in her voice.

"Lara," I said, softly, deliberately calmly. "Should I be worried about this?"

There was a pause on her end and that told me everything. "You did nothing wrong, Drake. You weren't seeing her. You never wrote those letters. There'd be no reason for you to keep it secret from me. I know everything about your past because I arranged it all. You would have told me if you were seeing Lisa."

"I would have," I said. "I only met my submissives through you."

"That's right. The cops may be on the wrong track for a while, but I'm sure they'll see the light soon."

With that, I sighed heavily, feeling like I needed to go for a run to work off some of my excess energy. The fact I hadn't had sex for months didn't help matters.

"What's the sigh about?"

"I need to go for a run," I said and shifted in my chair. "Hyped up tonight."

"Kate still not back to normal?" Lara said lightly. I knew what she meant.

"Not yet," I replied. "She's starting to feel better physically. I imagine once we know how Ethan's doing, she might be able to truly relax again. Things will get back to normal. Don't worry about me."

"I do worry about you, Drake. You're like my little brother."

"Ha!" I said with a laugh. "Some little brother, considering…"

"Yeah, I know. Maybe a stepbrother. Anyway, you have a good run. I'll talk to you tomorrow."

"Goodbye," I said and ended the call. I turned back to the screen and closed my email down then went to the bedroom and changed out of my clothes and into my sweats. The water was still running in the bathroom, so Kate was having a nice long shower.

I left a sticky note on the door to the bedroom with a hastily written note to Kate so she knew I was out for a run. I pulled on a light jacket and tied my running shoes and left the building, running down 8th Avenue on my usual route.

As I ran, I tried to focus on my technique, my stride, my breathing, my general form. I wanted to blank my mind of all the problems in my day – the case, Kate's trauma, Ethan, Lisa, but of course, my focus drifted from the pace I was keeping to my conversation with Lara. So, Lisa had been known as a bit of a problem... She'd asked that I be included in more of their play, but Derek had thought it best to let me take the lead. When she insisted, they broke up. She'd done some switching, training to be a part-time Domme? That suggested she wasn't entirely happy with being a submissive. That was fine – some people enjoyed taking both roles in their BDSM play, but with Lisa, it suggested to me that she was confused and unhappy. If Derek had broken up with her, ended their relationship because of her problems accepting his dominance, she might have been confused and thought of me as someone she could turn to. I was known as a lightweight in the community. Maybe she thought I'd be more flexible...

We hardly spoke when we were together back at Derek's mansion in Yonkers. It wasn't as if we had a social relationship and got to know each other personally. I topped her. That was pretty much the extent of our interaction, other than sitting down and talking beforehand about limits. She seemed to have none, and had been willing to do pretty much anything.

She was a mindless pastime to me and a chance to practice my rope technique.

If anything, Derek and I spent more time talking about mutual interests. He was a business man, wealthy from a family business like my father's business, although his was in some kind of specialized tools for building. He inherited his business from his father, as I did the corporation, so we had a lot in common. After we met via Lara, he became a wealthy donor to the Foundation.

I'd call Dave in the morning and see if he had any record of recent donations from Derek's corporation so we could get in contact with him about Lisa. I wanted to know what Derek thought about her, and what she'd said about me. I could at least know where things went wrong. I might be able to help prepare for any charges that might come against me.

I hoped, as I ran through the streets, that Lara was right – once the police had a clearer picture of who Lisa was, they'd know that she was mentally unbalanced and unreliable. Then, they'd stop looking at me as a potential accomplice and realize that I was totally innocent and a victim of her madness. I hoped that Lara could check the list of events Lisa claimed we met in secret so I could counter her claims. I knew that might be difficult. How could I prove that I didn't meet and have sex with her in the broom closet at an event we were both at?

The only way would be to have witnesses that saw me the entire time. I didn't usually use the washroom during a performance, but there had been times when my pager would go off in my pocket and I'd have to leave to take a call. My patients might have complications after a difficult surgery so I would respond, leave the event and return to the hospital to care for them. If I didn't have to leave, but consult, I would return to my place in the auditorium or theater. There was no way I could prove I didn't meet Lisa in the alley for a quickie, much as I had been with Kate that night at Carnegie Hall.

When I was finished with my run, I returned to my neighborhood and walked down the street towards the apartment. I glanced up at the windows and saw Kate standing in the kitchen with Sophia on her shoulder. Sophie must have woken up and needed another feed or change.

When I arrived inside, after taking off my running shoes, I went to the kitchen. Kate was speaking on the phone and turned when she heard me.

"Okay, thanks for calling," she said, her face pale. "Yes, I'm pleased to hear it. I'll see you tomorrow morning."

She ended the call and laid the cell on the island countertop. "That was Elaine," she said and patted Sophie on the back, who was now sleeping, her eyes closed tightly. "The phone rang and woke her up so I picked her up."

"What did Elaine have to say?" I asked softly, going over to them and bending down to kiss Sophie on her plump soft cheek.

"My father's awake and doing much better," she said and smiled, her eyes filling with tears of relief. "He was even cracking jokes."

I smiled at her. "That's a good sign."

"It is," Kate said and rubbed Sophie's back. Then, I followed her upstairs to Sophie's bedroom. Kate laid Sophie down in the bed and then leaned down to kiss her cheek, tucking the blanket around her. I followed suit and then the two of us stood and watched her for a moment, as we usually did. I was sure Kate felt as I did – amazed that this beautiful child was ours.

Kate left first, opening the door slowly so the sound didn't wake Sophie. I followed her out of the room and then made my way to our room to the master suite so I could have a shower.

"I'll be out in a minute," I said as Kate stood in the bedroom door watching me. "I need a shower after that run."

I stripped off my sweats and turned on the shower, waiting until it was nice and steamy before stepping in. Then, I lathered my hands and began to wash myself off, starting at my hair and working my way down. I was busy soaping my toes when the glass door to the shower opened and Kate stood there, naked, her eyes half lidded.

"May I join you?" she said softly.

I stood up and ran my hands under the stream of water to rinse off the soap. "You don't ever have to ask."

She entered the shower and stood next to me, the water running over her body, wetting her hair, her eyelashes, and then streaming over her shoulders and over her very ample breasts. While I watched, her nipples grew hard and my body responded like some teenage boy who hadn't been kissed before, my dick thickening, blood pulsing through my veins.

I looked in her eyes, hoping to see an invitation in them to do more than look at her longingly. Although I would usually initiate sex, I wanted her to invite me to touch her, to kiss her, to make love to her. I needed her fiercely, aching to lie on top of her and fill her up with my cock.

Instead, she stepped closer and placed her hand behind my head, pulling me down to her mouth for a kiss. That was all the invitation I needed. I kissed her deeply, then began to kiss her neck, dying to take her nipple into my mouth, but she stopped me.

"Here," she said and handed me a bar of soap. "I'd like it if you washed me off first."

"You don't have to ask me twice," I said, my voice thick with desire. I took the soap and lathered it between my hands, working up some nice slick suds which I then used to wash every inch of her body. Her delicious, curvaceous, bountiful body. My hands were shaking when I finally slid them over her shoulders from her neck to her breasts. Since Sophie had been born and nursed, I felt as if Kate's breasts belonged to her, and rightfully so, but now, they were mine.

I loved Kate's breasts, delirious from their heavy weight in my hand, the way her nipple responded to my touch. Usually light pink, they were darker now because of hormones, and they made my dick incredibly hard as they responded to my touch.

"You're so beautiful," I murmured against her neck when I bent down to kiss her.

She gasped when my mouth closed around one nipple, her back arching. At first, I worried that she'd be unresponsive because of being so focused on being a mother and nursing Sophie, but she was responsive. Very responsive, her eyes closing, her head falling back as I squeezed one breast in my hand and sucked on the nipple of the other breast.

She had recently nursed Sophie so was empty and we were uninterrupted by any milk leakage, which I was afraid would embarrass Kate. I moved very quickly from her breasts to her belly, which I kissed after the soap rinsed off in the stream of water. Below, her neatly trimmed thatch of pubic hair made my dick throb even harder. I loved it when she shaved, so I could see every-thing, but this was so primal. I slipped my fingers between her lips and stroked, the soap slippery. She spread her thighs so I could rinse her off, and then I pushed her gently back, lifting her thigh over one of my shoulders. She gripped the handrail in the shower and closed her eyes once more. Then, I covered her labia with my mouth, my tongue circling her clit softly.

"Oh, God," she groaned. When I slipped my fingers inside of her, stroking her firmly, sucking on her clit, I felt her spasm around them, her body shaking. "Oh, God, I'm coming already…"

"It's been a long time," I said with a smile. Then I kept licking her very lightly as her orgasm crested, her body trembling. I could feel her clit vibrate against my tongue and enjoyed the sight of her standing above me, her nipples hard as rocks, her belly muscles tight.

When she was finished, I stood and leaned over her as she recovered, smiling down at her. My dick was hard, throbbing, dripping with cum I was so ready, but I enjoyed watching her recover.

"I need you again," she said when her eyes opened. "Right away."

"I'm at your service," I said, unable to keep from laughing I was so pleased that my Katherine, my very aroused Katherine, was back and needy enough to ask, to demand. "See this?" I said and grabbed my cock, rubbing it over her pussy. "It's yours. Fuck me. Any way you want."

"I want to ride you on the bed."

"Your wish is my command," I said and turned off the water. Kate grabbed a towel off the rack, but I took it from her. "No," I said and took her hand, pulling her directly to the bed. "We don't have to dry off." Then, I crawled onto the bed and laid on my back, my hands held out to her. "Come and sit on my cock and fuck me until you come again."

She did, crawling on top of me, her eyes filled with need, her breath coming in short gasps she was so aroused. She laid her hands on my shoulders and as I held my cock for her, she slid onto it with a long slow gasp of pleasure.

"Oh, that feels so good…" she murmured, her eyes closed.

Then, she rode me, her breasts bobbing in my face as I helped her, my hands on her hips. I slipped a hand down and stroked my thumb over her clit as she thrust up and down on my cock. It took longer than her first orgasm, but it was even more shattering when she came, her face contorted in pleasure, her body shaking, quivering as she impaled herself on my cock. I sucked one nipple and then the other, trying to add to her pleasure and she shuddered, her mouth open, her eyes half-lidded.

Finally, she collapsed onto me, unable to maintain her position. On my part, I was smiling, my dick hard and deep inside of her. I wanted to enjoy the way her body pulsed with pleasure as her orgasm waned, her pussy clenching around my cock rhythmically.

I expected that she'd be ecstatic, as I was, but she wasn't. She was crying. I frowned and pulled away, trying to see her face, but she fought to keep hidden. When I rolled her over and leaned over her body, my thighs on either side of her hips, prying her hands away from her face, she finally made eye contact.

"What's the matter?" I asked, breathless, confused. "Why are you crying?"

She shook her head and then smiled. "I'm happy."

I finally came back to my senses. Of course, she was happy. Happy to be back as the old Kate. The Kate who loved sex and was easy to arouse and orgasm.

"I'm happy, too," I said and nuzzled her neck, my grin huge. "Believe me."

She laughed at that, understanding what I meant. I'd had the proverbial blue balls for months. Now, I might go back to being a man with a healthy sex life as well as a beautiful wife and baby.

"I was so afraid," she said, her expression serious, her brow knitted.

"What were you afraid of?" I asked, confused. "You didn't have a vaginal birth so there'd be no scar to hurt."

She shook her head. "I was afraid I'd spray you in the eye or something."

I laughed so hard at that, collapsing on top of her. The mental image that elicited was delightful, but I felt sorry for Kate, that she was so worried about her breasts leaking during orgasm.

"You were nearly empty so there was no pressure built up," I said and met her eyes. "Besides, some men would pay very richly to experience it." I wagged my eyebrows suggestively.

"Gross!" Kate said and grimaced. "It's embarrassing."

"It's *not* gross," I said. "At least not to those men who find it profoundly erotic. Although I have no predilection for being sprayed with breast milk during sex, some men love it." I took her hands in mine and leaned over her, looking into her eyes now that we were both calmer, the giggles having ended. "Women are our goddesses. You are *my* goddess. Nothing about your body is gross or should be embarrassing to you."

She finally relaxed, and maybe actually believed me. It was the truth. There was nothing about Kate or her body or her bodily functions that disgusted me or put me off wanting to have sex with her or sleep with her or do anything with her.

Nothing.

She was my goddess and I'd be happy to spend the rest of my life worshipping her and making her happy.

"I love you, Mrs. Morgan," I said, my voice soft. "Every inch of you."

"I love you, Dr. Morgan," she replied, a tiny hint of humor in her voice. "Every hard inch of you." Then she clenched her body around my semi-erect cock and I groaned, it felt so good. "Speaking of hard inches, what are you going to do with that?"

She squeezed around me once more and that was all the encouragement I needed to begin thrusting, slowly, deliberately, inside of her. Then, I had the idea of making her come once more. I knew I could do it, so I pulled out and began nuzzling her breasts, nipping at her until her nipples hardened.

"Drake…" she said, her voice soft. "Again?"

"Yes," I said, my voice firm. "Again. I've been sorely deprived of your orgasms. I need more."

She sighed as I licked my way down her body. "You can make me orgasm as many times as you want. My body is yours."

"It is," I said, trying to sound all Domish for a change. "And I'm going to make you come again."

So I did.

◦

AFTERWARDS, we lay with our arms around each other and snuggled, our bodies warm and still damp after the shower.

"I need another shower," Kate said and smiled up at me. "Care to join me?"

I laughed and pulled her closer. "If I see you all naked and wet again, there's no telling what I might do."

"Three orgasms are enough for me," she said with a smile. "If you want another, my body is yours."

I wagged my eyebrows. "I may have to take you again in the shower from behind."

That thought sent a jolt to my dick, which thickened once more.

Kate crept out of the bed and I followed her. We stood together in the shower and let the water slide over us. The feel of her soft wet body against mine aroused me once more and so I did what I suggested and turned her around, had her spread her thighs and arms, and I took her from behind, one hand holding her hip, the other covering her hand, which was splayed on the tile wall.

I did nothing to arouse her, knowing that she liked the idea of me using her body like that. It was the submissive part of her, desiring to be my object of pleasure and I wasn't going to argue with her, even though more and more we were becoming equals in the bedroom. I wanted her happiness and she wanted mine.

We'd work it out.

◦

CHAPTER 12 : KATE

My father slowly recovered over the next few days, and I spent as many hours as I could at the hospital without depriving Sophie too much of my company or breast. Drake and I took shifts, and I made sure to express breast milk when I was able so we had an extra supply for when Drake was at home with Sophie. Karen came over as well, for several hours each day, to let the two of us visit my dad in the hospital and cook a meal for us.

His progress was slow but steady, and soon, they had him sitting up on the side of the bed, then in his wheelchair. When he was well enough, they discharged him home, with a home care nurse to look after him and help Elaine with his care. On her part, Elaine rented a hospital bed and cleared out the living room so it could be converted to a hospital room. This way, my father could be in the living room with her and the two of them could watch television.

When he was well enough, over the next month, they hired physiotherapists to help him with his rehabilitation. He had lost some more function on his one side, and was not going to be able to walk any longer, but he was surprisingly positive.

"I like this chair," he said to me one afternoon when I came over with Sophia and Drake. "It has all the bells and whistles. I can use my good hand to move this joystick and it has great wheels that can go from hardwood to carpet to tile. "

"That's good, Daddy," I said and smiled as he demonstrated, turning his chair in a tight circle, going back and forth, a huge grin on his face. "I'll get one of those heavy-duty ones in the spring so I can go outside and terrorize 5th Avenue."

"You're so bad," I said with a laugh and leaned down to kiss his cheek.

I sat down on the sofa and he stopped the chair across from me, serious for a change.

"I've decided to write my memoir," he said, and I could tell he was trying to sound causal. "My days in Vietnam. My early days as an attorney. My time on the court."

"That's great," I said with a smile. "You could get a dictation software program and you wouldn't have to worry about hunting and pecking."

"That's a great idea," he said his eyes widening. "I was going to ask Elaine if she'd do dictation. She learned all that when she was in high school taking a business course, but I think the dictation thing might be an even better idea." He grinned for a moment. "I'm sure Elaine would prefer it to listening to me hem and haw as I try to remember my days in 'Nam."

"I'm sure Elaine would find it terribly interesting," I said.

"I already regaled her with all my tales," he said with a shrug.

"I'll get you Dragon Naturally Speaking," I replied and nodded, deciding then and there that I'd supervise my father's memoir writing project. "I can come over and help you get it set up and help you train your dragon."

"Train my dragon?" he said and laughed. "That sounds awfully hard for an old non-technical guy like me."

"Nonsense," I said and tucked his blanket in around his knees. The cold weather had arrived with a vengeance and the old apartment, while completely upgraded, still had an old steam boiler system and it was often drafty. "I'll bring Sophie over for a visit and we can work on it while she plays on the rug."

"Sounds like a plan," my father said and smiled softly. "What did I do to deserve such a good daughter?"

"You were such a good father," I said plainly.

"You didn't always think that," he said with a chuckle. "I recall there were years, when you were a teenager, that you thought I was an old curmudgeon. I know what you and Heath whispered about me. The 'Hangin Judge...'"

"You allowed us to dissent," I said. "I didn't realize it at the time."

"I tried," he said. "This stroke gave me a chance to look at my life and appreciate what I have had. I've been one of the luckiest men of my generation. Probably of any generation, when you think about it."

I nodded. "We've been very lucky as a family, even with the heartbreak," I said and thought of my mother and how she passed in so much pain. "That reminds me," I said and remembered that the concert on Veteran's Day that was coming up – the anniversary of my first real date with Drake. "Do you think you're up for a concert?"

He looked at me with narrowed eyes. "Is it that sad music you and your mother loved so much?"

I shook my head. "I wish it was, but no. It's only Mozart and Ravel."

"That's a special day for you two."

"It was Drake's and my first date," I replied, remembering the night with nostalgia "You invited him to sit with us and I was so mad at the time..."

"The boy was in love with you," my father said. "*Is* in love with you. You can't know how happy I was that the two of you got together. I only wish Liam were here to see you both. And little Sophie."

"And little Liam, too."

I thought of the picture of Liam and my father that Drake treasured so much. I wished I could have met Liam before he died. He sounded like such a gallant man, even if he was a very distant father for Drake.

"You two lovebirds will have to go alone," my father said, shaking his head sadly. "I'm not up to much yet. Maybe next year."

I sighed and leaned over to kiss him on the cheek. "Next year sounds good."

~

"ARE YOU EXCITED ABOUT TONIGHT?" Drake asked me as I stood at the vanity in the master bathroom and finished applying my makeup.

"I am," I said, butterflies in my stomach. I glanced at Drake. He was already dressed in his dark blue suit and white shirt, and was tying his tie. As usual, he looked like a billion dollars. Although the news coverage of his past had been a real source of stress, he still seemed to be able to rise above it and was almost perpetually cheerful.

"This is our first real date since Sophie was born," Drake said, meeting my eyes in the mirror. "I wish we could go to The Russian Tea Room first, but maybe after, we can stop and get some blini and drink some Anisovaya."

"Maybe," I said and put on my diamond earrings and diamond choker. "I don't want to be out too late. We don't want to take advantage of Karen."

"She said she'd be happy to stay until midnight, so we'll have time."

I nodded and watched as Drake ran a comb through his hair and smoothed an errant wave. He turned to me and smiled.

"How do I look?" He held out his arms and turned in a circle.

I laughed. "You look mahvellous, dahling. Mahvellous."

He came up to me from behind and put his arms around my waist.

"You look good enough to eat," he said, murmuring against the skin of my neck. "In fact, I think I will eat you when we come back and once Sophie's back to sleep after you feed her."

I smiled and tried to finish fixing my hair, but Drake was insistent, his hands squeezing my breast over top of my black velvet dress, the other sliding down over my belly to my groin, his fingers pressing against my clit. I closed my eyes and moaned softly. He knew right where to touch and what to do to instantly arouse me.

Downstairs, Karen was looking after Sophie, getting her ready for a feed before putting her down to sleep.

"Later," Drake said and caught my eye in the mirror. "We'll have a nice bath and you'll be so relaxed, you'll let me do practically anything to you."

"I will," I said and smiled to myself. "You always have your way with me."

Finally, after a kiss that promised so much more later, we pulled apart and each of us smoothed our clothes before going back downstairs. I was so glad I agreed to have Karen come and do nanny duties, and a little bit of housework, so that Drake and I could enjoy Sophie or take time to be alone.

We took my father's limo service to Carnegie Hall. I wished we could listen to Dawn Upshaw perform Symphony No. 3 by Gorecki but she wasn't performing it anywhere close to where we lived and I had no intention of flying to London or wherever she was. Instead, we would enjoy an evening of Mozart, whose music I loved, and Ravel, whose music I liked.

We arrived a bit early and stood in the foyer waiting to take our place in my father's box seats, when I noticed a few people staring at us while we stood together and talked. Drake was busy telling me something about Sophie when he must have noticed the same thing I did. I felt as if the two of us were surrounded by people talking about us. He stopped talking and glanced around, then turned back to me, his brow furrowed.

"I can't believe it," he said, his voice low and with a definite edge to it.

"What?" I asked, not wanting to admit that I felt people staring at us.

"People are definitely staring at us. A woman over to my left actually pointed at us and spoke to the other people in her group."

I took a quick peek and saw one of the women watching us intently. I wondered who she was and why she seemed so angry. The expression on her face, with her hair all done up in a tight ponytail, makeup heavy, wearing a gold sequined dress and high heels. She looked wealthy, her face pulled back by the tight hairdo and maybe some plastic surgery.

"She's definitely staring at us," I said.

Drake leaned down and kissed me purposely, then he took my arm and pulled me towards the auditorium. "Let's go. I don't need this."

We left the foyer and went to our seats, sitting in the front of the box so we could look out over the entire stage. They were great seats and we settled in. I was thankful that the lights were low so that we weren't all that visible, but still, as I glanced around, I felt a few faces looking up at us in the box and I glanced quickly away. Luckily, Drake was busy reading the program and didn't notice. I stared at him, feeling so bad that he had lost so much over the case – how he'd been forced off the board of the Foundation and the Corporation. How he'd given up his Fellowship to be with Sophie and me. How he'd taken a year's leave of absence from NYP…

He was no longer active in the BDSM community nor did he play with his band.

What was left for him but me and Sophie? The man who was so busy, his life so tightly scheduled with everything in such firm control was now changed. He was still as handsome, still as attentive, still as accomplished, but I felt like he was diminished. I wanted him to start playing with Mersey again, so at least he'd have his music and his friendships with the other band members to console him. I wanted him to finish his Fellowship as soon as possible, but would they invite him back after the case and all the publicity?

Would patients want him as their surgeon?

Worry about him and his future was a tiny black spot on an otherwise wonderful night – the first date we'd been on since before the accident. I wanted to enjoy every moment, but instead, I felt a touch of anxiety and sadness.

That wasn't fair to Drake, and so I took in a deep breath and put on a smile.

"What's the sigh about?" Drake said as he turned a page in the concert program. Then he turned to me, his blue eyes focused on me. "That sounded sad."

I raised my shoulder a bit, not wanting to reveal my real concerns. "It's strange being away from Sophie, I guess."

Drake took my hand and squeezed. "Karen is eminently qualified to sit in the living room while Sophie sleeps. In fact, she's probably the very best person we could have looking after her, other than a pediatric trauma surgeon, so relax."

I smiled and leaned back in my chair, squeezing his hand back. "I know. I will."

He leaned over and kissed me and then turned back to his program, reading over a paragraph about the conductor. I smiled again, and tried to enjoy my time out with Drake but as I looked at him – really looked at him – I felt some unaccountable fear. Fear that he'd be taken away from me. Fear that he'd feel cheated of his life, the life he had before I came along, and that he'd leave me – leave us – so he could be a neurosurgeon again. It was silly – Drake loved me and he loved Sophie. It was my postpartum PTSD brain, looking for something wrong when there was nothing.

By the time the performance started, I'd forgotten all about the rude woman who pointed at us. I sat back and enjoyed the performance, remembering back to the time I was here with Drake, when Dawn Upshaw was performing, and how I wanted him gone. Now, in contrast, I relished having him beside me, our hands clasped, his arm around my shoulder.

If I thought the evening was already perfect, other than the fact that people had been pointing and whispering about Drake while we waited in the lounge for the performance to begin, I was wrong. During intermission, Drake and I went to the bar for a drink. It was there, as we stood at a table and each drank a glass of wine, that Drake reached into his jacket pocket and removed a small package.

It was a gift from him for our anniversary. Small and square, wrapped in white tissue with a thin gold ribbon, the gift looked like a ring box.

"Drake, you shouldn't have," I said with a frown, even as I took the box eagerly.

"I should have and I did. You're my life," he said and took my hand, squeezing it, his eyes burning into mine. "You and Sophie have made my life full and real for the first time in a long time. For forever. I've never had a relationship like this with anyone – not Maureen, not anyone. This small token is nothing compared to what you've given me."

My eyes filled with tears at the sound of his voice, so low and full of emotion, and the words he spoke.

"Oh, Drake..." I smiled through my tears and we leaned closer to each other and kissed once more.

"Open it," he said, his eyes wide, his expression eager.

I did, pulling off the ribbon and removing the tissue paper. Inside was a white box and when I opened it, I gasped. The earrings were teardrop diamonds, that matched the teardrop necklace Drake had given me.

"They're beautiful," I said and looked up at Drake. He was smiling.

"I can't wait to see you wear them," he said and gave me a wicked smile. "Them and nothing else..."

"I can't wait to put them on. And nothing else."

Drake leaned in again and kissed me, the two of us smiling while we kissed. For a moment, there was only the two of us, and the rest of the world melted away as I held his gaze, feeling so happy and loved – really loved.

Then, the happiness was shattered.

"Disgusting," someone said – a woman's voice.

I frowned and turned to look in the direction of the voice and saw a middle-aged woman dressed in a black gown, her hair in a bouffant and her lips blood red. Jewels glittered on her ears, neck and wrists. She stood with a couple of other people – another woman and two men.

The woman turned back to her companions, and the four of them spoke amongst themselves, occasionally glancing at Drake and me.

I felt such hurt and anger at that moment, I wanted to go over and throw my drink in her face. What did she think? Did she believe that Drake was involved in the attack? Did she think he was a bad man because of his past in BDSM?

They knew nothing about Drake. *Nothing.*

Instead, I turned to Drake and shook my head quickly. "Let's go back to our seats," I said softly.

On his part, Drake stood a little taller, his back stiff. I could see his body tense and knew he was upset, but I took his hand quickly and squeezed it.

"Come on," I said again. "Let's go back to our seats."

I led the way and he followed me, my hand clasped in his. He was frowning, his handsome brow knit, his eyes dark. When we finally arrived back in the box, we sat down in our seats, and Drake glowered, resting his chin in one hand.

"Will I never be able to go out in public without people recognizing me and commenting?"

I took his hand and squeezed. "It'll pass as soon as the trial happens and Lisa goes to jail. People will soon forget as soon as the next scandal comes along."

"I hope so," Drake said. "If not, we're moving away."

"Where would we go?" I asked, surprised that Drake would consider leaving.

"I don't know," he said, his voice sounding tired and a little exasperated. "Somewhere else. California. South Carolina. Maine. Wherever you want to go."

"I don't want to leave my father," I said, unable to contemplate leaving him when he was so fragile. I should have humored Drake, sympathized with him, but the thought of leaving my father was too much to bear at that moment.

"No, no," he said and shook his head. "I'm sorry. Of course we won't leave Manhattan. We can't leave your father. I'd miss him too much. We'll stay and learn to ignore the idiots."

I nodded. "It'll pass, Drake," I said and squeezed his hand once more. "Like I said, as soon as the next scandal comes along."

He exhaled and turned back to watch the stage as the lights flashed to indicate the intermission was over. While people filed back in to take their seats once more, I saw a few heads turn to glance up at us.

Damn them.

Sadly, it wouldn't be the last time Drake and I became the object of public whispers…

MY FATHER gradually improved with each passing day, and I began to relax again, not filled with fear that he would die at any moment the way I had been after his stroke and hospitalization. As for me, my own life with Sophie was becoming more manageable as she grew and got into a routine of sleeping, eating, and spending time sitting on our lap or in her bouncer chair or swing. Despite being a preemie, she was growing like a weed and so I stopped worrying about her health as much.

Thanksgiving came and we spent the day with my family. My father and Elaine hosted dinner. Health and Christine came with their kids. It was a wonderful evening with turkey and all the trimmings. Sophie even sat with my father for a while, but he was still weak on his one side – even more so than before, and I had to sit beside him and help him hold her. He bent down and gave her big kisses on her plump rosy cheeks and did so again and again.

"She's a keeper," he said and smiled at me. "I'm so glad things worked out and you both were fine after the accident. What a wonderful gift, to have such a beautiful baby."

"I know," I said and smiled, my emotions still so close to the surface. My father's stroke was still so recent, and he was only slowly recovering function. My own recovery was complete, even if I still had a lingering fear of something happening to Sophie, but now at least Drake and I were closer than ever. I felt I could confide in him about my fears and he understood and always had calm words to comfort me.

The only dark cloud I felt hovering over me was the fact that Sophie would always be an only child. When I saw Heath's children playing so well together, I felt a pang of sadness that I would only ever have one child. I pushed that sadness out of my mind and heart and tried my best to enjoy what I did have. I had a lot to be thankful for and so for the rest of the night, I shoved all my usual sadness and anxiety aside and tried to live in the moment, and enjoy what I did have instead of being sad for what I would never have.

Seeing Drake holding Sophie and how comfortable he was with her, how easy he was holding her and playing with her, caring for her and feeding her a bottle, made it all worthwhile.

If only the police would clear Drake of any suspicion, we could finally move on, but the case seemed to be taking forever. That darkness I couldn't escape, although I was determined not to let it ruin my holiday and so I shoved that thought to the back of my mind and turned to watch my husband and my sweet baby, sitting with the rest of my family.

CHAPTER 13 : DRAKE

As Christmas approached, Kate and Sophie and I went to Macy's in mid-December to do the usual window shopping and to buy gifts for each other.

"I have to get something for you," I said, after we spent some time checking out the displays. "You two stay out here while I zip in and get my gift for you. I don't want you peeking."

"Okay," Kate said and kissed me when I leaned in. I kissed Sophie's cheek and then went inside, looking for the locket I wanted to get for Kate. I'd drop it off at a special jeweler in Chelsea and get it engraved with the words I'd chosen. I wanted this gift to be special – a sign that I was hers and she was mine. I'd chosen the line from the chorus of *And I Love Her* by the Beatles. She loved that song and it had special meaning for us.

The locket was still there in the display case. It was from an estate sale and was a beautiful antique with burnished gold and a delicate filigree. It would look wonderful against Kate's skin. I paid the clerk and pocketed the tiny box, eager to see Kate's face on Christmas Eve when she opened it. I had already bought a gift for Sophie – a $10,000 bond that would gain interest over the years so that she could do whatever she wanted with it when she came of age – go to college, invest in a business – travel the world, but I wanted something special for Kate.

I made my way outside to find Kate and Sophie standing in front of one of the displays. I kissed them both.

"There you two are," I said and brushed a flake of snow off Sophie's rosy cheek. "My two girls." I kissed Sophie's forehead once more. "The loves of my life."

I looked in Kate's eyes only to find that she had been crying. "Hey," I said, frowning. "Why do I see tears?" I pulled her into my arms and held the two of them, repeatedly kissing them both, trying to understand if Kate was upset.

She smiled. "It's nothing," she said and laughed. "I just miss my mother. We used to come here every year…"

"I know," I said softly and wiped a tear from her cheek. "I miss my father. We didn't have this kind of happy tradition, but I always spent my Christmas Eve with him, going out for dinner and then to look at the lights."

She laid her head on my shoulder for a moment of comfort while Sophie sucked away on her pacifier noisily.

"So, are we going to Dad's for supper?" I asked as we started walking down the street to where our car was parked.

"Yes," Kate said and took my hand. "We can go any time. He'll probably have his ear attached to his phone, but we're always welcome to drop by early. I can help Elaine with supper and you can take Sophie to see dad."

"Sounds like a plan," I said, smiling with delight that I finally had a real family.

~

WE HAD a wonderful meal with Ethan and Elaine. Ethan had recovered a bit of function, but still had to stay in his motorized wheelchair, using his good hand to move the joystick, so he could travel from room to room. He kept busy on the phone, which he had rigged up to his cell with an ear piece so he could carry on conversations despite being unable to hold a phone to his ear. Dinner was exceptional as usual, and we returned home after tea and conversation. Sophie had fallen asleep in the car and so after Kate put her to bed, she had a warm bath while I checked my mail and tried to catch up on what Dave reported on the foundation.

I finished up and went into the bathroom, to find Kate stepping out of the tub. I helped her dry off.

"What do you think, Mrs. Morgan?" I said, standing behind her, my hands roving up her body to cup a breast. "Shall we take advantage of this time and fuck like bunnies?"

She laughed but I could see the look of desire in her eyes, which were heavy.

"Whatever you say, Doctor Morgan," she said, closing her eyes as I pushed my hips against her, my cock already hard and pressing against her buttocks.

Just then, Sophie woke up and let out a massive scream. Immediately, Kate's body responded and milk sprayed out of one of her breast – no doubt the one that had been drained the least and so had filled up the most since her last feed.

We laughed so hard, Kate standing there with her fingers on her nipples, trying to stem the tide, so to speak. She grabbed some tissue and held the pieces over her breasts to stop the milk from spraying all over everywhere.

"My god, you're lush," I said, wrapping the towel around her while Kate pressed the tissue against her nipples. "It's such a waste that I don't have a lactation fetish, because you would be my goddess." I kissed her briefly. "You are my goddess even so."

On her part, Kate smiled, and slipped into her nursing nightgown, designed to make breastfeeding easier. Then, she went to Sophie's room, picked her up out of the crib and sat on the chair to feed her.

I followed her and helped her get situated, with a knitted blanket over Kate's shoulder to keep her warm.

"Do you want some tea?" I asked from the doorway. "I feel like a cup before we go to bed."

Kate yawned. "Not for me, thanks. I'm way too tired."

"Decaf," I added. "You need to keep your fluids up."

"Okay, Doctor," she said with a smile. I went to the kitchen and put on the kettle, arranging a couple of cups and saucers and fixing the tea pot. When I was finished, I peeked into Sophie's room again and saw that Kate had her up on her shoulder for a burp.

"Here," I said and reached for Sophie. "Let me do that. You go and get your cup of tea."

I took a receiving blanket over my shoulder and placed Sophie onto it, patting her back to bring up a burp so she could go to sleep.

Finally, she rewarded me and let out a serious belch, her eyes still closed.

"Like clockwork," I said and stood by the window, rocking her for a while before I put her down.

Kate went to get her tea and returned with a cup in hand, leaning on the doorjamb while I continued to rock Sophie on my shoulder. Finally, I laid her down in her crib and tucked a blanked behind her. Then, I went to Kate and together, we stood in the doorway and watched her.

"She's a keeper," I said and pulled Kate closer to me.

"She is."

We went downstairs to the living room and I put on some music while Kate sat on the sofa and drank her tea.

"I had hopes of making love to you earlier, Ms. Bennet," I said and sat back beside her. "Are you too tired?"

"I'm never too tired for you," she said and smiled up at me.

"I don't believe a word you say," I replied, knowing she was just being agreeable. "I saw you hide your yawn."

She smiled guiltily. "I'm sorry, but I'm just exhausted tonight for some reason. Maybe the cold air. It often makes me really sleepy at night when we go out for an evening walk."

I kissed her cheek. "I'll have to remember that. No more evening walks when I want to make love to you."

"I'm sorry," she said and made a pouty face. "It's just I feel like I need to sleep when Sophie does so I can wake up and feed her. I can lie quietly while you take your pleasure.".

"Don't worry about it, and don't apologize," I said and leaned in to kiss her. "I understand completely and you should sleep when she does. Besides, taking my pleasure always means giving it to you. Here," I said and took her empty cup. Then, I pulled her up and into my arms. "You go and get into bed. I'll join you in a few minutes. I need to send an email and turn out the lights."

I went back to the office and opened my email while Kate went to our bedroom and got into bed. I wanted to give her the chance to fall asleep if she wanted, without worrying about me.

About fifteen minutes later, I returned to the bedroom and sat on the side of the bed to take off my socks. Of course, she woke and rubbed her eyes.

"Sorry I woke you," I said softly.

"It's okay. I wanted to talk to you before we go to sleep. Something happened tonight while you were in Macy's."

"What?" I asked, removing my watch and placing it on the nightstand. When I was naked, I slipped into bed beside her.

"Maureen and Liam are in town. I saw them in the crowd while you were shopping."

"What?" I said, a shock going through me. I leaned up on my elbow and looked into Kate's eyes.

"Yes," she said softly. "I went over and said hello. Chris and Maureen broke up when Chris got a job in Borneo. Maureen probably didn't want to go because of Liam's health."

That surprised me, for I thought that Maureen would never want to separate Liam from Chris. "Is he sick?"

Kate shook her head. "He looks great. He's grown taller and his hair has grown in. He looks so much like you."

"I wish," I said, but stopped myself. I was going to say that I wished I could get to know Liam – that I could be a real father to him.

"What?" Kate asked, moving closer.

I sighed and rolled onto my back. "I wish Maureen would let me see him. If Chris and Maureen have broken up, he has no father." I turned back to look in Kate's eyes. "*I'm* his father. I should have visitation rights."

She nodded. "You know you'd have the best lawyers in the country working to get you access, if you want to push for it."

I sighed heavily. "I don't want there to be hard feelings between Maureen and me. I wish she could understand that I'm not some dirty old man who would corrupt him. I want to get to know him, and be his father. The way I should be."

"You should be," Kate said. "Maybe you should call her, talk to her. She's staying at her mother's place for Christmas."

"Maybe I will," I said and took in a deep breath. "The worst she can do is say no again. Given it's Christmas, maybe her cold hard heart will be filled with comfort and joy and she'll let me see him."

"Maybe." Kate stroked her hand over my bare shoulder. That aroused me, her touching me combined with the news, and my sense of sadness that I wasn't in Liam's life made me feel very needy. I turned over and pulled her against my body. She didn't resist in the least, perhaps knowing I needed her now more than ever. We kissed deeply, and soon, she warmed up underneath me, her body responding to my touch, to my mouth, and my fingers. To my surprise, she rolled over on top of me and rode me with no words being said and soon, very soon, she orgasmed, her body clenching around me.

When she was finished and collapsed against me, breathing heavily, a smile on her face, I rolled her onto her back and began to thrust, needing the release to ease the sadness I felt at the news about Liam. I watched my cock slide in and out of her body, her breasts moving each time I thrust, and soon, I was there, my orgasm cresting.

"Oh, *God*," I groaned, pleasure coursing through me, washing away some of my sadness. Finally, I lay on top of her and recovered. "That was…"

"So good," she said, finishing my sentence, smiling. "Poor deprived daddy. Not getting enough sex because he's up too late feeding his baby every night while his wife sleeps, and nothing kinky for months…"

I smiled at her and kissed her deeply. "Not deprived. Just in need. And very thankful, kink or not."

As we lay in bed with the moonlight from the window falling across the blanket, I thought about Liam and wished that someday, Maureen would soften and allow me to become a real father for him.

∾

CHAPTER 14 : KATE

My father told me to be happy.

I was determined to do that – be happy. I had every reason. A beautiful baby and a handsome – gorgeous – husband. Although I had taken a leave of absence from finishing my Master's, I could go back and complete it any time I wanted. I was creating art again – when Sophie slept and when I felt an urge. My father was slowly recovering from his latest bout with a stroke.

The only downside to our lives was the case. The police should have cleared Drake of any involvement in Lisa's plans to kill me, but they hadn't – not officially, although they hadn't interviewed Drake again nor had they spoken to me for a few weeks. Christmas was fast approaching and I wanted everything to be perfect for Sophie's first Christmas.

As Christmas approached, I felt certain that they'd let us know that Drake was no longer a suspect, but they were silent on that. The only other sore point in my life was how Maureen was still unwilling to let Drake into his son's life. One afternoon later that week, when Drake went out to get us coffee and Karen had the day off, I called up my father and talked to him about the issue.

"He'll have to go through a series to tests and interviews, to confirm his suitability for visits with Liam."

I sighed. "Drake's going to be a pediatric brain surgeon. If anyone can be trusted with his own child, it's Drake."

"Sorry, sweetie, but that's not good enough. Of course, Drake can be trusted. You know that and I know that, but we have to prove it to a judge."

"I know," I said with a heavy sigh.

"Drake will have to prove paternity," he said firmly. "Once he does, he can request a judge grant him access. The first thing is to talk to Maureen and see if she understands how important it will be for Liam to know his real father, especially now that Chris is out of the picture."

"I know, but will she? She *hates* Drake…"

"The law doesn't care if she hates him," he said. "The law only cares that he's the boy's father and is a member of the community in good standing."

"He's a pediatric neurosurgeon, for God's sake," I said, shaking my head.

"What's wrong with the woman?" my father asked.

"I know." I rubbed my forehead. "You'd think she'd want some help now that she and Chris have split, but no. I feel so bad for Drake."

"Let me know what I can do. I have a few connections." Then he asked about the case, but I had nothing new to tell him.

"Tell me about this Lisa woman."

I didn't go into specifics. "Drake had a few encounters with her when he was single and never went any further than sex. She took advantage of that prior relationship to emotionally blackmail Drake, demanding to be treated as a special friend, and using the threat of exposing Drake's past to force him to comply."

I could hear my father sigh on the other end of the line.

"We'll deal with this, but the case won't help Drake get access. It might complicate things."

"I was afraid of that," I said and felt gloom descend over me. Drake might never get access because of the case. I could imagine some case worker in a dingy office reading the headlines about Drake, the BDSM Doctor, and stamping REJECTED on his case file…

"Don't you worry," he said as if he read my mind. "I have many connections and am friends with powerful people. We'll make this work."

"Thanks, Daddy," I said and hung up.

Thank God we had lawyers like my father and Lara in our private circle so we had good legal advice at least.

I sat for a moment in silence, watching the snow fall outside my window. At least we'd have a white Christmas, but it would be a sad one for Drake if he couldn't even see Liam…

I made a decision and went to our storage room, to find some of the boxes that Drake brought from his apartment. I remembered seeing a file on his divorce when we were packing up his place so I spent the next hour looking for it. I wanted Maureen's maiden name so I could look up her mother.

Maybe she'd listen to reason…

$\sim$

AN HOUR LATER, I sat on the floor in the living room with the file in one hand and my cell in the other. Part of me hesitated to call, but the other part of me – the part that felt Drake was being treated badly – decided to take a chance and call. I found Maureen's maiden name -- Becker – and her mother's name on a wedding invitation.

Mr. John Becker and Mrs. Brenda Becker
  request the honor of your attendance
  at the wedding of their beloved daughter
  Maureen Becker
  to
  Dr. Drake Morgan
  on...

I SEARCHED for her mother's phone number and dialed, not knowing what to expect. Would she hang up in my ear or would she listen to reason?

A woman answered, her voice warm.

"Hello?"

I took in a deep breath and started my spiel.

"Hello, is this Mrs. Brenda Becker?"

"Yes," she said. "This is she."

"We've never met, and I know this call may seem out of the blue, but I'm married to Dr. Drake Morgan. I'm calling in the hopes of talking to you about letting Liam and Drake meet and get to know each other, as father and son. I know Maureen is in town for Christmas and that Chris and Maureen have separated. It would be great—."

"Let me stop you right there," Mrs. Becker said, her voice firm.

"Okay," I said, biting my bottom lip, waiting for her to give me a hard time.

"I'm *completely* sympathetic to Drake seeing Liam. Unfortunately, Maureen's very stubborn and nothing I've said has seemed to work. I'm trying, honestly, but she's still so adamant that Drake is a bad influence, although I've never understood... I always liked Drake."

"Did Maureen tell you why she thinks he's a bad influence?"

There was a brief pause on the other line.

"Well..." Brenda said, her voice trailing off. "She said he was into some kinky stuff and felt he was an inappropriate parent. I tried to tell her that it was more important what kind of father he was, not what he did in the bedroom, but she's like her father. Very stubborn. I tried... We'd love for Drake to get to know Liam, especially now that Chris and she..."

Her voice trailed off and she exhaled as if she'd given up.

"Anything you could do to convince her would be great," I said. "Drake saved Liam's life and I think it would be wonderful for them to get to know each other. Even if Liam doesn't learn about Drake being his father this year, at least try to persuade Maureen to let Drake *see* him. Invite Drake over for a visit if she's concerned about him, and let Drake see how he's doing. I saw Liam with his mother the other day and he's grown so much."

"He's doing well," Brenda said, a smile in her voice. "We're so thankful that Drake did the transplant. You can't imagine how shocked we were that Drake was the father, although I always thought how much he reminded me of Drake."

"Liam does look a lot like Drake," I said and smiled to myself. "I was able to get a photo of Liam for Drake and he cherishes that picture. It sits on his desk and I often catch him staring at it. I feel so helpless, like I know what the right thing to do is, but I can't do it."

"Let me see what I can do," she said and I could hear determination in her voice. "I'll try to arrange something. We're having a Christmas Eve get together with family and I'd love if Drake could come over before. Maybe five o'clock? I know that Maureen is going to be out with some of her old girl-friends from the hospital in the afternoon so if Drake came by while she was out..."

I frowned. "Do you think that's wise? Won't it make Maureen mad if she finds out?"

Brenda sighed. "Yes, but if she won't listen to reason, I'm willing to take that risk. Let me see how things go and I'll call you back."

I gave her my cell number and my email and we said goodbye. I moved from the floor to the sofa and sat there, looking out the window, wondering if I was going to regret contacting Maureen's mother but something had to give. While I tidied up, putting the box away, I thought that Drake should be spending time with Liam now, while he was in Manhattan. Maureen had to grow up and do what was best for her son, not what was best for her.

DRAKE ARRIVED HOME a little later and bent down to kiss me when he came into the living room.

"What have you been up to?" he asked, plopping down on the sofa beside me. "You have this look in your eyes."

"What look?" I said, trying to look all innocent.

"*That* look," he said with a laugh. "Is it the gift you got me for Christmas?"

I smiled and slipped my arms around his neck when he pulled me onto his lap.

"Something like that. It's a gift I *want* to give you, but things might not work out. Best laid plans and all that..."

"You don't have to give me a gift," he said and kissed me. "You being my wife and the mother of my child is all I need for Christmas."

He laid me down on the couch and kissed me once more, his kiss warm and loving. He pulled away and brushed hair off my forehead, smiling as his gaze travelled down over my face and down to my cleavage.

"How close to a feed are you?" he asked, and I knew why he was asking. If I was too close to a feed, my breasts would be filled with milk, which would leak out while we were having sex.

"I fed her before you went out, so it's been over an hour."

"Good," he said and pulled down my sweater to bare one well-supported breast in a nursing bra. "I can nuzzle you without getting sprayed in the eye."

"Oh, *Drake*," I said and made a face, my cheeks hot. "That's so... not sexy."

"Don't kid yourself," he said and laughed. "There are grown men who would pay lots of money to be sprayed with milk during sex."

We laughed together and I got over my reticence when he started to nuzzle my neck, one of his hands slipping down between my legs to stroke me over my yoga pants.

"Can I persuade you to let me fuck you before she wakes up?"

"Have you been a very good man this year?" I asked playfully.

"Very, *very* good," he said and narrowed his eyes.

I closed my eyes and let him take me where he wanted me to go, and over the next hour, he proved that he was right.

He was a very, *very* good man.

THE NEXT DAY passed with no word from either Brenda or Maureen and I was beginning to give up hope that Brenda had any success with her very unreasonable and stubborn daughter.

Finally, Brenda sent me an email and I opened it with trepidation.

I covered my mouth and my eyes filled with tears. This would be the best Christmas present Drake could get this year and I couldn't wait to tell him. Then I had an idea – I printed a copy of the letter off and decided I'd slip it into a big empty box filled with tissue paper and put it under the tree. Drake would open it up on Christmas morning at my Dad's place and it would make his day. Hell. It would make all our days.

I smiled to myself as I searched through the pantry for an empty box, so pleased to be able to give Drake this gift on Christmas Day.

CHAPTER 15 : DRAKE

The Thursday before Christmas, I spent my afternoon at the Foundation, finishing up some paperwork for a project in Africa providing equipment and supplies to a field hospital near the war zones in Sudan. Although they had removed my name from any promotional materials, I still wanted to be involved. Dave was there and updated me on his recent work. After our business was finished, I said goodbye and made my way to a jeweler not too far from the 8th Avenue apartment to see about my gift for Kate.

It was the same jeweler where I got Kate's diamond collar and her anniversary earrings – a family business that went back to the 19th Century and was owned by old Mr. Naismith. This time, I was getting an antique locket inscribed for Kate.

We bent over the locket, which was underneath a magnifying glass. The locket was an estate piece that I bought at Macy's. It was gold and had delicate filigree engraving on the front. Oval in shape, it was on a thin gold chain and would come to rest right above Kate's delicious cleavage. The locket opened and I wanted to enclose a photo of Sophie and one of Kate's mother, but I was having difficulty getting images of the right size. Mr. Naismith said he'd have his grandson resize the photos I brought to him.

"Did you decide on an inscription? It can't be too long," Mr. Naismith said as we examined the locket. "There's not much room."

"I have," I said, remembering Kate's favorite song that Mersey played. "And I love her."

"Ah," Mr. Naismith said, nodding. "The Beatles? A great choice and a great song." He smiled and peered down at the locket. "It'll be tight, but I'll make it work."

"You liked the Beatles?"

"I heard them play when they came to New York, in fact." He smiled at me.

"I know it's late but I appreciate your work."

"No problem," he said and waved his hand. "You've been a very good customer these past two years. I'm glad to do this for you. It'll be ready tomorrow afternoon. We're open until five thirty."

"I'll be back," I said and we shook hands.

Then I went out into the snowy Manhattan evening and home to my beloved wife and my sweet baby.

THE NEXT DAY, I swung by Naismith's to pick up the locket and Mr. Naismith came out from the back of the store with the locket in a nice black velvet box, displayed with the locket open so I could see both tiny pictures inside. We stood at the counter and I bent down to examine the locket under his magnifying glass. One picture was of Sophie at about three months, taken just a few weeks ago. The other picture was of Kate's mother, from a McDermott family Christmas picture, taken before she became ill. I turned the locket over and saw the delicate script:

And

I

Love

Her

It was beautiful. I hoped Kate would love it as much as I did.

"Thank you so much," I said to old Mr. Naismith. I was so pleased with the results. I shook his hand and clapped him on the back when he came around the counter to hand me the box.

"My pleasure, Dr. Morgan."

I tucked the box into my jacket pocket and left, satisfied that my gift shopping was all done and I had the perfect gift for Kate. I'd put the other gift under the tree – a beautiful cream satin and lace nightgown and robe along with a pass to the day spa she liked.

Kate had been a bit bedraggled after the accident, and then the adjustment to nursing, and getting used to Sophie's sleeping and feeding schedule. I wanted to pamper her so I had ordered a day trip to the spa for her and Elaine and Christie, so the three of them could relax while I looked after Sophie. I included an additional gift certificate so Kate could buy whatever she wanted – soaps, lotions, and all the other products they sold at the spa gift shop. I wanted Kate to feel pampered like a queen when she returned.

I wanted her to slip into bed, wearing that beautiful full length lace and satin nightgown with spaghetti straps and a low bodice, so I could very slowly and very deliberately run my hands all over it. Then, I planned to strip it off her luscious body before making her come very hard while restrained with my new lamb's wool cuffs for her wrists and ankles. They would be under our tree, not Ethan's, on Christmas morning. I realized they were as much for me as Kate, and smiled when I thought about reintroducing a bit of kink back into our sex life, now that Kate was pretty much fully recovered from the accident.

Until now, I had been so careful with her, not demanding anything from her, letting her take the lead when it came to reestablishing our sexual and D/s relationship in the bedroom. Kate was ready to begin again and so was I, my body warming just at the thought of tying her up again. I was certain it would happen one day very soon, when I felt and she felt the time was right.

~

WHEN I ARRIVED home that night, Kate had a radiant smile on her face, and Sophie was bright eyed and smiled when she saw me. The two of them like that, greeting me when I got home after being away all day, did something to my insides. I almost felt like I had to pinch myself to be sure this wasn't some fantasy I'd concocted when trying to get through the day.

It was real. Kate and Sophie were real.

"My two loves," I said and after I hung up my coat and took off my boots, I went right over to them, pulling them into my arms for a hug and kisses. "How did I ever get so lucky? What did I do to deserve this happiness?"

"You were *you*," Kate said and kissed me again. "You deserve to be happy. You deserve a family who loves you totally and completely, Drake."

I squeezed her and then took Sophie from Kate, carrying her to the kitchen while Kate went to the stove and tended something in a pot. It was Karen's day off so Kate was cooking.

"What's for dinner?"

"Braised beef shanks Cuban style," she said. "I've been watching Anthony Bourdain and it looked so good, I had to try it. There's smashed potato with garlic and fresh steamed broccoli."

"Smashed potatoes? Sounds delicious. What about Sophie?"

"She's too young for beef shanks," Kate said and then turned around to give me a huge grin before turning back to the stove.

"Oh, you," I said and pinched her ass. "You know what I mean."

137

"It's the breast for her," she said and took Sophie from my arms. "I need to feed her and then she'll go down for a nap. Then, we can eat."

"I want to eat *you*," I said and pulled her against my hips. She laughed and wriggled out of my arms, and I managed to tickle Sophie as Kate went by. I was rewarded by a big smile.

"My girls," I said, following Kate to the living room. Kate took a seat on the sofa and opened her sweater, pulling down the flap that covered her nipple. She had a breast pad on marked with an X so she could keep track of which breast Sophie fed from first. Finally, she got Sophie settled in the crook of her arm, fed her a nipple and Sophie was off, one hand on the soft swell of Kate's breast, her eyes latched onto Kate's.

What a beautiful sight. It choked me up with happiness, seeing the two of them doing so well. Only a few months earlier, it could have all ended in tragedy.

I checked my watch. Christmas was on Sunday and Christmas Eve fell on Saturday.

"Are we going to St. Stanislaus on Christmas Eve?" I asked, stroking Kate's hair. "I loved it last year."

"I'd love to. We'll have supper at my Dad's as usual and then open a present. Then we can go to the cathedral to listen to carols."

"Sound like the perfect Christmas Eve."

I smiled and leaned in to kiss Kate, and couldn't imagine that anything could make me happier.

I RACED AROUND on Christmas Eve day and did some last-minute shopping, picking up some wine for Christmas Eve dinner at Ethan's, fresh cream and a baguette from our local grocers, and some bagels from the deli down the street. Then, I went home and changed into a suit and tie for dinner at Ethan's.

Kate was wearing a nice new black taffeta dress with bare shoulders and a built-in bra, plus black sheer stockings, her black lace garters and thong underneath.

"I feel way too sexy, Dr. Morgan," she said as she pulled up one nylon and attached the garters.

"I know," I said with a lascivious grin. "I remember another day a couple of years ago when I first saw your garters. I think I was a goner at that moment. Yep," I said and licked my bottom lip slowly when she met my eyes. "Captured and tamed at that precise moment."

"You're crazy," she said with a laugh. "It took more than that."

"No," I said and shook my head. "Seriously. I had two prospective subs lined up, both of whom were very desirable, but all I could think of was you and those bloody knees and torn nylons with your black lace garters..."

"Really?" she said and stood up, straightening her dress. "Two?"

"Yes," I said, remembering them. "I turned them both down because what I wanted was to capture you and debauch you, convert you to my depraved ways so I could tie you up and make you scream out my name."

I grinned at her and she smiled back, wagging her eyebrows. "Caught, debauched and converted," she said with a light laugh. She came to me and slipped her arms around my waist, pulling her hips against mine. "Waiting impatiently to scream out your name again and again."

I pulled her into my arms and we kissed. On her part, Sophie bounced in her bouncer, a wet drooly smile on her face. I held my hand beside my mouth and whispered, pretending to keep Sophie from hearing.

"Tomorrow night, if you're up for it. I have something special planned..."

She grinned. "I'm almost always up for it," she said, grinning as she leaned up and kissed my jaw.

"You are," I said and returned her grin. "And I'm a very happy man as a result."

～

Dinner at Ethan's and Elaine's was perfect, as usual. The apartment was decorated in reds and greens and golds, and the meal was delicious. All my life, I'd wanted a real Christmas, the kind with gifts and a fireplace and a tree, roast turkey and all the trimmings. Most of all, I wanted a family who loved me.

I had all that now. Besides Ethan and Elaine, Heath and Christie were there with their two kids, and so with Kate, Sophie and I, we were a very loud and happy dinner table. Sophie took turns sitting on Kate's and my lap, and occasionally, when she got fussy, she spent time on Elaine's.

Ethan sat at the head of the table in his wheelchair, with Kate on one side and Heath on the other, and we took turns speaking about our year, and our hopes for the future.

Kate took my hand. "I couldn't be happier," she said. "Life's so good."

I squeezed, smiling at her. "Life's the best."

We opened presents after dinner and Kate was very happy with her gift of the nightgown and robe and the spa passes. She got me a great volume of Sherlock Holmes stories, which she saw me eyeing during a trip to a local bookstore. That plus several framed rock band posters for my office featuring Cream, The Beatles, The Stones and a few others. I couldn't wait to hang them, and listen to their music while I worked on my fellowship research paper. Although I had taken a leave of absence, I wanted to continue working on the research paper to keep my mind fresh.

Once we were finished with the presents, and after tea and coffee, we left the apartment and made our way to St. Stanislaus's for late mass and the choral music Kate loved. Kate would have liked for Ethan to come but he was still too immobile and didn't want to go to all the fuss so the three of us went alone.

It was perfect. The perfect family Christmas. The only two things that would have made it better would be if my father had been alive, and if Liam had been part of my life, but I didn't want to feel ungrateful.

I was a very lucky man, and I knew it. It was all because of Kate – and Ethan. I had one resolution for the new year. I would never let either of them forget how much I appreciated and loved them both.

CHAPTER 16 : KATE

O n Christmas morning, I woke to bright sunlight streaming in from the window. Drake was asleep beside me and I could hear Sophie sucking her pacifier over the baby monitor on my nightstand. I snuck out of bed and went to the bathroom to shower and brush my teeth. Then, I went downstairs to the kitchen and put on a pot of decaf coffee from Starbucks, before squeezing some fresh orange juice for our breakfast. I pulled out some bacon and eggs, planning on a special breakfast for us.

When I heard Sophie cry out over the second monitor we had in the kitchen, I put down the handful of green onions and went to Sophie's bedroom, to find her rolled over into the corner, her head pressed against the bumper pad.

"Hey, baby girl," I said when I went to her, picking her up out of the crib. "How's my little one?" I kissed her cheek and took her over to the change table, to get her out of her wet diaper. She kicked and flailed her arms around while I changed her and put her in a clean romper for the morning. I'd bathe her later and get her ready for dinner at my father's later in the afternoon.

I fed her quickly, moving her with ease from one breast to the other, burped her, then I put her into her jolly jumper swing downstairs in the kitchen. Then, I proceeded to make an omelet for our breakfast. I chopped up green onions, green pepper, and bacon, and then beat the eggs in a small mixing bowl. The scent of frying bacon mixed with the aroma from the onions and peppers smelled delicious. It was enough to make my mouth water.

Just then, Drake came out of the bedroom and peeked into the kitchen at Sophie and me.

"There's my two girls," he said with a smile. "It smells great in here."

"There's coffee," I said and gestured to the pot. "Decaf, but if you pour me a cup in my mug, you can make some hi-test."

"I might do that," he said as he washed out my coffee mug and poured me a cup. Then he made regular coffee.

"Shall we open a present here first?"

"You're eager to get to the presents?" I asked, smiling at the happy expression on Drake's face. He loved Christmas. He ate it up, loving everything about it – the decorations, the lights, the gift buying and giving, the big Christmas dinner.

"I am. I can't wait to see what you think of my gift."

"I can't wait for you to get my gift." I smiled, thinking about it. My gift would make Drake's Christmas.

With Sophie still in her swing, we sat beside the tree which was decorated all in gold and red, and Drake handed me his gift. I was eager to see what it was and quickly tore the paper off to find a pair of lamb's wool ankle and wrist cuffs. Seeing them sent a jolt of excitement through me. We hadn't done anything kinky since the attack.

"So this is what you had planned for tonight, hmm?" I said, wagging my eyebrows at him.

He grinned. "Guilty as charged."

I tried one cuff out to see how it felt, imagining Drake tying me up and making me come again and again.

"I'm looking forward to Master D making an appearance," I said and bent over to kiss Drake. "He must be feeling very deprived with his very vanilla lifestyle lately…"

"Not at all," Drake said, ever the gentleman. He turned my face to his and looked deep into my eyes. "I thought you might like a little spice now and then. I'm perfectly happy the way things are, but don't want you to feel cheated out of the man you married."

"I don't feel at all cheated," I said, and I meant it. I knew that we had been way too busy dealing with the attack, Sophie's premature birth and the aftermath to be involved in the lifestyle. When we had more time, I looked forward to us returning to our previous interests. I even imagined attending a dungeon party, if one were available.

Next, Drake handed me another gift. I opened it, realizing as soon as I saw it that it was a jewelry box. I pulled off the wrapping and opened it. Inside was a beautiful gold locket on a thin gold chain.

"Oh, Drake, it's beautiful. It looks ancient."

"It's from an estate sale," Drake said. "I like the delicate filigree. Open it up."

I did open it. Inside were two tiny pictures. One of Sophie and one of my mother.

"It's beautiful," I whispered, tearing up.

"Look on the back," he said, his voice soft.

I turned the locket over and in tiny script was engraved *And I love her*. I covered my mouth to stop from sobbing.

"Thank you," I managed, before pulling him close so I could kiss him. "You are such a beautiful man." We pressed our foreheads together for a moment and I wiped my eyes. "I love you."

"I love you."

When I had recovered, I pulled my gift for Drake from under the tree. "This is for you."

"Another present?" he said, opening it eagerly. Inside was the action figure I'd bought for Liam, on the hope that Maureen relented and allowed Drake to see Liam during the holidays.

"Iron Man?" he said, his expression confused.

"Read this," I said and handed him the card I received from Maureen's mother, Brenda. Drake opened cautiously, a frown on his brow.

"What's this?" he said and glanced at me. He pulled out the folded letter and read it, his mouth open. The letter had come only a few days earlier. I was afraid it would never come but it finally arrived and it announced we were on for a visit before supper on Christmas Day.

Today.

"Does this say what I think it says?" Drake asked, looking up at me from the letter.

I nodded, my eyes welling up with tears at the expression of shock on his face.

"Yes," I said. "The present is for Liam. We can wrap it before we go."

"What?" he said, still confused.

"Maureen's mom was able to talk with Maureen and convince her that this is the right thing to do for Liam. We're invited to come over this afternoon. Maureen is going to talk to Liam before and let him know that you're his biological father."

Drake shook his head. "Today? This afternoon?" He read the letter over again, and I could tell he was still in disbelief.

I nodded. "Yes. Before dinner. Around five o'clock." At that, I couldn't hold back any longer. Tears spilled down my cheeks and I had to cover my mouth to stop from sobbing out loud. Drake pulled me into his arms and buried his face in the crook of my neck.

When he glanced up at me, his eyes were filled with tears as well.

That was the greatest gift I could have received – to see Drake with tears of joy in his eyes because he was finally going to see his son on Christmas

Day. That Liam would know Drake was his biological father. Most especially, because he could start to be a real father to Liam.

LATER THAT AFTERNOON, after Sophie had a bath and nursed, Drake and I stood in our bedroom and dressed for the evening.

"How do I look?" Drake asked, standing in front of the floor length mirror. He adjusted his tie and buttoned his jacket.

"You look fantastic," I said, for he did look wonderful "But don't worry. You could be wearing jeans and a t-shirt. Liam won't care what you look like."

"I want to impress Maureen so she's happy she agreed to the meeting."

I tucked a handkerchief into his suit pocket and brushed a few strands of hair off his forehead. "You look like a rich, well-educated, highly skilled pediatric neurosurgeon. You'll do fine. Be yourself."

"Maureen hated my *self.*"

"She didn't hate you," I said, frowning. "You two weren't right for each other."

Drake sighed, and I knew he was nervous. I took his hand and led him to the door where I had left Sophie already asleep in her car seat, pacifier in her mouth, her white angora mouse hat so cute she looked like a Gerber baby.

Drake slipped on his coat and boots. He held my coat out for me, pausing to embrace me from behind, kissing my neck.

"Thank you," he whispered in my ear. I smiled and turned into his arms for a brief embrace.

Then, Drake picked up Sophie's car seat and Liam's freshly wrapped Iron Man action figure, and we left the apartment.

WHEN WE ARRIVED at Maureen's mother's apartment, I could hear Nat King Cole singing Christmas tunes from under the door.

"This is it," Drake said, inhaling deeply. He looked a bit nervous.

I leaned up and kissed him, trying to allay his fears. "You'll do fine. Smile."

He smiled and squeezed my hand, but I could feel his nerves in his grip, which was tighter than needed. I knocked at the door and immediately, the volume of the music dropped and I heard footsteps that announced Maureen was coming to the door. When the door opened, I was surprised to see Brenda instead of Maureen.

"Drake!" she said and held open her arms. Drake embraced her, but I could tell from the expression on his face that he was surprised by the warm welcome.

Then, she turned to me. "You must be Kate," she said with a smile. "So glad you took the initiative and contacted me. This is going to turn out to be a great Christmas after all. Liam was pretty upset to not have Chris here, but with Drake coming, he may feel happier."

"Does he know?" Drake asked softly, handing her the present.

Brenda nodded. "Come in," she said and reached out to take the present. "You two take off your coats and boots and come on inside." She pointed to the closet. "Hang your coats there and come into the living room."

Drake helped me with my coat and then slipped out of his own. I saw him smooth his freshly washed hair, a nervous expression on his face.

"How do I look?" he asked once more when I stood up from removing my boots.

"You look *mahvelous*, dahling. *Mahvelous*." I grinned and finally, Drake smiled in return.

"You're too young to know that reference," he said and squeezed me, pulling me briefly into his arms.

"I have a father who loved Saturday Night Live," I said. "We watched re-runs and so I know them almost as well as him."

Drake picked up Sophie's car seat and together, the three of us went into the living room. Inside, Liam sat on the floor, surrounded by a model train set.

I took Sophie out of her car seat and held her, while Drake went further into the living room. I'd dressed Sophie in a black velvet and lace dress that made her look like a little porcelain doll.

"Where's Maureen?" Drake asked, glancing around.

"She had a previous engagement," Brenda said and raised her eyebrows. She pointed to the sofa. "Kate, please come in and sit down. Drake, I'd like to introduce you to Liam." She turned to Liam and gestured at him to stand. "Liam, this is Dr. Drake Morgan. Your mother told you about him earlier."

Liam stood and wiped his hands when Drake extended his for a shake.

"Hello," Liam said.

I stood with Sophie in my arms, a choke in my throat to see them together – father and son. So much alike. Both had jet black hair, fair skin and very blue eyes rimmed by thick, dark lashes.

"You're my bio-logical father," Liam said simply, as if it were nothing too monumental.

Drake leaned down and shook Liam's hand.

"That I am," Drake replied, his voice thick with emotion. "You're my biological son. Pleased to meet you."

"Here's a present from Drake and Kate, Liam," Brenda said, handing Liam the wrapped toy. "Why don't you open it?"

Liam sat down and quickly ripped the wrapping off.

"Wow," he said, an expression of surprise on his face. He held up the boxed Iron Man figurine. "It's Iron Man!"

Drake knelt and helped Liam remove Iron Man from of the box, which was no easy feat, given all the plastic wrap and wires to prevent theft. Finally, he had it done. "Here you go."

Liam examined it carefully, moving the arms and legs into various positions.

"Thank you," Liam said finally. Drake nodded, smiling as he watched Liam fly Iron Man through the air.

We all sat on the two couches and watched Liam for a moment. Drake was focused on Liam, his expression intense as if he couldn't believe it was real.

"That's a nice train set," Drake said and knelt back down beside Liam. "Can you show it to me?"

"Sure," Liam said and put Iron Man down. Drake bent onto one knee and watched as Liam turned to the train. "I got it from my grandpa and grandma for Christmas. It's a Thomas the Tank Engine set. I watch Thomas on TV."

The next hour was taken up by Drake making small talk with Liam about his toys and how he felt about being in Manhattan. Meanwhile, Brenda and I talked about Sophie and how she was doing after the attack.

I overheard Drake and Liam talking and it made my eyes well up.

"My mom said you're the man who gave me stem cells," Liam said while he moved Thomas the Tank Engine along the track.

"I did," Drake replied. "We were lucky that we were a match."

Then, Liam picked up Iron Man and flew him around some more.

"Do you have any questions about me?" Drake asked, his voice soft. "Anything you want to ask? It must be strange to find out I'm your biological father."

Liam continued to play for a moment, making the sound of a plane as Iron Man flew around.

"Are you going to marry my mom again?" he asked, his little face serious, brow furrowed.

I felt a knot in my gut as I watched Drake. He glanced at me and then Brenda before turning back to Liam.

"No," Drake said softly. "We got divorced before you were born. I'm married to Kate now. Sophia is our daughter and your half-sister."

"I have a half-sister?" Liam asked. He turned and looked at Sophia, his eyes wide.

"Yes," Drake said. "She's my daughter and you're my son, so you two are half-brother and half-sister to each other."

"Will she come to my birthday party?" Liam asked, his eyebrows raised. "We don't know anyone here."

"Of course she'll come if you want her to," Drake replied.

"She's kinda young to play with my toys, but she could hold something." Liam went to a box of toys at the side of the room and removed a stuffed Minion. "Here," he said, bringing it over to where Sophie sat with me. "She could hold this."

Sophie was busy sucking away on her pacifier but she stopped sucking and smiled when he came over.

"She likes me," Liam said and turned to Drake.

"She does," Drake said with a smile.

"Here you go, Sophia," Liam said. "Here's a Minion. He's Herb Overkill. He has only one eye."

On her part, Sophie reached out slowly and grabbed Herb Overkill, bringing him immediately up to her open mouth.

"She's trying to eat it," Liam said. He pointed at Sophie and turned to Drake. "Babies always try to eat everything."

"No, no, sweetie," I said and tried to take Herb away. "You shouldn't get Liam's toy all wet with drool."

"That's all right," Liam said, sounding officious. "She can have it. I already have another Herb Overkill. It's a present."

Drake smiled and ruffled Liam's hair. "That's very nice of you, Liam."

"She *is* my sister."

"She is," Drake replied, his voice low and filled with emotion.

For the next few moments, the three of us adults and Liam watched while Sophie chewed on Herb Overkill. Then, she reached for Iron Man, when Liam held him out.

"No, you can't eat Iron Man," Liam said and pulled him gently away. "He's too strong. He'd break your teeth."

"Luckily, she doesn't have any teeth yet," I said with a smile. "We won't let her get Iron Man all wet."

Of course, at that pleasant moment, the front door opened and Maureen walked in, her arms full of shopping bags.

"I'm home," she said and removed her coat. She turned to us and saw Drake on the floor with Liam. "You're still here."

"We should go," I said to Drake and stood up. "Sophie needs to nurse."

"Yes," Drake said, his voice filled with obvious reluctance. "We should be going." He turned to Liam. "It was nice to meet you. I hope we can get to know each other better now that you're living in Manhattan.

"Will you bring Sophia?" Liam asked as he handed Sophie Herb Overkill once more.

"We sure will," Drake said. "Maybe next time you could come to our house."

"Maybe," Maureen replied. She walked over to Liam and stood behind him, holding onto his shoulders protectively. "We'll have to do some planning about this."

Drake nodded. "Whatever you think is best."

On my part, I put Sophia's snowsuit back on and got her into the car seat while Drake pulled on his boots and coat.

Liam came over to the door, Iron Man clasped in his hand, watching while Drake tied his scarf.

"Well, Liam," Drake said. "I'm glad I met you. I hope we can see each other again soon." Drake glanced in Maureen's direction. She didn't look entirely happy, and was probably hoping to have missed the three of us.

"Yes," she said. "I'll call you and let you know what time is good. Sorry I didn't get back in time to visit."

I didn't believe her for a moment. Finally, after a brief hesitation while I dressed in my coat and boots, we went to the door. Drake turned around and waved at Liam as we left the apartment.

Brenda winked at us as she closed the door. I was glad we had her on our side.

Drake put his arm around me as we went to the elevator.

"That went well," I said and smiled at him.

"It did. It went very well." He didn't say much, but I could tell from the expression on his face that he was ecstatic. Liam knew Drake was his father. It didn't mean much at this point, for Drake was a stranger. To be a real father, Drake would have to spend time with Liam, be there for important occasions and hang out with him. They would have to build a relationship slowly, over time.

Finally, the elevator bell rang and the doors slid open. We rode it in silence, but when I glanced at Drake, he looked so happy, a smile lingering on his face. It made my heart swell with love for him.

"I got my wish," he said to me when we walked along the street to the parking garage.

"I'm so happy for you, Drake," I said, tears in my eyes.

"Thank you," he said, his voice breaking. "It was all because of you that I even had the chance to see Liam." He leaned down to kiss me. "I love you more than anything."

"I love you more than anything," I replied. I meant it. At that moment, I felt as if all the bad things that happened over the previous six months were forgotten, pushed back into the darkness. There was only today, and Drake, Sophie and me. Soon, Liam would be part of that small circle.

Drake kissed me and then we continued to the parking garage and drove off into the growing darkness of the Christmas Day night.

~

CHAPTER 17 : DRAKE

The first few weeks after Christmas were uneventful, and I almost forgot about the looming trial and the investigation into the attack. It all came back again to interrupt my time of marital and parental bliss when I got a call from Detective McDonald to attend a meeting at the precinct.

"What's the meeting about?" I asked, annoyed that they still hadn't cleared me of any involvement in the attack on Kate.

"We need you to answer a few questions."

"Is this really necessary?" I said, impatient, not wanting to go back to the precinct yet again. "You charged Lisa. Why am I still being questioned?"

"Because we have more information, more dates to check, and need to get your response."

"Can't you forward a copy of your questions and the dates to my lawyer? She and I can go over them and provide any answers you need."

"We'd prefer if you could come down in person," McDonald said curtly.

"All right," I said. "I have to coordinate with my lawyer to arrange a time she can attend."

"Please call me back as soon as you have a time. We'd appreciate it today or tomorrow at the latest."

"I'll try," I said and ended the call, in no mood to be polite. If the cops had done their job, I should have already been cleared. I had no idea how they could believe that I had been involved with Lisa and was conspiring with her. It beggared belief.

I left my office and went to the living room, where Kate was reading the daily paper and Sophie was in her Exersaucer.

"What's up?" she said when I leaned down to kiss her. "You're frowning."

I took in a deep breath and tried to calm myself. Kate had enough on her plate. She didn't need to deal with a frustrated husband.

"Detective McDonald asked me to come down to the precinct to answer some more questions," I said and plopped down beside her on the sofa. "I suppose that Lisa's claiming we were together on some new dates."

"You're kidding," Kate said and frowned. She moved closer and ran her fingers through my hair, her green eyes so sympathetic. "I'm so sorry." She leaned up and kissed me on the mouth. When she pulled back, she shook her head. "She's completely insane if she thinks she can make those claims and that they'll stand."

"She's mentally unbalanced," I said with a nod. "I still wonder if she's delusional or whether this is to punish me. She couldn't have me so neither could you and when that didn't work, she's trying to make trouble for me. I should track down Derek Richardson up and talk to him about her. I called and left a message but he hasn't returned my call. He could corroborate the fact that I didn't want to get involved more than just a one-off at his dungeon parties. And he offered."

"You should give his name to the police. Let them know."

"Apparently, he moved to Malaysia. I'll try to reach out to him again, but it may be difficult to find him."

Kate made a face. "Whatever she is, I hope the police figure this out so we can move on. I don't even want to think about the attack." Kate shivered visibly and moved closer. I put an arm around her and pulled her against me, kissing her temple, her cheek, her mouth.

"Don't worry," I said and squeezed her. "They'll have to realize she's crazy sooner or later."

"I hope so. Are you going to ask Lara to go with you?" she asked, her eyes moving over my face. "She can corroborate a lot of dates for you. She knew who all your submissives were, didn't she?"

I nodded again. "Yes," I said and pulled out my cell. "I'll call and she if she's available."

I made the call and held the cell up to my ear. It rang twice and finally, Lara answered.

"Drake Morgan, MD. Just the man I wanted to speak to."

I smiled, glad to have her on my side. "What did you want to speak to me about?"

"I spent some time talking to a few subs I know who are familiar with Lisa. Apparently, she was collecting stories about you and your activities during the past few years."

"Yeah," I said and rubbed my eyes. "I got a call from Detective McDonald about coming down to provide my whereabouts on about some more dates."

"When do they want us down there?" she asked, and I heard the sound of paper shuffling on the line. "I'm in court later today, but I'm off tomorrow morning. We could go then."

"They said today or tomorrow at the latest. I'll call McDonald back and tell him we'll be by tomorrow."

"Okay," Lara said and exhaled. "Do you want me to call them?"

"No, I can do it. I don't want to seem like I'm not cooperating. But hey," I said, thinking about Derek. "Have you had any luck contacting Derek Richardson? He could back me up that he offered for me to be a regular in their play, but I refused."

"No," Lara said, her voice sounding hesitant. "I haven't been able to track him down. I've contacted someone I know who works in Kuala Lumpur to try to find him, if he's in Malaysia. Derek is free to do whatever he wants whenever he wants. He's hands-off when it comes to the business so he might be traveling, according to his manager of US operations."

I sighed. "Okay. We'll have to deal with the dates alone, I guess."

"Yep," Lara said and I heard the papers shuffle some more. I knew she was busy getting ready for court and felt bad I was bothering her. "I can go over around eleven. We should meet first and talk about the past few years. Get things straightened out. Bring your calendar if you have one. Bring your surgical calendar as well so we can know when you were in surgery, and when you had office or clinic hours."

"Will do. Shall we meet at your office or the coffee shop?"

"Oh, let's go to the coffee shop. I've got cabin fever, after working for weeks on this other case. I'll have my own little black book of information since I was your pimp, so to speak."

"I appreciate it, Lara. You're a godsend."

She laughed lightly. "That's why you pay me the big bucks."

I ended the call and turned to Kate, who watched me with raised eyebrows.

"So?" she said, waiting for me to fill in the blanks. "What did Lara say?"

"We're meeting tomorrow at 10:00 and will go to the precinct at 11:00. I'll call McDonald and let him know." She nodded and kissed me before I stood up. "I'll go into my office."

"Okay," she said and forced a smile. "Come back when you're done and read the paper. I'll make some regular coffee for you."

I nodded and left the room, returning to my office and the business card Detective McDonald gave me with his direct line at the precinct.

~

I MADE arrangements and then joined Kate and Sophie in the living room, fresh cup of coffee in hand. I should have pushed thoughts of Lisa and her machinations out of my mind, and tried to enjoy my time with my beautiful wife and daughter, but I felt a sense of dread come over me at the prospect of yet another meeting with the detectives at the precinct.

I must have looked as dismal as I felt for Kate put her section of the paper down and turned to me. "Drake, you have to let it go. You did nothing wrong. I have faith that the police will soon clear you. They're following procedures."

"I know, I know," I said with a sigh and ran my fingers through my hair. "It's just that there have been people wrongly accused of murder, who've gone all the way to prison before they've been cleared, spending years in jail."

She shook her head. "That's not you. Those people were poor and uneducated, easily confused and with poor lawyers." She frowned. "You're a well-educated, wealthy professional neurosurgeon who has a great lawyer. There's no way you're going to spend a day in jail or even be tried. They'll figure it out soon. Really," she said and squeezed my arm. She gave me a small smile, as if she was trying to force it.

I kicked myself mentally for even talking about my anxiety. The last thing Kate needed was a husband worrying about being wrongly accused of a crime. I had to be strong for her. I wanted to be strong for her and Sophie, not weak or anxious. I couldn't figure out why it was taking so long to clear me.

"Forget it," I said and stroked her cheek. "Let's go out and have a nice walk through the park after lunch. The snow's stopped and I bet it's beautiful."

She smiled, a real smile this time. "That sounds wonderful. I love Central Park when the trees are all covered in frost."

THE NEXT DAY, I went to the coffee shop and sat down at a table at the back of the room across from Lara. The table was where we usually sat to avoid anyone overhearing our conversations. The table top was covered in papers, and Lara was on her cell. She stood and walked over to the far window and kept speaking, her voice soft. I tried not to listen, but couldn't help overhear parts of the conversation.

"Yes, isn't *that* interesting? What's the connection again? Through an aunt?"

She stood looking out the window, her hand on one hip, the other cradling the cell to her ear. A waitress came over to the table to take my order. I asked for a latte and then scanned the papers Lara had spread out while she finished her conversation.

Dressed in a sober black business suit with her platinum blonde hair pulled back into a severe bun, she was a formidable looking woman. I'd be intimidated by her if I hadn't been her friend for years and her once upon a time Dom-in training.

"That explains it," Lara said. "They don't want to think of their little girl doing anything on her own like this."

I wondered if she was talking about Lisa, so I listened more closely.

"I will tell him. He's right here, in fact. We're getting ready to go to the precinct to speak with the detectives on the case."

She turned and glanced at me, smiling briefly as if to reassure me.

"Okay, I will. Thanks so much for calling. This is indeed an interesting turn of events."

She ended the call and returned to the table, sitting back down on her chair, her back straight, a look on her face that was inscrutable.

"*Apparently*," she said and opened a file. "Our Miss Lisa has a family member on the NYPD Major Crimes unit."

"Ahh," I said, finally understanding. "And that someone is hoping that Lisa's allegations hold up because then they can lay the blame on me instead of their delusional family member..."

"Precisely," Lara said. Her wide eyes were the only hint that she was excited about this development. Other than that, she was as composed as ever. "We're going to have to tread very lightly, if that's the case. People can get very pig headed when family is involved. This will require a deft hand with the NYPD. I have a few markers I can call in – a few backs I've scratched before. Don't worry," she said and closed a file. "We can deal with this."

"I sure hope so," I said, leaning back in my chair, exhaling heavily.

We spent the next hour drinking down coffee and poring over my schedules, re-checking for any time I had gone to a dungeon party, a night out at the opera or theatre, and any fundraising activities with DWB. I marked down every night I worked late on an emergency surgery. Dates that I was involved in board meetings at night for the corporation. There were a lot of dates. I was a very busy surgeon, executive and philanthropist. Plus, I brought along my schedule of dates I played with *Mersey*.

"God, I didn't realize until now how busy I was back then," I said and shook my head. "I was out more days than I stayed at home. Pretty much every evening was taken up either practicing, performing, at some function or working late. I don't know when I could have squeezed in a mistress on top of a serious girlfriend, fiancé and then wife."

"Too busy," Lara said. "Once we can check the new dates she gave the police, we can probably rule out all of her claims that you were together."

"How can I prove I didn't meet her secretly in the broom closet at Carnegie Hall?"

Lara shrugged. "We'll find something. One date we can prove you were not with her, then all the other dates become suspect."

"I hope so," I said and checked my watch. "Looks like we have to get going."

Lara checked her watch and nodded. "Okay, handsome," she said and smiled at me. "Let's go slay some dragons."

"You can lead," I said and helped her with her coat.

She grinned. "As always."

MCDONALD AND ST. JAMES met us in the waiting area and escorted us into a larger conference room. It was not at all like one of the smaller interrogation rooms I had been in before. It made me feel less like a suspect and more like a citizen who had to clear up a few details before the case could move forward.

At least, that's what I hope it meant.

McDonald sat across from me and put a piece of paper on the table, pushing it towards me with a placid expression on his face.

"You are familiar with the list of dates that Dr. Monroe claims you were together. I would appreciate it if you could provide us with your whereabouts on those additional dates," he said and pointed to a half-dozen new dates appended to the bottom. "If there's anyone who can corroborate your details, we'd appreciate their name and phone number so we can contact them to clear this up."

I nodded and took the sheet of paper in hand. Lara scooched closer, and spied the sheet after putting on her horn-rimmed glasses. The dates were spaced out over the period, with a notable blank space during the time Kate and I were in Africa, but there were a few dates each year that supposedly, Lisa and I were together.

Lara had a list of dates in her hand.

"That," she said and pointed to a date two years earlier. "That was the fundraiser for Doctors Without Borders." Lara glanced up at the detectives.

"I was there with Dr. Morgan," she said. "I didn't see her that night and I would have known if she was there."

"You're his lawyer," St. James said, his tone dismissive.

"I'm also his friend. I know both Lisa Monroe and Derek Richardson. I'm sure once you get ahold of Derek, he'll tell you that Drake was not interested in Lisa beyond a couple of times they were at parties together. In fact, Mr. Richardson offered to involve Dr. Morgan more intimately, but Dr. Morgan declined."

"Is that so?" McDonald said and glanced at me. "So do you think her," he said and paused, "focus on you began at that point in time?"

"Yes," I said, glancing at Lara. "It must have. I wasn't interested in her as a submissive or in becoming more involved with them. You can talk to

Richardson about it. He knows how I felt. In fact, I talked to him about her after I started in the fellowship program."

"Mr. Richardson has been a difficult man to find. He's out of the country right now, according to his lawyer, so we can't confirm your story. But we will, once we're able to contact him."

I leaned back. "I'd be happy for you to contact him, because he'll corroborate my story."

McDonald nodded. "When was the last time you spoke with Richardson?"

I thought back to my call to him after Lisa started the program. "I believe it was in early fall after I started my fellowship and realized Lisa was in the program."

"Tell me," St. James asked, leaning in. "Why *weren't* you interested?" His voice sounded doubtful. "She's a very attractive woman. She was offering herself as a partner."

I shook my head. "They were interested in things that I wasn't."

"Such as?"

I glanced at Lara, wondering how deeply to get into BDSM play with the officers. I expected they'd already heard pretty much everything. She nodded.

"They were into breath play. I wasn't."

Lara was busy cross referencing dates with our list.

"Here's one," Lara said and glanced up from her list. "She claims she was at Carnegie that night you met Ethan and Kate there. That's one we can cross off."

Lara handed me the sheet and I checked the two lists. Sure enough, she had indicated she was at the performance where Kate and I had our first real date.

"I sure didn't see her there," I said, unable to keep a scoff out of my voice. "Does she have a ticket to prove it?"

"Do you have tickets?"

"I have credit card receipts."

"Were you in the theatre the entire time?" St. James asked. "Sitting with your party and can they confirm it?"

I thought back to that night. I had left the box where Ethan and Elaine and Kate were seated, but only for a short time. I found a different empty box and sat there so I could watch Kate. I was only away from their box for fifteen minutes.

Kate even saw me at the end, after the performance, before the intermission.

"I stepped out for fifteen minutes, and sat in another location."

"Why did you leave?"

"My wife, Kate," I said, frustrated that I had to explain my absence. "It was our first date and she asked me to leave because she became very emotional during the performance. You see, she went every year with her mother and--."

"So you were away from their box for fifteen minutes," St. James said, interrupting me. "Did you sit with anyone?"

"I was sitting in an empty box nearby. One of the ushers let me sit there when I explained to him why I left my own seat."

"Do you remember which usher?"

I frowned and rubbed my forehead. "It was two years ago. I don't know what usher it was. Some young guy with dark hair," I said, struggling to remember. "Looked like a college student. Tall and skinny with a bad case of acne."

"We'll check it out."

I turned to Lara right. "Do you have any other dates?"

She pointed to one. It was a night I was playing with *Mersey*.

"I was playing with my band, *Mersey*, that night," I said and showed Detective McDonald. "We were playing at O'Riley's. I stayed after and had a drink with my band mates. Then, I went home and got up early. I had office hours that next morning."

"Can your band mates confirm this?"

"Yes," I said. "Of course. Lisa was never there. I never saw her in the audience and I never spoke to her."

"Do you always keep track of every audience member?" St. James said, frowning.

"I never saw Lisa that night. I never spoke with her. You can ask my band mates. I'll give you their names and addresses. They'll back me up on this. I went right home after we finished closing the place up. Lisa was not there."

"We'll check it out," McDonald said. At that point, I realized that I'd have to come clean to the O'Riley's about my personal life, who Lisa was and how I met her. While I was sure they already knew some of it, because of all the press, I had never said anything to them directly about my past and how it played into all this.

I did not look forward to that reality.

There were three other dates that Lisa claimed she was with me that conflicted with my calendar entries. One was an evening that I had surgery late.

"I went right home after I finished checking on patients," I said. I shrugged, because I had gone right home and after showering, went right to bed. I'd played racquetball with Dave that morning and was exhausted after a long day of surgery.

I couldn't prove Lisa hadn't come home with me. Except...

"There's a security guard on staff at my building in Chelsea. There's also video of the block but would they still have it on hand or would it have been written over? I can't imagine tapes would still be available this long after the date…"

I glanced between McDonald and St. James.

"Would the guard remember me coming home alone?"

St. James shrugged.

"Is it even still the same man?" I added. "I haven't lived there for a year or more."

"We'll check it out," McDonald said, "but from what I am hearing, there's at least a few days you can't prove you weren't with Dr. Monroe. Am I right?"

"She can't prove she was with me either," I said, my voice defensive. "It's her word against mine."

"Precisely," St. James said.

"Dr. Morgan is a highly esteemed neurosurgeon," Lara said. "He owns a business and runs a charitable foundation. He's very respected."

"He's also involved in a subculture that often involves sexual violence," St. James said pointedly.

"It's entirely consensual," Lara protested. "Everyone involved in the life-style signs contracts to that effect when they become involved. What they do is not illegal."

"It's also not respected or esteemed by the general population," St. James said.

"Are you going to charge Dr. Morgan with a crime?" Lara said, her voice icy. "If not, we have to go."

"No, we're not going to charge Dr. Morgan," Mc Donald said testily. "Not at this time. We wanted to check out the new dates Ms. Monroe provided." He turned to me. "You're free to go, but please, don't leave the state. We may have more questions."

"Of course," I said and stood up, buttoning my jacket. "I understand you're merely doing your jobs."

With that, I helped Lara with her coat and we collected up our papers. I kept the copy with the new dates Lisa had claimed we had been in contact.

"If you can think of anyone else who can confirm they were with you on those other dates, you have my number," McDonald said with a perfunctory smile. "Give me a call."

"I will," I said and forced a smile back that I didn't feel any more than he did.

Lara and I left together, my hand on Lara's waist as she led us down the hallway to the exit.

"Well, I'm glad that's over," I said with a sigh. "I hope that they'll realize she lied about the dates. There's no way she was at that fundraiser. I never saw her there. I was with Dave the entire night."

"Don't worry," Lara said. "I'm sure we've provided enough for them to stop looking at you as a suspect. Dave will corroborate your story."

I nodded. Dave was another person I'd have to come clean to. Although we'd been friends for several years outside of work, I had never divulged anything about my secret life. He knew what was being said in the news articles, and he was trying to play it down to the board members and donors but I would eventually have to provide an explanation.

I opened the door, and together, Lara and I left the precinct. As I walked down the steps, I felt a little less gloomy.

We stopped on the street outside the precinct.

"I wonder where Richardson is."

Lara shrugged. "He's a free spirit. I'll call his lawyer and speak with him. It would be nice if the detectives could talk to him. Once they talk to Dave, he'll confirm that you were together for the entire evening at the fundraiser. When they get a couple of falsehoods from her testimony, it'll put all the rest of her dates in doubt."

"I hope so," I replied. "Dave will confirm that we were together the entire evening. I even dropped him off before I went home. Unless there was someone who could confirm that Lisa was there, she could provide no evidence that she was even at the event."

Lara nodded. "I'm going to walk the rest of the way," she said and squeezed my arm with affection. "You go home to your beautiful wife and baby and forget about this, okay? I'll take care of this list."

"Thanks," I said and leaned down to kiss her cheek. "You're the best."

She smiled. "I am, aren't I?"

We laughed and then parted. As I walked down the street to the parking garage, I was glad Lisa picked an event that I could account for every minute of my time. She made a big mistake. She lied about everything, of course, but that lie was one I could prove. That had to count for something. If she lied about that, why believe anything else she said?

I arrived at my car and got in just as a light snow started to fall. Eager to get home to Kate and Sophie, I was glad that the meeting was over. I'd do my best to forget about it, like Lara suggested, but I doubted I could. Not until they officially cleared me.

Until then, the case was a dark cloud over my day.

When I got home, I saw that Kate and Sophie were taking a nap so I went to my office and sat down, flipping through my contacts so I could find Richardson's cell and call him. It was a long shot, since he was probably out of the country and using a different cell, but I thought I'd give it a try.

I dialed the number and got an answering machine.

A female voice gave a message:

Mr. Richardson is currently out of the country on business. Please leave your name and
number and a brief message and he'll get back to you as soon as possible.

The voice sounded a bit throaty, and I tried to remember if I'd met any of
his staff but came up empty. Whatever the case, I left a message and hoped
that he'd call me back the next time he checked his messages.

CHAPTER 18 : KATE

Over the next week, Drake was in a different mood – one that I hadn't seen before during the entire time we were together. He seemed on edge, his silences prolonged, his focus on making sure that his dates and the dates Lisa provided the police were taken care of. I tried to assure him it would all turn out in the end, but he seemed unsure.

On Friday, after Drake arrived home from a trip to meet with Lara, we sat in the living room after Sophie had gone down for a nap, before eating the dinner Karen had prepared. I'd sent her home early, having had a nice nap and feeling more like I could handle things on my own. He'd come in, his shoulders covered with snow, and plopped the mail onto the table in the entry. I met him at the door and helped him off with his coat.

"How did things go?" I asked when we went to the living room. He sat down in the middle of the sofa and spread his arms out over the back. His face was a bit flushed, like he was upset.

"All right, I guess," he said, his voice discouraged. "How can you prove a negative? Lara and I have been combing over all my schedules, cross matching with the dates Lisa claimed we were having our secret trysts, but it's impossible to prove I wasn't with her on some of the dates."

I knelt at his feet, my hands on his thighs, trying to encourage him.

"Drake," I said imploringly. "You weren't with Lisa. Period. Once you cross off enough of those dates on the list, the police will know. McDonald will know and they'll clear you of any involvement. You have to believe that."

"I do," he said and pulled me up off my knees and onto his lap, where I sat with my arms around his neck. "There's so much fallout for me due to the case. The news reports are brutal. The stories she's telling people, which are being leaked to the press…" He shook his head. "It makes me look like a bad guy. Doctor Dominant. Doctor Dangerous. Doctor Discipline. People in the public believe that if you're a man and in the lifestyle, you're a sadist. They don't listen once they hear Dominant."

He sighed and glanced away, as if he couldn't face me.

"Don't worry about those descriptions of you. They're great for headlines," I said and brushed hair off his forehead, "but they're not true. Anyone who knows you, knows they're exaggerations." He finally turned back and met my eyes. "You're Doctor Delicious. Nothing more," I said and kissed him. "You should be Doctor Pleasure and Doctor Multiple Orgasms, if the truth were told."

He smiled a bit at that. "I wish Richardson would get in contact and confirm what I told the detectives.

"Did you try to call him again?" I asked.

He nodded. "I did, but he's still out of the country, apparently."

"He'll get in touch and he'll confirm everything."

I could tell he didn't believe it. I remembered way, *way* back when I first saw Drake in the bar before I went to my father's fundraiser. Dawn had said he was *Doctor Dangerous*. He was anything but dangerous. With him, I had felt so much pleasure. I found myself when I was with him. I felt safe. I knew I was loved. My insecurities and self-doubt vanished, because he helped me to see my strengths. Now, I had a family and a budding future as an artist. My MA was almost finished. Once it was, I could probably get a job at a newspaper or online as a journalist.

"Oh, I almost forgot," Drake said and raised his eyebrows. "There's a letter in the mail for you from the Ballantine Gallery."

"What?" I jumped up and went to the entry to retrieve the letter. It was in a white, letter sized envelope with a logo for the Ballantine Gallery on the front. It was addressed to Katherine McDermott Morgan.

I sat beside him and ripped it open, frowning, for I hadn't contacted them and hadn't even heard of the gallery before.

Dear Katherine McDermott Morgan,

Thank you for the submission of your artwork titled "Scenes From Africa" for our consideration. Our board reviewed your work and think it would be perfect for an upcoming theme of naturalist and wildlife art. We would like to invite you to exhibit all five paintings at the gallery in February. Please call me at the gallery and we can arrange the details.

Yours truly,

Celine La France, Curator

The Ballantine Gallery

"What does it say?" Drake asked. I handed him the letter, totally confused about it.

"How did they get hold of my artwork?" I asked. "Did you send them images?"

He shook his head. "No," he said and handed the letter back to me.

"Tell me the truth. Did you know about this?" I said, catching the grin on his face.

"I might have *known* something about it, but it wasn't me who came up with the idea. I was a co-conspirator." He smiled and pulled me back onto his lap. I continued to hold the letter in disbelief.

"Who did this? Was my father?"

"Why don't you ask him yourself?" he said, grinning widely.

"Drake!" I squirmed out of Drake's arms and went to get my phone out of my bag. I called my father's cell phone and waited. It rang twice and then he picked up.

"Hello, dear," he said.

"Did you send the Ballantine Gallery pictures of my artwork from Africa?"

He chuckled. "Not even a *hello, father, how are you?*"

"Daddy!" I said, unable to keep from laughing. "When did you do it?"

"Elaine and I talked about it with Drake a while back. Elaine met Celine LaFrance at some fundraiser or other and said you were a wildlife artist. She suggested that you send in some examples and they'd check them out. We knew you wouldn't do it on your own, so we conspired to do it for you."

"That's so wonderful of her," I said, my eyes welling up with tears. "Of both of you. Of *all* of you," I said and glanced at Drake, who sat smiling like the Cheshire Cat. "I can't believe it."

"Apparently, you *can* believe it," my father quipped.

"They want to include my paintings in an exhibit featuring naturalist and wildlife art in February."

"That's so great to hear," he said, and I could hear the pleasure in his voice. "I'm so proud of you, sweetie, but you have to thank Elaine. It was originally her idea and she did the legwork. Drake and I went along for the ride. I think she took photos of your paintings when we babysat for you once, if I'm not mistaken."

"That night Drake talked me into going out for dinner, when you and Elaine came over and babysat?"

"Exactly," he said with a laugh. "We're a conniving bunch when necessary."

I turned to Drake and stroked his chin affectionately. "What can I say but thank you so much. Maybe the four of us can go out and have dinner to celebrate? The Russian Tea Room?"

I looked pointedly in Drake's eyes and he nodded. I knew he'd always be happy to go there.

"Any excuse for some blini and vodka," my father said with a chuckle. "I'm able to get around with a wheelchair and I believe The Tea Room has an elevator and is wheelchair accessible."

"It is," I said and kissed Drake on the lips briefly. "How about next week? They're probably all booked up this weekend, but Drake could probably get us in next weekend if he calls."

"Sounds perfect. Come by this weekend if you have time and see your old man. We'd love to see Sophie and you two."

"I'll talk to Drake and we'll come by."

"Love you, sweetie, and congratulations once again. You deserve it. I'll talk to you later."

"I love you too, daddy. Tell Elaine thanks. I'll call her later."

We both hung up and I turned to face Drake, who was smiling widely.

"You and my parents..." I said with a smile. "Why didn't you tell me?"

Drake shrugged. "Didn't want you to be upset if they turned you down."

I glanced at the letter once more and sighed. "I'll call Celine on Monday." Then I put the letter down and turned back to Drake, who was leaning back, his gaze on my face. "How can I thank you?" I said, immediately thinking of making love with him.

"You don't have to thank me," he said and stroked my cheek. "I should have thought about it myself, but thankfully, Elaine is on top of things."

"She's wonderful," I said, shaking my head. "But I want to thank *you*. Tell me what I can do."

He cracked a grin. "Well..." he said and raised his eyebrows. "A nice hot bath and massage might be in order. I haven't seen my little slave girl for quite a while..."

"This one would love to provide her Master with a bath and massage," I said, dropping my eyes and trying my best to look demure and submissive.

When I snuck a glance, he was smiling, his eyes narrow. "Going to be pretty tough for you to fall into submissive mode after all this time," he said softly.

"This one definitely needs practice," I said, and tugged at his tie, not meeting his eyes. "If it would please her Master, she'd love to go and run a warm bath. Then, she could undress him and bathe him, if it pleased him."

"It would please me very much," he said, his voice thick.

Then, he reached out and squeezed one of my breasts, which was hard and full of milk. "How close are you to feeding Sophie again?"

"Oh, *damn*," I said and frowned, realizing that Sophie had been asleep for more than an hour and would need to be fed first. "I should wake her up and feed her first. But then she'll be awake until bedtime." I looked in Drake's eyes. "Can you wait until then?"

"Of course," he said. "I'd wait forever for you."

"Luckily, you don't have to wait forever. Only until after nine."

I leaned forward and kissed him. He pulled me against his chest, one of his hands still squeezing my breast, the other tangled in my hair. His kiss was warm and deep, and I melted against him, wishing we could have made love then and there. When I pulled back, I smiled.

"I better go wake her up now or else she won't be tired until late."

"Let's go get her," he said and nodded. "I'll hold her while you get ready. I haven't seen her since this morning."

I stood and went to her room, which was dim, the curtains closed. It was nice and cool in her room and she was asleep on her stomach, her little butt in the air. She looked so cute like that. I stood over her crib and stared at her, thankful that I had such a beautiful little child.

I felt Drake join me, standing next to me at the crib. "It's a shame to wake her when she's sleeping so nicely," he whispered. "Here, let me get her." He leaned over the bed and pulled back the blanket. Then, he picked her up and kissed her cheek before holding her in his arms. She woke up and stretched, arching her back. Drake was quick to slip her pacifier into her mouth and she sucked on it happily.

"Hi, sweetie," he said and kissed her cheek once more. She smiled, her pacifier almost falling out of her mouth. Almost seven months old, she was getting so accomplished physically. When she saw me, she smiled as well. She was such an easy baby, always smiling and happy when she woke up from her naps. From what my mother used to tell me, I had colic and was a hell-raiser from birth. Sophie must have inherited her temperament from her father, for it seemed he had been a placid baby, and had always been self-soothing.

"Do you want to feed her in here or in the living room?" Drake asked. "I can start supper."

"The living room," I said and followed Drake down the stairs to the living room. I sat down on the sofa and removed one of my breast pads, pulling open my nursing blouse to expose one of my breasts. Drake handed Sophie to me and in no time, she was on the breast and eagerly nursing.

"What do you have in mind for supper?" Drake asked as he watched us.

"There's leftover pasta," I said. "You could make a fresh salad."

He nodded and went to the kitchen while I sat and nursed Sophie. I could see him from where I sat, enjoying the ability to watch his domesticity.

It was while I was focused on Sophie that Drake's cell rang.

He answered and I heard him say, "Oh, hi, Lara. What's up?"

He listened and then came around the island to pick up the television remote control off the coffee table.

"I'm turning it on now," he said and clicked on the flat screen.

I turned to face the television. As I watched, a scene came into view of a forested area next to a lake, the video taken from a helicopter. Below, was a white tent-like structure and several figures dressed in white suits that were used for crime scenes.

"Oh, my *God*," I said when I read the subtitle. *Derek Richardson, of Richardson Securities, Confirmed Dead, Autopsy To Be Conducted.*

Drake stood in shock, his cell up to his ear, the remote in his other hand. "I'm watching now," he said to Lara.

We listened to the television for a while. The news anchor said that a staff member went to the billionaire's cabin to do a routine check of the premises as part of a security detail of the property. While there, the security guard noticed that a door had been unlocked and there were signs that someone had been living in the residence. In the basement of the property, there was evidence of a struggle so the police were called. Evidence led to the boat house, where a significant quantity of human blood had been found, suggesting a murder had taken place. Police divers checked the lake but found nothing. Searchers scoured the nearby forest and found a body in a shallow grave less than one hundred yards from the cabin.

The body was identified as Derek Richardson.

The coroner's report would indicate how long the body had been in the grave, giving a better idea of when Richardson had been murdered, but the preliminary report suggested it had been months due to the advanced decomposition.

"Drake," I said, turning to watch him. He was frowning, his jaw clenched, his cell at his ear. "Do you think Lisa…"

"Lisa's been in custody since they arrested her soon after the attack," Drake said. "How *could* she do it?"

He listened for a moment and then nodded. "I'll call you back," he said and put his phone onto the table.

"Do I think Lisa killed Derek?" he said, walking to the sofa and turning the volume up. "I think Lisa killed Derek or had someone kill him for her."

"But how?" I asked, confused. "She's been in custody since the attack. They didn't let her out on bail, did they?"

"Not that I know of," Drake said. "Lara said she was held at Bellevue for a psychiatric evaluation and then was held in general lockup because she was not given bail due to evidence gathered when they arrested her. It must have shown she planned the attack."

I put Sophie up on my shoulder for a burp, and thought back to the weeks after the attack. I saw a brief video of her being escorted into the courthouse. She was wearing prison orange.

"Maybe someone else killed him," I said. "He's very rich. He might have been killed during a robbery or something."

"Seems far too coincidental," Drake said and finally sat down beside me.

"They would have found out sooner if that was the case. I thought he went out of town."

He seemed stunned, his eyes wide as he watched the video of the crime scene taken from a helicopter.

"Well, we know she has it in her to try to kill someone, so why not have Derek killed as well? But why would she? What did Derek do that would make her want to kill him?"

Drake shrugged. "You know," he said softly, "there was a moment – several moments back when I was trying to deal with Lisa that I got this bad feeling about her. The way she looked at me – there was this madness in her eyes. This threat. I never thought she could actually harm you."

"You did want the added security," I said. "You must have sensed some danger from her."

"Yeah, but this? I mean, I could blame her attack on you as a moment of hot blood, a crime of passion, but killing Richardson suggests something more calculating. She overheard me talking to you the day she attacked you. For her to get someone to kill Richardson suggests something more..."

"More evil?" I said, finishing his sentence. "I saw her in the club that night Mersey played. The way she looked at me actually made me shiver."

Drake sighed. "I guess we were right to be worried about her. I wonder what Richardson did. I called him back when I first learned that she was in the Fellowship program and was pushing me for a relationship. I told Fred Parker about her and I might have mentioned Richardson in the discussion. I wonder if he didn't contact Richardson for more information and she found out."

"Let's hope the police figure it out."

"Richardson was a decent guy," Drake said. "He didn't deserve this. He tried to help me. Maybe he contacted her and told her to stop, and she killed him."

I turned to Drake and ran my fingers through his hair. "Don't worry about it. If she killed him or if she had someone else kill him, the police will find out. She may be smart, but she was caught right away after the attack. If she did this, the police will know."

Drake leaned his head into my hand, then took it and kissed my palm.

"I could have stopped all of this if only I'd quit back in September."

He looked in my eyes, and his were so pained that his expression brought tears to my eyes.

"Oh, Drake," I said and turned to him. "Don't put this on your shoulders. It was her and her alone. You did everything you could to placate her. She's crazy and that's all there is to it."

He closed his eyes and then moved closer, taking me and Sophie into his arms.

"I'm so sorry," he said. "You were almost killed. Sophie was almost killed. Derek is dead…"

We kissed briefly and then he kissed Sophie's head.

"If you had quit, there's no certainty that Lisa wouldn't have stalked you anyway. She could have still done harm."

Drake shook his head. "No," he said. "Everything I did encouraged her. You can't encourage a crazy person. They don't react the same way that a sane person does. We were assuming she was sane and that she'd get the message, get the picture, but she couldn't. Derek broke up with her and said she had become a switch. That means she discovered her dominant side and enjoyed using it. I think she's probably bi-polar and once she gets an idea into her head, she can't let go and becomes obsessed. When she finally realizes she can't have what she wants, she becomes violent."

"Do you think she actually killed Derek?"

Drake shrugged. "She would have the element of surprise. Derek probably wouldn't expect that she'd be violent."

I sighed and turned back to the news, which was now on a different story – thank God.

"We have to let the police figure this out."

We sat there and watched the news for a while, but a darkness descended over Drake that threw a damper on our evening together.

I hoped the police would soon discover who killed Derek, and if it was Lisa, perhaps they would finally realize that Drake was totally innocent when it came to Lisa's lies about him.

I hoped that would be the case, but I had a bad feeling about the whole business…

~

CHAPTER 19 : DRAKE

The news over the next few days kept getting more and more morbid. I tried not to watch except in private, when Kate was sleeping, but she was as interested as I was in the murder of Derek Richardson and whether Lisa was involved.

On the following Wednesday, my cell phone rang while I was sitting in my office reading news headlines while Kate and Sophia slept.

I checked the caller ID and saw that it was McDonald.

"Hello," I said and braced myself. "Drake Morgan speaking."

"Hello, Dr. Morgan," Richardson said, his voice sounding calm but firm. "Detective McDonald here. I take it you've heard about Derek Richardson's murder?"

I sighed. "Yes," I said and rubbed my temple. "I've seen the news coverage."

"We were wondering if you could come down to the station, give us a statement about your whereabouts the week before your wife was attacked."

A surge of adrenaline went through me, making my heart pound.

"I already gave a statement about that week."

"Yes, but we want to check out a few details that were a bit confusing. Can you come down this afternoon?"

"I'll have to check to see if my lawyer is available."

"If you insist. Call me back when you have a time."

I hung up and dialed Lara. Luckily, she wasn't in court and answered on the second ring.

"Drake," she said, and I heard papers flipping in the background. "What's up? Everything all right?"

"The police want me to go to the station and go over my statement," I said with a sigh.

"When?"

"This afternoon," I said and checked my calendar. Of course, it was empty. I hadn't planned on doing anything but stay home with Kate and Sophia for the next month.

"It's your lucky day. I'm free from 3:30 until the end of the day."

"Okay," I said. "Let's go there for 4:00. Then we can go for a drink afterwards."

"Sounds good. Will you pick me up?"

"Yes. See you at 3:30."

"And Drake?" she said, her voice sounding firm. "Don't worry. You had nothing to do with this. There's no evidence that you were involved in any way. This is routine."

"I know," I said. "You'd think they would have cleared me by now."

"They will. I'm certain of it. Maybe even today, after they talk with you."

"I hope so," I said and exhaled at the thought of being cleared once and for all. "I don't want anything to worry Kate. She's still a bit delicate because of everything she's be through. I want her to stay as relaxed as possible."

"Me, too. I'm glad she finally came clean about her depression."

"I think she's better now. It was temporary, due to the trauma."

She said nothing for a moment and then spoke once more. "If she has PTSD, this could be a longer-term thing."

"I know," I said, remembering my training in psychiatry and psychology. "I'm on top of it."

"Good," Lara said. "I'm extraordinarily fond of Kate. She's such a sweet loving person. I hate to see her suffering."

"I'm doing everything in my power to make her happy."

"I know you are," she replied. "I knew you two were perfect for each other the day I met her at the café. Just your type."

"Exactly my type."

With that, we ended the call and I returned to the living room. I clicked on the television, keeping the sound muted, so I could check the headlines. There was nothing on Derek's murder, so I went upstairs to the bedroom where Kate and Sophie were napping. I set my watch so that I didn't oversleep and crept in beside Kate where she dozed, Sophie asleep beside her. Luckily, I didn't wake her. Instead, my body gradually warmed as I lay spooned against hers.

As I lay against her, I thought about the whole situation. Part of me kicked myself mentally for becoming involved in BDSM in the first place. I knew it was a risk when I met with Lara that first time and we talked about me training to be a Dominant. She told me as much, advising me to keep that part of my life completely and utterly separate from my public persona.

"Don't ever become involved with anyone from the hospital," was her first bit of advice. "Even when things are consensual, people change. They change their mind about kink and what's acceptable. If you become involved with a colleague, you run the risk of losing reputation if they ever turn on you or betray your privacy."

How I wish I had been more careful. It was a total coincidence that Sunita was involved in the lifestyle and that we met at a dungeon party where there were no masks. She was already involved in the lifestyle, but was looking for a partner at the time I became involved with her. I was a new Dominant, still learning, and she was a willing participant, but she wanted more pain than I was willing to give. I could happily administer a spanking for punishment if needed, to reinforce the submissive's sense of submission – which is what they desired after all. However, I could not go into inflicting real pain for pain's sake. I was into pleasure and control. I liked the way women looked when tied up and helpless before me, allowing me – wanting me to do what I would with their bodies and mostly give them intense pleasure.

Sunita and I did not work out, but she felt cheated and held a grudge. A grudge that almost caused me to lose Kate. It was likely Sunita who fed information to Lisa about me, and the media, sharing the video she made of us. How much I regretted allowing her to make a damn video! Live and learn... When I made my photo albums of my submissives, I made sure to hide my own face so that I couldn't be easily identified. There was nothing particular about my body that could be used to identify me so I felt secure. The only people identifiable in the photos were the submissives themselves and they wanted the images.

Finally, I gave up thinking about everything, and beating myself up, and tried to count my blessings instead of all the negatives. I had Kate. I had Sophie. I still had my license to practice medicine. I was still a top surgeon in my field. My services would be in demand once all this cleared up.

Soon, I began to relax. It was a good thing, because I was stressed about the case, and the fallout for my reputation. I yawned and pulled Kate closer, closing my eyes and drifting off to sleep.

I woke up to my alarm, surprised at how fast thirty minutes passed. Kate woke up as well and rolled over onto her back to look at me.

"There you are," she said and smiled, rubbing her eyes. Beside her, Sophia rustled, and sucked at her pacifier with her eyes closed. We were all warm and snug together, and I felt my heart swell. If only the three of us – and maybe

Liam – could be happily together like this all the time, my life would be perfect.

Then, reality crept back in and I exhaled.

"What's the matter?" Kate asked and brushed hair off my forehead. "That sigh means you're stressed or unhappy."

"McDonald called and wants me down at the precinct this afternoon. I'm going with Lara."

"Drake!" she said and frowned. "What the hell is going on with the police? How can they still think you have anything to do with this? Why are they still calling you down to the precinct over this? You're as much a victim as I am."

"As Lara told me months ago, the police always consider the husband for any harm that comes to the wife. Always. They're usually right. It's the rare case when a wife is attacked or killed and it was not the husband."

"But there should be evidence," she said, her voice rising a bit, making Sophie squirm beside her, her eyes still tightly shut, the pacifier still in her mouth. "There is no evidence."

"There's he said – she said. Lisa claims we met in secret and planned the attack. How can I prove we didn't? We were alone together a few times – in the car when I drove her home, in her apartment when I attached the flat screen, in the hallways at the hospital. In my office. According to her, we were apparently at the same social functions at the same time. She could claim that we talked when we were alone and I encouraged her to kill you so we could be together."

"Anyone who knows you, who knows us, knows that's full of bull." Kate shook her head and sighed. "The police will figure it out."

"I'm neat and tidy. Who else do they have to go on?"

I stretched and lay on my back, my arm around Kate's shoulder, pulling her against me. We lay in silence for a few moments, both of us no doubt thinking about the case, about Lisa, and how we got into this mess.

Beside Kate, Sophie rustled, changing position, her eyes still closed. After a brief stretch, she went back to sucking on her pacifier contentedly.

"We're damn lucky she's such a good baby," I said and kissed Kate's forehead. "What if she'd had colic or some developmental delay? All the rest of this BS would be even harder."

"We *are* lucky," Kate said and squeezed her arm around my waist, smiling up at me. "We have to forget the case and let it play out. You'll be cleared, Drake. They'll figure it out."

"I hope so," I said and kissed her again. "I'm not as confident as you are. Even if they do clear me, there's still a lot of fall out for me in terms of reputation. I've already removed myself from the Foundation board of directors. What's next? Will I lose my surgical privileges at NYP?"

"Over your sex life before you were married? Are they that small?"

"Who can say?" I shrugged, not having a clue about why a surgeon could lose their privileges. I didn't have any plans to do surgery during the coming year, but what about when I felt able to start practicing medicine again? Would NYP take me back?

"Maybe you could talk to the head of neurosurgery at NYP and see what he has to say."

I took in a deep breath and rubbed Kate's shoulder affectionately. "Don't worry about it. You have enough on your plate to think about."

I checked my watch and saw that I should get up and start getting ready for the meeting.

"Will you be all right while I'm at the police station?" I asked and looked into Kate's eyes for a clue about how she was feeling. "I wish you would keep Karen on for a while longer. I hate to leave you alone."

She smiled and squeezed her arms around me again. "I'll be fine. I don't need Karen any more, except for date nights. Sophie and I will cook supper while you're out. I'll put her in her Jolly Jumper swing and she can watch me in the kitchen."

"She loves that thing," I said and smiled back. "Before we know it, she'll be rolling all over the place. Then, we'll have to be on our toes. Baby-proof the place."

"We will," Kate said. "I already ordered those safety plugs for electrical outlets and those plastic thingies to keep the cabinet doors closed."

"Thingies?" I said with a grin, squeezing her again.

She grinned back. "That's scientific terminology, I'll have you know."

I laughed and pulled her over on top of me, and we lay for another few moments like that. Of course, I couldn't help but think of fucking her later, after we put Sophie down for the night.

"This is nice..." I murmured against the skin of her neck.

"It is," she said and let out a long sigh.

We remained like that for another minute or two. Finally, I realized I had to get going.

"I better get ready," I said and rolled her off me. I sat up on the side of the bed and adjusted my clothing. "Don't want to keep Lara waiting."

"Thank God for Lara," Kate said with a sigh.

"That's for sure." I rubbed her knee. "Will you be okay by yourself?"

"Of course," she said and sat up, running her hand through her hair. "I have everything under control. I have the best baby in the world and a wonderful warm home. I'll rustle up some grub for you while you're gone fighting battles..."

"Rustle up some grub, huh?" I said and grinned at her.

"I watched *True Grit* while you were out yesterday," she said and laughed lightly. "I always wanted to use that line."

I stood and left the room with reluctance, enjoying the quiet domesticity of the scene. I went to the bathroom and combed my unruly hair, tucked my shirt back into my slacks, and gave my teeth a quick brush. Finally, I went back to the bedroom and saw that Kate was propped up in bed, a Kindle in hand, reading.

She smiled up at me when I came over to the bed.

"Gotta go," I said softly, noting that Sophie was still sleeping, on her back, her hands in tiny fists, her pacifier in her mouth. I bent down and kissed Kate and then touched Sophie's plump cheek, which was soft and warm to the touch. Her cheeks were a bit flushed, but she was sleeping soundly, so I didn't kiss her.

"See you later," I said and Kate nodded and blew me a kiss.

I left the apartment after getting my coat and scarf, and took my car to Lara's office to pick her up. I texted her once I arrived and she was down in a flash, dressed in her wool coat with a fur collar.

"Hello," I said when she slid into the passenger seat. "Thanks for this."

"You're welcome," she replied. "Anything for you and Kate."

"So," I said and cleared my throat, trying to be nonchalant. "Do police always interview the husband three times in a typical investigation?"

"It depends on the investigation and the detectives," Lara answered. "They interview you once to get down your basic account of the event. They may interview you again if and when new evidence arises. They may interview you once more to push you for inconsistencies in your story, before letting you go and clearing your name or arresting you. In fact, they can interview you as many times as they want."

"So what is the purpose of this interview?"

Lara smiled. "I'll bet you a thousand dollars that they're going to clear you and maybe inform you of how the case is going, seeing as you're innocent."

I nodded. "I hope so. I like the precinct and all, but I'd rather be at home with my wife and child."

WE DROVE in silence and although she had tried to reassure me about the purpose of the interview, I couldn't help wonder.

"What's the chance they arrest me?"

"Drake!" she said and frowned at me. "Of course they won't arrest you. They have absolutely no evidence except the hearsay of the accused."

"I was joking," I said and laughed ruefully, although there was this tiny part of me that imagined everything going sour. I did not want to spend any time in jail, even if I ended up being found innocent of accessory to attempted murder.

"No, you weren't," she said and gave me a scolding look. "Don't worry. I'm serious. There is no way you are on the truly looks-guilty list. Most women who are victims of an attack or are killed, it's by the hands of their partners, husbands, current or ex. They have to give you a good look or they wouldn't be doing their job."

"So you keep saying." I stopped the car and glanced out at the grey sky.

She reached out and squeezed my arm. "Trust me. In a few days, maybe even today, you'll be officially cleared. Then, we'll go out for a drink and celebrate."

"We will for sure," I said. "Now that we have a babysitter that Kate trusts, we can go out once in a while."

"It's a deal."

Finally, we arrived at the precinct and I parked in the visitor's parking lot. I opened the door for Lara and we walked into the building. I glanced around and decided that once this was all over, I'd send Lara on a trip to Bermuda, which was her favorite vacation spot. A week in the sun would be a nice treat and a way to thank her for everything she had done to help both Kate and me during our crazy time both before and after the attack.

We checked in at the front desk and were greeted by a young female detective in business casual, her Detective shield hanging on a lanyard around her neck. Her dark eyes appraised me, giving me the once over.

Detective Susan Mahood.

"Detective McDonald will be with you in a moment," she said, her voice pleasant while she led us to a conference room. "In the meantime, can I get you a coffee or water?"

"No thanks," Lara said.

I shook my head. "We'll be fine."

Lara and I took seats on one side of the table and waited. Across from us was a two-way mirror the size of a picture window in a house.

I unbuttoned my jacket. Neither of us spoke, waiting for the detectives to arrive. After fifteen minutes passed, I sighed and turned to look at Lara.

"Shall I go ask about the delay?" she asked, raising her eyebrows.

"No, it's okay." I shifted in my chair, tense.

Finally, the door opened and in walked Detective McDonald, accompanied by Detective Mahood. McDonald had a file in his hand and a paper bag in the other. His jacket was off and his tie loosened. He appeared to have been busy and rushed in.

"Sorry to be late," he said and sat across from us. Mahood took a seat beside him. "Another case, another interview ran overtime."

"No problem," I said, although I felt a bit upset at the wait.

He opened his file and flipped through it. "I have a few questions to go over, if you don't mind."

"Ask away," I said and folded my hands on the tabletop.

"Is there anyone besides your wife who can corroborate your whereabouts on the night of June twenty-sixth?"

I frowned and tried to recall that date.

"Let me refresh your memory," McDonald said. "That was a Friday, before the attack."

"Let me check my phone," I said and removed my cell. I scrolled through my calendar. "I had a meeting with the manager of special projects at the Foundation that afternoon. We played racquetball and then had a drink. I went right home. Parked my car in the parking garage. Went into our building. Didn't go out again until the next morning – probably to get our paper and some fresh bagels from the bagel shop a block down the street. That's our usual Saturday morning routine."

"If you could give us the address of your parking garage, I'd appreciate it."

"Is there some reason that date is important?" I asked, curious about it.

"I'm unable to reveal that information, but it's related to the disappearance of Derek Richardson."

I shrugged. "Other than spending the afternoon with Dave Mills, I was with Kate the rest of the day and night."

Lara leaned forward, her brow furrowed. "Can I ask whether you plan on clearing my client of any suspicion in the case?"

"We're almost ready to make an arrest in the case, but have a few more details to check before we move forward."

It was then Detective Mahood sat forward. " I would like to ask Dr. Morgan if he recognizes this," she said and reached into the paper bag at her elbow. She withdrew an object and placed a small paperweight on the desk between us.

It was a paperweight from my office at NYU. A gift from my father when I was in college, the paperweight featured a tiny African landscape with a baobab tree inside. The inscription on the base read KENYA.

"That's my paperweight, if that's what you mean," I said. I reached out to pick it up but Mahood took it back.

"And when was the last time you saw this?" she asked, placing it beside her on the table.

"Where did you get that?" I asked. "It's from my office at the hospital where I was doing my fellowship."

"Do you remember the last time you saw it?" she pressed.

I shrugged. "I can't say. It was on top of my inbox, but I haven't used that office for months because I'm on a leave of absence from my fellowship because of the attack...."

"It was found at the cabin where Derek Richardson was murdered."

"What?" I said and glanced from McDonald to Mahood and back. "Are the cases connected?" I asked, wondering about Derek's fate.

"You were friends," Mahood said, as a statement of fact rather than a question.

"Yes," I said. "Acquaintances. We ran in the same circles. I already told you that I contacted him when I found out Lisa was in the NYU neurosurgery program."

"You were concerned about it and felt he could provide you with some information about Dr. Monroe?"

I nodded. "I wondered what she'd been doing since the last time I saw her, which was more than a couple of years before."

"Why were you interested?"

I sighed. "She was pushing things between us. I wanted to get a sense of her mental state from Derek. They'd been involved for quite some time. If anyone knew her, it was him."

"What did he say?" she asked, her face impassive.

I shifted in my chair. "He said they had broken up not long after our last meeting. She was no longer happy; he was no longer happy. She had another involvement soon after."

"Do you know the name of this involvement?"

I shook my head. "No, but from what I understand, he was her submissive partner."

"He liked to be submissive?" Mahood said, her face not changing expression. Beside her, McDonald tried but failed to hold back a smile, turning away slightly to hide his grin.

"Yes, Detective," I said, unwilling to pretend I was embarrassed. "Some men like to be submissive in a relationship."

"But not you," she said, turning back to me, a barely-suppressed smile on her lips. She was unable to hide the contempt she felt in the sound of her voice, which was lightly mocking. "You were the one who liked to be dominant. You want – you demanded that things go *your* way."

"In my relationships within the community, yes," I said. "They were all safe, sane and consensual. Every single partner I had consented to our relationship. I take pride in that."

Lara laid a hand on my arm as if to warn me not to get too emotional. I tried to relax and sat back in my chair, breathing in deeply.

"Dr. Morgan, we're very close to making an arrest in the murder of Derek Richardson," McDonald said and closed the file. "You can imagine we're curious how your paperweight came to be at a crime scene."

"Lisa Monroe must have taken it from my office at NYU and placed it there," I said and glanced at Mahood. "She had the opportunity. Then, I remembered the time I found her in my office after I had left for a brief moment to speak with a colleague down the hall and hadn't locked my door.

"Why would she leave it there?"

177

I shrugged. "Maybe because she wanted to implicate me?"

Mahood looked back down at her file and flipped a page. "We have a few suspects, based on previous relationships with Dr. Monroe. When we arrest someone, you'll be the first to know."

"So I take it that means Dr. Morgan isn't a suspect?" Lara said, her voice insistent.

"I didn't say that," Mahood replied and glanced up at us. "I didn't say he was a suspect either. You know well enough that we must explore every avenue in murder cases like Mr. Richardson's. Very often, the intimate partners are our first persons of interest. Friends, spouses or lovers."

Lara shook her head in disgust and met my eyes. I could see fire in them. She wanted to argue more with Detective Mahood, but she gritted her teeth and exhaled instead.

"Are we finished?" Lara said acidly.

"Yes," Detective McDonald said, his voice pleasant. "Feel free to leave."

"Stay in town, Dr. Morgan," Mahood said, her voice dripping with warning. "Now is not the time to be going on business trips or anything."

"I have no plans to leave," I said, trying hard to keep the acid out of my voice, but I mostly failed. "I'm waiting to hear who you finally arrest. Derek was a friend, even if we didn't speak much for the past couple of years. We were both busy with our lives."

"Understood," McDonald said and stood. "Thank you for coming down."

He flashed me a brief smile that said nothing. I stood as well and buttoned my jacket, then offered my arm to Lara, who stood beside me, glowering at Mahood. They were playing good cop-bad cop, and Mahood seemed to like to play the bad cop.

I knew it was a tactic used to get cooperation with suspects, but it still grated.

Once we were outside, Lara practically exploded. "I could strangle that Mahood. She was so damn rude."

"She's playing a role," I said and let out a long breath I'd been holding without knowing it. "You know, the old good cop-bad cop routine."

"I know that more than anyone," she said and sat in the passenger seat after I opened the door for her. "It still gets me."

"Me, too," I said and went around to the driver's side. I slipped into my seat and closed the door, heaving a sigh of relief now that the interview was over. "Let's go get that drink."

"Absofuckinglutely," Lara said. It was uncharacteristic of her to swear so I could tell she was angry.

We drove in silence for a moment, and then she turned to me.

"I'm sorry all this is happening to you. There's no way you should still be a person of interest in Kate's case. That paperweight means nothing, although I admit that it does look suspicious. You were never at Derek's cabin, so your DNA won't be there at all – unless that bitch Lisa gathered hair from your chair and took it out there to plant. There's absolutely no evidence you were involved in any way with Derek's murder. You shouldn't be hauled down to the precinct office to be interviewed like this. It's only because of your BDSM history. Cops don't understand."

"I know," I said and squeezed her arm. "I had to be prepared for something like this when I became involved. We all do."

"Still, they should do their damn jobs and clear you."

"They will," I said, trying to sound more positive than I felt. McDonald had to know I was innocent, and that I was not involved with Derek's death. They had to know. They couldn't tell me yet who they were going to arrest and so kept us all in suspense. "It'll all work out fine. You wait and see. This time next week, we'll hear back from McDonald that they arrested someone in the Richardson case and that I'm cleared of any suspicion in Kate's attack."

"You're right. I'm frustrated that the wheels of justice don't move more quickly."

We drove to a little pub we both liked off Madison Avenue, and went into the darkened interior. An old Irish Pub, with dark wood paneling and burnished brass fixtures, it was a throwback to something you might see during the heyday of the Irish Mafia.

We sat at the bar side by side and when the bartender came over, white bar cloth in hand, Lara ordered for us.

"Two Irish whiskeys, best you have, neat."

"Will Powers John's Lane do?" the bartender asked.

"Hit us," Lara said and removed her jacket, slinging it over the back of her stool. "Then give me another."

The bartender poured us two shots, and we downed them together. I enjoyed the warmth as the whiskey burned down my throat. So, Lisa had tried to frame me for Derek's murder?

I had a feeling it was going to be a long night.

CHAPTER 20 - KATE

Drake had more than a little hangover the next day. When I got up with the sunlight, he grimaced and turned over onto his stomach, pulling the pillow over his head.

"Oh, God," he groaned. "That's way too bright at this time of the morning."

I laughed softly and pulled the drapes closed more tightly. I usually liked waking up to the light, but given Drake's condition when he came home close to nine the previous night, I decided to close them in pity.

"I'll bring you some more aspirin."

"Bring me another brain," he said, his voice muffled under the pillow. "Preferably one that no longer drinks Irish whiskey."

"No way," I said and rubbed his back with affection. "I like the current brain. It needs to unwind now and then – especially when it thinks it's a murder suspect. And drink vodka instead of Irish whiskey."

He reached out and groped around the bed, looking for me. I took his hand and he squeezed.

"I love you," he murmured.

"I love you, too," I replied and squeezed back. Then, I pulled my hand away and got up, leaving the bedroom so I could get him some aspirin and water. I padded down the hallway and peeked into Sophie's bedroom, where she was sleeping soundly. I decided to go inside and check on her and when I got to her bedside, I felt her forehead and got a shock. She felt hot to touch.

I bent down and pressed my lips against her forehead and sure enough, she felt distinctly hot.

Since she was sleeping well enough, I left the bedroom and went downstairs to the medicine cabinet. In addition to the aspirin and glass of water, I took the ear thermometer with me and returned to the second floor.

I went into the bedroom and put the aspirin and water on the bedside table.

"Sophie feels hot," I announced, and felt a surge of unease go through me now that I said it out loud. "I'm going to take her temperature."

Drake pulled the pillow away, a frown on his forehead.

"What?" he said and sat up. "She's got a fever?"

"I haven't checked yet, but I'm going to," I said and held up the thermometer.

"Give that to me," he said and downed his aspirin and water. "I'll do it."

"You're the doctor," I said and forced a smile.

Drake slipped out of bed and pulled on some boxer briefs, before taking the thermometer out of my hand. I followed him to Sophie's bedroom.

I didn't like the idea that Sophie was hot. It was cool in her room – not cold but not too warm either. We hadn't had any visitors to give her any kind of virus – except for Karen but she had been fine.

Once inside, Drake bent down and kissed her forehead the way I had.

"She does feel warm," he said in a soft voice. Then he tilted her head to the side and placed the tip of the ear thermometer into Sophie's tiny ear. He activated the thermometer and it flashed briefly into her ear. Sophie stirred but didn't wake up. She merely sucked more intently on her pacifier for a moment.

Drake examined the thermometer.

"She has a fever. It's pretty mild, but it's up a degree."

He looked at me in the dimness of the room. "It's probably a simple virus. She'll be fine," he said, but his voice wavered a tiny bit. Of course, my mind went to the worst thing that it could be – influenza or one of the childhood illnesses. She'd been vaccinated, her first shots, but that only gave her partial protection.

Drake put his arm around my shoulders and pulled me out of the room. "Whatever it is, we should let her sleep. Come out and bring the baby monitor to the living room so we can listen in."

I nodded and went to the bedroom, retrieving the monitor so we could listen to her while she slept, in case she woke up or was having difficulty breathing.

Drake went right to the shower, so I went downstairs to the kitchen and made some decaf coffee and started to cook some bacon for our breakfast. My father always told me that you need something hearty after a night drinking to fight the hangover, so I thought a good British breakfast would help Drake recover. I sliced tomatoes, popped in some toast, heated up a small can of baked beans, and then cut up some leftover baked potatoes in butter. It would be a feast.

Drake came downstairs in his sweats, his chest still bare, toweling his hair. "That smells fantastic," he said and bent over to kiss my cheek. He went to the baby monitor on the island and upped the sound, then turned to me, forcing a smile. "I checked on her again and she's sleeping quietly. No need to worry."

"But you turned the sound up anyway, right?" I said, and exhaled, trying not to get too nervous.

"All babies get sick eventually," he said and sat at the island. He draped the towel over his shoulders and ran a hand through his hair, smoothing it with his fingers. He looked delicious, sitting there half dressed, his hair wet, his cheeks a bit rosy from the heat of the shower.

If I hadn't been busy cooking, and if he didn't have a hangover, I'd have wanted to go back to bed with him, see what developed, but not that morning. Instead, I admired him, my eyes lingering over his well-developed chest and abs, and the tiny trail of dark hair than led from his navel beneath his sweats. God, he was gorgeous...

"What's on the agenda for today?" I asked, flipping the bacon over and moving the potatoes around in the frying pan.

"I'm going to spend the entire day with my two favorite people," he said and drank some of the orange juice I'd squeezed. "The three of us, all day. No corporation, no foundation, no surgery. Just us."

I sighed and turned to face him. "I'm sorry that your board members felt the need to kick you off the boards. I think it's highly unfair."

"It's all about perception. I don't want their reputations to be harmed by association. The most important part of the corporation and foundation is what they do, not my part in them."

"That's awfully big of you, but you enjoyed your work with them. It meant something to you. Now, what will you do?"

He shook his head and reached out, took my hand. "I have you. I have Sophie. We have our place here. That's all I need. The rest is window dressing."

I nodded and turned back to the stove, flipping the bacon again and stirring the beans. I cracked two eggs and watched them bubble in the pan beside the bacon.

"You never told me how it went last night," I said and watched him from the stove. "You kind of stumbled into bed after you and Lara had a late dinner. What did the police want to talk about?"

Drake made a face. "Sorry about missing dinner with you, but it was a difficult meeting. Lara took me out for a drink and it turned into five and she fed me so I wouldn't absorb all that alcohol."

"It's fine," I said and smiled. "Why was the meeting so bad?"

Drake sighed. "They had a paperweight of mine. Apparently, they found it at Derek's cabin."

"What?" I said and put down the fork. "How did it get out there? No, wait," I said and leaned against the counter. "Let me guess. Lisa took it from you and planted it there. Was it the one from Africa that your father gave you?" I said, remembering seeing it in Drake's office when I had visited.

"Unfortunately, yes," Drake said and frowned. "What was she thinking? Did she take it as some kind of weird memento? Or did she actually plant it at the cabin to implicate me?"

I shook my head and turned back to the stove. "Who can say? She's crazy."

"She is." Drake got up and went to the coffee maker, pouring my decaf into a carafe and making a pot of caffeinated coffee for himself.

"So, to completely change the topic, what are your plans for your art? The gallery said it wanted to see more of your work. What's next?"

I shrugged. "I don't know yet," I said. "I'm busy with Sophie and the house. Honestly, it takes all my energy to look after her."

He nodded and watched me as I plated out his meal. "Pretty soon, you'll have more time. When she stops nursing, you can get me to give her half her bottles."

I put his plate down on the island in front of him. "I don't want to stop nursing yet," I said. "I have to carve out some time to myself. If she slept through the night, it would be easier. I'd feel more awake during the day."

Drake cut up his eggs and dug into his meal. "You have to do what works for you," he said. "Whatever you decide. I'll support you."

I nodded. "Thank you," I said. "Sophie's still too young to stop nursing. The doctors all said six months at least. Since she was premature, that means eight months for Sophie since she was premature. I have some time to go. I'd like to nurse her for a full year, if I can."

Drake dragged his toast through his eggs. "Like I say, I'll support whatever you decide."

"Thank you," I said again. In all honesty, I wasn't ready to go back to painting. I'd been preoccupied with the trial and how my father was doing. While he'd been recovering nicely from his stroke, he was still frail and was at risk for small strokes, called TIAs. I wanted to spend as much time with him and Elaine as we could. Almost losing him like I did made me realize how much a part of my life he was and I wanted to keep it that way.

"I was going to go to dad's today, but if Sophie's sick, I don't think I should."

"No," Drake said. "Go if you want. I'll stay home with her."

I shook my head. "I'd be too worried," I said and fixed my own plate.

"Hey," Drake said when I sat beside him. He put his hand on my shoulder and leaned in to kiss my cheek. "In case you forgot, I'm a pediatric neurosurgeon, or would have been one already if it weren't for Lisa Monroe."

We kissed and I forced a smile. "I know. Maybe I'll go over later if Sophie's okay."

"Up to you."

~

AFTER WE FINISHED OUR BREAKFAST, I went into Sophie's room, deciding to wake her up and feed her so she wouldn't sleep too long. She groused a bit when I picked her up, snuffling, her tiny fists beside her head as she stretched. Her pacifier was still clamped in her mouth when she smiled at me.

"I guess you're not feeling too bad," I said and kissed her rosy cheek. I brought her downstairs to the living room where Drake was sitting, having dressed in his bath robe, a cup of coffee in his hand. He was watching CNN and reading the newspaper.

"There's my girl," he said when I sat beside him on the sofa and adjusted Sophie in my arms so she could nurse. "Time to wake up, sleepy head."

Drake leaned down and kissed her forehead and then watched while I got her latched on.

"You do that like a pro," he said and smiled.

"It hurt like hell for weeks," I said, remembering all the times I fed Sophie with tears in my eyes. "But once I got it right, it stopped hurting completely."

He stroked Sophie's head and then brushed hair off my cheek, smiling as he did.

"My two girls," he said softly. "I wish my father was alive to see you two."

I smiled at Drake, a sense of regret filling me that I'd never met the legendary Liam Morgan.

"I wish I'd known him."

"He would have charmed you," Drake said. "He was a lady's man. You would have loved him."

"Like father like son," I said with a laugh.

"I am *not* a lady's man," Drake said with a mock-frown. "I'm a committed married man and father of a beautiful daughter."

~

LATER, when I was finished nursing Sophie, I laid her down on the floor on her blanket for some tummy time. Drake sat beside me, reading the paper.

"Oh, I forgot," he said and left the room, taking the stairs to the second floor. "Stay right where you are."

"I'm not going anywhere," I replied, smiling at the look on his face. I wondered what he was doing, but he came back down quickly and had his hand behind his back.

"I guess you forgot what day it is," he said as he stood across from me, his hands behind his back.

"What do you mean?" I said and frowned, trying to remember but failed. "I'm drawing a blank..."

"You've been preoccupied, so I don't blame you, but I remember. Here," he said and knelt in front of me, on one knee. "This is for you."

He held out a small present, the size of a ring box wrapped in white paper with a big pink ribbon.

"Oh, my God," I said, finally realizing the fact it was Valentine's Day. "I forgot all about it. I didn't even get anything for you. Not even a card..." I glanced at his face, but he was smiling, apparently too excited about me opening his present to care about the fact I'd forgotten to get him anything. "I'm so sorry..."

"Don't say a word," he said and held out the box. "This is a small token of my love for you."

I finally took the little present and gently pulled off the ribbon and paper, to reveal a black velvet ring box as I suspected. When I opened it, my eyes almost bugged out. It was a huge pink diamond cut in a marquise shape set in white gold.

"Drake, you shouldn't have," I said and slipped it on my other finger. It fit perfectly, of course.

"I most certainly *should* have and wanted to," he said and took my hand, kissing my palm before turning my hand over so he could admire the ring. "It's a very rare pink diamond that I found when I was looking for something for you."

I admired the ring. It was beautiful. "Was it very expensive?"

"Not really," Drake said. "I mean, not compared to some. Colored diamonds are less valuable because they're flawed. But I thought this would be perfect for you. It's so pretty."

I smiled and pulled closer up for a kiss. He leaned over me, his hands on either side of me, his body between my thighs. Of course, in that position, my mind went immediately to what else I'd like that body of his to do and I wrapped my legs around his hips.

"Mmm, Ms. Bennet," he murmured against the skin of my neck. "This position gives me many ideas..."

"Me, too," I said and smiled when he began kissing my chin, my throat and nibbling on my ear. "Maybe when Sophie goes to sleep..."

"Count on it," Drake said. "I'll run a nice bubble bath with candles and we can indulge."

"It's a date."

We kissed once more and although I would have been happy to make love with Drake right then and there – if Sophia was asleep that is – I let him go and he sat beside me on the sofa, adjusting himself, and picked up the paper once more.

～

CHAPTER 21 - DRAKE

Kate had been on edge ever since Sophie ran the fever.

We spent the morning as we usually did, breakfast together followed by watching the news and reading the paper. Sophie was still sleeping, but soon, she'd wake up and Kate would feed her. Then, she'd spent time on the floor with her toys for tummy time.

In the meantime, Kate brought in a couple of mugs of coffee for us and placed them down on the coffee table.

"Did you get a call from Detective McDonald about the case?" she asked when she sat beside me.

"Not yet, but he said they'd call as soon as they arrest someone. Not that it will do me any good, now that someone leaked the fact that one of my possessions was found at the crime scene."

Kate sighed and sat closer to me. "I'll be glad when it's all over," she said and put her arm around my shoulders, her face next to mine. "I hate what this has done to you."

I leaned back and put my arm on the back of the sofa behind her. "I'm alive, I have you and I have Sophia. I'm rich as fuck and can go anywhere in the world that I want. What else do I need?"

"Drake Morgan?" Kate said, a look of surprise on her face. "Rich as *fuck*? I've never heard you talk like that..."

"It's true. I guess I'm angry that everyone's so quick to dissociate themselves with me over this. You sure learn who your true friends are."

Kate nodded and ran her fingers through my hair. "The O'Rileys are true friends. I was afraid that Mrs. O would be too shocked to be able to stay friendly with us, given the BDSM. I mean, they're a big Catholic family."

"Thank God for Mrs. O. She invited us to Sunday dinner, if you want to go."

Kate shook her head. "Not this week. Maybe when Sophie's all better. She's still got the sniffles and I don't want her going out in the cold."

I nodded and heard her stirring on the baby monitor. "Speaking of Sophie, she's waking up."

I stood up, wanting to go and check on her since she'd still been a bit cranky for the past few days. I thought she was over her cold, if that's what she had, but it seemed to linger. I didn't want to worry Kate, so I said nothing, but I kept a close watch over her temperature, checking it when Kate was busy so I didn't set off alarm bells.

I went up the stairs to Sophie's bedroom, which was dim and cool. She was lying on her back, sucking on her pacifier, her eyes still closed. She was snuffling. I bent over her and kissed her forehead and knew immediately that she was hot.

She coughed, her cough wet and raspy, and I frowned. I went to the change table and retrieved the ear thermometer from the top drawer, taking her temperature. It was up two degrees.

She was sick. Kate came into the bedroom and saw me with the ear thermometer. Immediately, her face fell and she came right over to the crib.

"Does she have a fever?"

"It's up a bit," I said, trying to keep my voice calm. "I'll get her some Tylenol."

"Aww, poor baby," Kate said and picked Sophie up. She opened her eyes and wasn't her usual self. Usually, she'd smile at us, but this time she sucked her pacifier and struggled to breathe through her tiny nostrils. Then she coughed again and started to cry.

"Drake," Kate said and laid her down on the change table. "She's sick."

"I'll be right back with the Tylenol. Change her and put her in something light. We need to keep her cool."

I went to the kitchen and found the baby Tylenol and then retrieved my medical kit from the hall closet where I kept it in case my skills as a doctor were ever needed. I sprinted upstairs and arrived while Kate was finishing changing Sophie, dressing her in a thin cotton onesie.

"This won't be too hot, will it?" she asked, her eyes wide with anxiety. "It's light cotton."

"She'll be fine," I said and tried to sound confident so Kate could relax. "I don't want her wearing anything too warm. Our apartment is nice and warm so she doesn't need anything heavy."

I put my medical case on the chest of drawers and opened it up, taking out my stethoscope so I could listen to Sophie's heart and chest.

"Is that necessary?" Kate asked, alarm in her voice.

"I do this for all my patients," I said, and unzipped Sophie's onesie pajamas. I listened to her chest, which was clear, and her heart sounds were normal, so she didn't have bronchitis or pneumonia. At most, I suspected she had a rhinovirus, with some post-nasal drip that made her cough sound wet.

"She has a little fever and a touch of the sniffles," I said and picked up my otoscope so I could check her tympanic membrane for any inflammation. Sophie's tiny ear drums were pink and healthy. "So far so good. What she has is likely a virus that will run its course in a few days. No need to worry. She might be a bit fussier because of it but she should be back to normal in a few days."

"Poor baby's not feeling good?" Kate said in a sympathetic voice as she bent down over Sophie. "We'll be sure to give you lots of TLC until you're better."

Kate picked Sophie up while I put away my otoscope and closed my medical kit.

"How come she got sick?" Kate asked, frowning. "Neither of us are sick. Karen wasn't sick."

"We all carry around a lot of viruses that don't make us sick. When we're out, we touch things, bring them into the house. There's nothing you can do except wash your hands carefully every time you come in from outside."

"I hardly even go out," Kate said and I could tell she was starting to get a bit more worried than I thought she needed to be.

"I go out frequently, but I always wash my hands before I pick up Sophie if I've been outside."

Kate nodded and we went down to the main floor, where Kate got situated on the couch and proceeded to nurse Sophie. It was a bit difficult for Sophie to feed, due to her stuffy nose and she had to stop and catch her breath on and off, fussing at the breast as a result.

"Her nose is so stuffy," Kate said and turned to me, her brow furrowed. "Is there anything you can do?"

I went back to my medical kit and took out a nasal bulb syringe. I checked its size and it seemed too big for Sophie's little nose but I tried it anyway.

"Here," I said and took Sophie into my arms. I laid her on the couch beside me and poked the end of the deflated nasal bulb into her nose, sucking the mucus out of one tiny nostril. Sophie coughed and sputtered in response. I did the same with the other nostril, and soon, she was breathing more clearly. "There," I said and smiled, handing Sophie back to Kate. "A little procedure to clear her nose. That should help her breathe more easily."

Kate put Sophie back onto her breast and sure enough, Sophie could nurse without stopping for breath.

"Thanks," Kate said and turned to me, her expression more relaxed. "I'm so glad I have an honest-to-God pediatrician as my husband."

"You do," I said and kissed Kate's palm. "At least, one in the middle of training. If I ever finish, that is…"

"You will," Kate said. "As soon as things are back to normal."

I sighed and settled back, watching Sophie feed enthusiastically. "If they ever go back to normal."

"The new normal," Kate said. "Both of us have a new life, with Sophie." Kate turned to Sophie and took hold of her tiny hand. "She's our focus now."

I leaned over and watched her nurse, enjoying the sight of my beautiful wife and baby in such a calm domestic scene. As long as Sophie had nothing serious brewing in her, I felt like Kate and I could finally – finally – put the case and all the fallout around it to bed.

OF COURSE, things didn't work out quite the way I thought they would.

That night, we woke to Sophie snuffling and coughing, her tiny voice magnified over the baby monitor, which Kate had set to its highest volume level. We both woke up abruptly, and when I switched on the lamp by the bed, I saw Kate's face was blanched with fear.

"She sounds terrible," Kate said, throwing back the coverlet and jumping out of bed. She pulled on her robe and rushed out of the bedroom before I could even pull on my boxer briefs. I ran a hand through my hair and went to get my medical kit, running back up the stairs from the hall closet where I kept it.

When I got to Sophie's bedroom, Kate had Sophie up and on her shoulder and was rocking her back and forth.

"Poor baby," Kate said, her brow knit in anxiety. She glanced at me. "Her cough is worse. She's sick."

"Let me have her," I said and took Sophie from Kate, laying her down on the change table. I quickly checked her temperature and sure enough, her fever had spiked, this time considerably higher than earlier in the day.

"We need to give her some more Tylenol." I grabbed the bottle off the chest of drawers and measured out the right amount for her age and she sucked on the dropper. Then she coughed and coughed. And cried. I quickly changed her to get her out of her wet diaper and put her in a fresh onesie. Kate reached in front of me and wanted to pick Sophie up, no doubt wanting to comfort her, but I stopped her as I pulled out my stethoscope and listened to her chest, to make sure she hadn't developed a chest infection.

Luckily, her lungs were clear and so I assumed it was more post-nasal drip. I gently suctioned her nose once more to clear her nasal passages and then handed her over to a clearly distraught Kate.

Kate took Sophie and held her to her shoulder, rocking her gently.

"I never realized how scary it is to have a sick child."

"I know," I said and stroked Kate's cheek. "You have me. I'll be here to watch over her. You don't have to worry."

"Why does she have a fever?" Kate asked, frowning. "And why is it higher than before?"

"Babies' fevers often spike. It's their immature immune system overreacting to an infection. The Tylenol will take it down in about forty minutes."

"Forty minutes?" Kate said and then sat down on the glider rocking chair she used to nurse Sophie at night. She pulled open her nursing nightgown and gave Sophie the breast, getting her latched on and feeding in short order. However, Sophie still struggled to nurse because of her stuffy nose. She cried in between gasps for air, and between coughs.

"She's having a hard time nursing," Kate said and looked at me in alarm.

I took Sophie once more and suctioned her nose again, before handing her back and sure enough, that worked. Sophie was now able to nurse without any problem. The two settled in and Kate began to rock back and forth slowly. I watched for a while, then went back to the bedroom and pulled on my robe and watch, and retrieved my cell. I went back to check on them, as Kate was changing breasts, and I stood in the doorway.

"Do you want me to get you anything to drink?"

Kate glanced up. "What time is it?"

I checked my watch. "Four-thirty."

"Maybe some water," Kate said. "She'll go back to sleep soon."

I went downstairs to the kitchen and poured Kate a glass of water and decided to stop and check my emails on my cell. I had twenty-two new emails.

I checked the main email for my Drake Morgan, MD account and there, the second from the bottom, was an email from Maureen's mom, Brenda Becker.

~

FROM: Becker, Brenda
    TO: Morgan, Drake MD

RE: Visit

Hey, Drake, hope this finds you well. Maureen is out of town and will be away for the next week if you want to come by and spend some time with Liam. Call me.

Brenda

I REPLIED RIGHT AWAY EVEN though I knew Brenda wouldn't see it until later in the morning.

FROM: Morgan, Drake MD
　TO: Becker, Brenda

RE: RE: Visit

Hi, Brenda – thanks so much for writing and offering. I would love to spend some time with Liam. At the moment, Sophie's sick with a cold so Kate will probably stay home with her, but I'll be glad to pop by. Where's Maureen?

Cheers,
　Drake

THEN, I sent it off, glad at the chance to see Liam. I hoped to be able to spend time with him, but Maureen seemed reluctant to arrange anything in advance. I wondered if she had gone to Borneo to be with Chris, which meant that she wanted to get back together with him. I hoped not – I did not want her taking Liam out of the country, especially not to a place like Borneo.

I was reluctant to go the legal route, wanting to create as much good will with Maureen as possible and I didn't think forcing the issue was the way to do that. So, I held off applying for shared custody.

I may have to rethink it if Maureen was even seriously thinking of moving to Borneo to be with Chris.

There was nothing to do about it until Brenda returned my email, so I went back upstairs to Sophie's room. Kate was laying her back down in her crib, and Sophie had her pacifier in her mouth and was sucking away much more easily, her eyes closed already. Kate tucked the light blanket around Sophie and then glanced quickly at me.

"That's not too warm, is it? That blanket?"

I shook my head and leaned down beside Kate, helping to tuck in the blanket.

"No, she should be fine. The Tylenol will kick in soon and she has only a light onesie on. We don't want her to be cold. If she has a fever, she'll feel chilled and will be uncomfortable. The light blanket will keep her warm enough."

Kate nodded and together, we stood and watched in the dim bedroom lit only by a Peter Pan nightlight, stars twinkling on the ceiling from the lampshade. I took Kate's arm and pulled her out of the room. She stopped me in the doorway, and I knew she was reluctant to leave.

"She's fine," I said, trying to comfort Kate, whom I knew would be on high alert because of Sophie's fever.

"I know," Kate replied, her voice soft. "I'm anxious because she's a preemie. I read that their immune systems are often underdeveloped."

"She's not a preemie anymore. She's now officially an infant instead of a neonate. Babies get fevers all the time in their first couple of years, as their bodies encounter and fight off every virus that circulates in the population."

She nodded, but remained in the doorway, her arms folded around herself.

I took her in my arms and we embraced, both of us watching Sophie from the door. I was sure that this one was no different from any other rhinovirus, and that in a few days, her nose would be clear again. I'd keep a close watch on her fever and check her ears and throat for any signs of infection, but I fully expected she'd be better in a matter of days.

"Let's go back to bed," I said softly, pulling Kate down the hallway. "You need to sleep. We both need the rest."

Kate sighed heavily. "I'm afraid she'll have trouble breathing," she said, her voice wavering.

"We'll hear every little sound on the monitor," I said and pulled Kate a little more firmly down the hall. "I promise she'll sleep well for the next few hours and so should you so you can be refreshed for the day ahead."

"Okay, doctor," she said finally, following me when I took her hand in mine. "You're the boss."

"I am," I said in an officious voice. "Oh, yeah," I said, remembering Brenda's email. "I got an email from Brenda inviting me to come by and visit with Liam. I guess Maureen's out of town and so the coast is clear..."

Kate crawled into bed beside me as I held open the coverlet so she could slip underneath.

"You'll have to go by yourself," she said, her voice doubtful. "I can't take Sophie out when she's sick." Kate lay on her side, her back to me.

"Of course," I said and pulled Kate against me so we spooned together. "I'll go by myself. I haven't seen Liam since Christmas. I want to be more than a stranger to him so I'm glad Brenda contacted me."

"Me, too," Kate said and yawned. "You have to file for shared custody. You know my dad would help with his contacts."

"I know," I said and snuggled down, closing my eyes. "We'll play it by ear."

I lay beside Kate and wondered what the morning would bring, how Sophie would be and whether Liam would be receptive to seeing me.

I fell back asleep with thoughts of what kind of gift I could get him, struggling to choose between an action figure or a Lego set.

～

A COUPLE OF HOURS LATER, I got up and went to check on Sophie, careful not to wake up Kate. I checked her throat, her ear and her eyes, as well as taking her temperature, which – thankfully – was down to almost normal.

When I returned to bed, Kate stirred.

"Did you check on Sophie?" she asked and rubbed her eyes.

"Yes. She still has a bit of a fever, but it's being controlled with the Tylenol, so if we give her a regular dose, she should be fine," I said, trying to calm Kate, who still had wide eyes. "I don't see any sign of an ear infection or throat infection, so she's probably brewing a virus."

"I hope so," Kate said.

Later, we both got up and while Kate gave Sophie a sponge bath, I put my medical kit away. Kate got Sophie dressed in a clean pair of pajamas after putting on a fresh diaper, and then carried her downstairs. I had a quick shower and went to check my email to see if Brenda had replied. Sure enough, there was a response waiting in my inbox.

FROM: Becker, Brenda
    TO: Morgan, Drake MD

RE: RE: RE: Visit

Come on by this morning whenever you can. Liam has a doctor's appointment this afternoon so we'll be out then. Liam's home and is bored, so now would be a good time for you to pop by. Maureen is in Borneo with Chris, apparently trying to work things out. Looks like they might get back together and Chris is considering moving back to California. I'm not too happy about them leaving, but if Maureen's happy, I'm happy. I'm sure you won't like it, but Chris is all Liam has known in his life and he misses Chris a great deal as you can imagine.

Talk to you this morning,

Brenda

I REPLIED that I'd be over in a short time and got dressed, and went to the kitchen island to drink my coffee and down a bowl of oatmeal.

"You going out?" Kate asked, Sophie in her arms.

"Yes," I said and handed her a mug of decaf coffee. I bent down and kissed Sophie on the cheek. "I'm going to run to the drug store and get a toy for Liam. I saw it there the other day. Brenda replied to my email, inviting me over for coffee this morning. I guess Liam has a doctor's appointment this afternoon, so the morning works out best."

"It's so nice of her to offer," Kate said and smiled, no doubt amused at how eager I was to see my son. "I hope Maureen's willing to let you see Liam more."

I sighed. "She's in Borneo with Chris, so I guess they're reconciling. Chris wants to move back to California."

"Oh, Drake, you didn't say anything about that," Kate said, frowning. "That's too bad for you. Here I thought you and Liam would be able to establish a relationship."

I shrugged and put my empty bowl in the dishwasher. "I don't want to deny Liam access to Chris. He's the only father Liam has known."

I went over and kissed Kate while she put Sophie in her high chair. On her part, Sophie was a bit fussier than usual, but that was to be expected. The Tylenol seemed to keep her more comfortable so I checked the time.

"Can you give her another dose of Tylenol?"

Kate nodded. "Yes, she's due."

I went to the door and started to pull on my boots, eager to go to the store and buy Liam a toy.

Kate took the bottle of Tylenol and measured out a dose and Sophie was only too happy to suck it down out of the dropper. When she was done, Kate left her and came to the door to say goodbye.

"Say hello to Brenda for me," she said after we kissed.

"I will, and thank you," I said as I pulled on my coat and scarf.

"You don't have to thank me," Kate said, adjusting my scarf.

"I do. You contacted Brenda back before Christmas." I smiled and I remembered Christmas Day when I could see Liam. "It's because of you that I'm even able to go and see him."

"I'm glad I did," Kate said. She kissed me once more and then opened the door.

"See you in a couple of hours," I said.

"Have fun and give Liam a hug for me."

"I will," I said and with one last glance at where Sophie sat in her chair in the kitchen, I was gone.

~

My visit with Liam was enjoyable and made me think of how much I had missed of his young life because Maureen had been unwilling to let me know he was mine. She had suspected as much, but given our separation, and her affair with Chris, she had hoped the child was his.

I could understand that, but I still felt cheated of years I could have spent with him. I understood only too well how it felt to not have a father around and wanted to make sure that whatever relationship I had with Liam, I would make the best of it.

"Where's Sophia?" Liam asked when I entered the apartment. He glanced around me as if looking for her and frowned when he didn't see her.

"She couldn't come today," I said and handed Brenda my coat and scarf. While I removed my boots, I smiled at Liam. "She has a cold but as soon as she's better, I know she'd like to see you again. Maybe we can get together."

"Before we go back to California," Liam said and nodded.

I handed him the gift I'd bought him – a Lego Star Wars plane. "This is for you."

Liam took it and went to the living room, where Brenda had a tray with coffee and cups set out. There were small cinnamon buns on a tray as well.

"Have a seat," Brenda said. "Can I pour you some tea?"

I nodded and sat to watch as Liam unwrapped the gift and then stared at it wide-eyed. "It's an X-Wing," Liam said, his voice sounding impressed. "Can you help me put it together?"

For the next hour, Liam and I put the Lego spaceship together, with Liam telling me about Star Wars and him flying it around the room once it was finished. As I watched him play, I couldn't help but think about him moving back to California with Chris and Maureen, once they returned from Borneo. I felt a pang of regret that all this time had been wasted and Liam and I had barely gotten to know one another. When my time was up, I rose to leave with reluctance.

"When is Maureen back?" I asked quietly while I went to the closet to get my coat.

"Next week," Brenda said, helping me with my scarf. "They'll be here for a while to help pack up and then Chris will go back to California and open up the house. Liam and Maureen will fly back once he's settled in."

She raised her eyebrows at me suggestively. "I feel bad about all this, Drake. You've only met your son, officially, and now you'll be losing him."

I took in a deep breath, and nodded. "I know," I said. "I don't want to interfere, because Chris has been his father all Liam's life, but I do want to keep a relationship with Liam."

"You should," Brenda said. "I'll put in a good word with Maureen. At the least, I'll email you and let you know what she says."

"Thanks," I said and gave her a quick hug. I turned and glanced back at Liam, who was lying on his back, the plane in his hand.

"See you later, Liam," I called out to him. He turned to see me and jumped up, running to the door with the plane in his hand.

"Thanks for the X-Wing. Will you come by and bring Sophie with you?"

"I'll talk to your mom and as soon as we can, we'll come over and see you again."

Liam nodded. I extended my hand and we shook. I wanted to hug him, but I felt that would be premature. He knew I was his biological father as an idea but it meant nothing to him yet. That would take time. Time that I apparently didn't have.

I left, a lump in my throat at the sight of him standing there, a sprig of black hair sticking straight up, his blue eyes so much like mine.

My *son*.

I'd only gotten to know him. Now, I'd be losing him again.

I walked out into the cold February morning and wished things had worked out differently.

~

WHEN I ARRIVED home from my visit, Kate was waiting for me. I took off my coat and boots, and threw my scarf into the bin in the closet and then went right to Kate, who stood beside the entry watching me.

"How did it go?" she asked. I said nothing. Instead, I took her into my arms and pulled her tightly against me. Momentarily, I felt overwhelmed with emotion and the sense of loss that Liam would be going back to California.

"Oh, Drake, I'm sorry," Kate said softly as I pressed my face into the crook of her neck, unable to speak.

I shook my head and took her hand in mine. When I checked the living room to see where Sophie was, I saw that she wasn't anywhere in sight. She must be upstairs in her bed napping.

"I need you," I said and pulled Kate against me once again.

"I'm yours," she said, knowing exactly what I meant.

I needed to lose myself, and get rid of this sadness I felt.

I'd lose myself in her.

~

CHAPTER 22 : KATE

Sophie improved over the course of the next few days, and soon, her sniffles were gone and she was back to her old self, trying to crawl around, mostly pushing herself back.

One morning, Drake and I were sitting in the living room while Sophie played on a blanket on the floor on her tummy. While she played, I read the paper and watched the local news, hoping to catch a report about Lisa's trial and Derek Richardson's murder case.

Drake's cell buzzed from where it lay on the coffee table. He picked it up and checked the caller ID.

"Lara," he said and answered, holding the phone to his ear. "Hello, Mistress Lara," he said with a smile on his face. "How is my partner in crime today?"

He listened and then the smile fell off his face. He picked up the remote control and switched the TV to another local news channel. On the screen was the image of a man with a shaved head and a thick black beard. He had his hands cuffed and was being walked up the stairs to the police station, a detective dressed in a suit and tie escorting him in. Beneath the image was a caption.

Suspect Arrested in Richardson Murder Case.

Drake turned up the volume and we listened as the reporter announced that a man had been arrested and charged with first degree murder.

Drake looked at me. "Lara says that's Lisa's submissive."

"What?"

I turned and watched as the doors to the police station closed and photographers left the scene.

"Okay, I'll tell her. Yes, she'll be pleased. Thanks again, Lara. You're the best."

At that, Drake ended the call and put his phone down. We listened to the reporter, who went over the details in the case once more before the news story ended and they moved on to another case.

"Well?" I said, impatient to hear what Lara told Drake. Whatever it was made him happy. "What did Lara say?"

Drake muted the volume on the television and turned back to me, smiling.

"I'm finally, officially, no longer a suspect," he said, his smile turning to a wide grin.

"Oh, that's so great, Drake! Wonderful!"

"Finally," he said and leaned over, picking up Sophia and kissing her head and then me on the mouth. "No longer a suspected attempted-murderer. Now, merely a kinky Dominant."

"*My* kinky Dominant," I said and laughed, so pleased that the police finally decided to take their focus off Drake and put it where it should be. "What happened?"

Drake handed Sophie to me for a feed and leaned back, his arm on the back of the sofa. "They finally found Lisa's submissive partner, and when he saw them, he ran. The police found incriminating evidence, tools in the back of his vehicle, that link him to Richardson's murder. A crowbar that was used to kill him and a small gardening tool that he used to dig the shallow grave they dumped him in."

"They?" I said and frowned while I got Sophie latched on. "Lisa and him?"

"Yes," Drake said, his eyebrows raised. "The week before she attacked you, they apparently took Derek out to his cabin and held him there. They made Derek withdraw money from his bank and send messages to friends and colleagues that he was going out of town for months and wouldn't be in touch for a while. Not to worry, that kind of thing. Then, when Derek tried to escape, he and Jones got into a fight and Jones killed him, buried him in the forest behind the cabin. Jones lived there for a while after Lisa was arrested. He's claiming it was self-defense against Derek, but that's pretty damn weak. There was enough evidence left at the cabin to identify him. They eventually found him at his mother's place in upstate New York."

"Wow," I said and switched Sophie to the other breast. "And Lisa was involved in that murder, too?"

"Apparently, yes," Drake said and shook his head in amazement. "When she was called into the office at NYU the day she attacked you, Derek was already dead. She thought she could go out there and hide with Jones after she attacked you, but she made the mistake of delaying her trip out there and was caught before she could leave. When Jones realized she was in custody, he hid at the cabin." Drake sighed. "It all started when Derek called Lisa and talked to her, threatening to report her to the university if she didn't leave me alone. That's when they went to his mansion and took him hostage."

"Unbelievable." I sat there dumbfounded. "Who would ever think she was capable of something like that?"

"She's vengeful. She wanted to make Derek pay and then make me pay. Jones was her little servant. He was so enamored with her that he'd do anything for her."

"Even kill for her," I said.

"Even that," Drake said. "Some people are so needy, and so empty inside that they only feel whole when someone powerful takes control of them."

I glanced at Drake. "Not all submissives are like that," I said softly.

"No," Drake said quickly, as if he didn't want to hurt me and realized how his words might be taken. "Not all are like that. Probably only a very few. But just like there are a few sadists among Dominants, there are also people who can be easily manipulated among submissives. You have to hope you meet someone who isn't going to hurt or use you."

I leaned over to him and hugged him with my free arm, kissing him on the cheek. "I'm so lucky I contacted Lara that day about the interview. What would have happened if I'd met someone who was a sadist? I hope I would have run away, but what if he was really persuasive?"

"You were lucky that Lara is such a good judge of character. She knew when she met you that we were right for each other and that I'd love you. She even said that to me. She said *You'll love her.* I told her I didn't want to love someone. How wrong I was. And how right she was."

I put Sophie on my shoulder to pat her on her back. After she burped, I got up and put her in her Jolly Jumper for a bit of play time. She loved that jumper and I watched her for a few moments as she bounced around, smiling at me.

On his part, Drake came up behind me and put his arms around me.

"I'm so glad this nightmare is over," he said and kissed the back of my neck. I turned around in his arms and he pulled me against his body. We kissed and it was warm and tender. I felt such relief that they had finally decided to end their investigation into Drake, and realized that it was Jones who was the one being manipulated – by Lisa. Not Lisa being controlled by Drake.

We stood there, in each other's embrace, and enjoyed the moment. If Sophie hadn't been so wide awake, I would have taken Drake's hand and lead him into the bedroom, but that would have to wait until later when she was down for a nap. Whatever the case, I knew we'd make love sometime later in the day. I felt a deep ache in my body when Drake pressed his hips against me. I knew he felt it, too.

So much stress over the past weeks and months since the attack and since the police refused to clear Drake of any suspicion.

"Later," I whispered in Drake's ear. I looked at his face and he quirked a smile.

"Say the word," he said in a deep husky voice, "and I'm your man."

"You *are* my man," I said and smiled back, narrowing my eyes. "Every delicious hard inch of you."

He laughed at that, his eyes twinkling. "You ain't seen *nothing* yet."

"I hope to see something," I replied, trying to keep up with the playful banter. "I hope to feel something, too. And taste something."

"Mrs. Morgan, I believe you will give me terrible blue balls unless you follow through with your seductive promises."

"I will follow through," I said and pressed my hips against his again. "I need you. I need this. After this hell we've both been through, we need each other."

"More than ever," Drake said, his voice filled with emotion. He bent down and kissed me again, then pulled me deep into his embrace, his lips at my neck. Then I heard him chuckle softly. "Even if you smell a bit like baby puke…"

I laughed and pulled away. "I'll have a shower first, I promise. This afternoon, when she goes down for a nap."

"It's a date."

IT WAS PRETTY THRILLING to hear the details of the arrest and arraignment of Jones, Lisa's submissive partner in crime. Cases like theirs didn't happen often and so I felt quite like a voyeur as I listened to the reporters talk about Jones and the details police were releasing. Someone had found images of Jones online and posted them, and they were quite explicit. The pictures showed him naked from the waist up, his chest bare, except for some large tribal tattoos, and a very well-developed six pack. He was good looking in a rugged sort of way, and I wondered if he realized what he was getting into when he first sighed up to be Lisa's submissive.

At that, my cell phone rang and I pulled out of Drake's arms with reluctance. "I'll have to get that. It's probably my father or Elaine."

I went to my phone and sure enough, it was my dad's number.

"Hi, Daddy," I said and smiled when I heard his voice.

"Hi, Sweetheart, your old man calling to say I heard the news that they finally arrested someone in the Richardson murder case. What do you know?"

I sat on the sofa beside Drake. "Apparently, Lisa and her boyfriend kidnapped Derek with the idea of extorting money from him and Jones killed him when he tried to escape. Jones confessed everything to the police, according to Drake's lawyer. It was enough to clear Drake of any involvement so they won't be pursuing him as a suspect in my attack any longer."

"That's good. I knew they'd clear him eventually, but I was surprised it took so damn long."

"Yeah," I said and turned to Drake, brushing hair off his cheek. "I knew they would, too, but it was still annoying and pretty much ruined Drake's year."

"It's such a shame they kicked him off the board," my father replied, his voice sounding tired. "Hey, look Sweetheart, there's another reason I'm calling. Elaine and I have been talking about finding another place in a warmer climate. Since the stroke, it's hard for me to get out and during the winter, I'll have an even harder time getting fresh air. We thought we might find a place Somewhere in California. What do you think?"

"What do I think?" I said, a shock of adrenaline going through me. "I don't want you to leave Manhattan!"

"We'd keep the place here but spend most of the year there. We were thinking Monterey. Somewhere with good weather, and somewhere more wheelchair accessible.

"Monterey?" A wave of sadness went through me at the prospect of not having my father around all the time. "That's so far away…"

"It's only a few hours by plane. Of course, you and Drake and Sophie would be welcome to come and stay with us any time you want. We'll get a place big enough to have you and Heath come to visit. We'll get a place with a pool, and have a nice yard. Think of it – barbecues every night under the stars. The ocean, the beach. It'll be great."

"Aww," I said and actual tears sprung to my eyes and my throat was all choky with emotion. "I'm going to feel so lonely if you go…"

Drake looked at me, his brow furrowed. "What?" he asked softly.

I covered my phone with my hand. "Dad and Elaine are thinking of moving to Monterey, California."

Drake nodded and rubbed my shoulder affectionately. "That would be good for him."

"I don't want you to move away, Daddy," I said and I realized I was whining, but I truly felt sadness at the prospect of not having him there for me whenever I wanted to pop by and see him.

"We can Skype anytime you want," he said, his voice soothing. "I'm tech savvy for a half-paralyzed old coot. Plus, you can text me or email me and we'll be connected on Facebook…"

"I'm so sad," I said again, and blinked back tears. "But I understand it would be good for you. Of course I'll come and visit. Drake and I have the year off so why not? It would be nice to visit the ocean and see the sights."

I looked in Drake's eyes. "Tell Ethan I'll miss him," he said. "He's the only father I have now."

"Drake says he'll miss you, too. He said you're his only father."

"I'll miss him," my father replied. "But I expect the three of you to come and stay for a good long time once we find a place."

"Okay, Daddy," I said and smiled to myself, trying to accept it, wiping moisture off my cheeks. "Thanks for calling."

"Give Drake a hug for Elaine and me and give that pretty baby of yours a kiss for me."

"I will," I said and ended the call.

I turned to Drake after I put my phone down. "I don't want them to go."

"Of course you don't," he said and pulled me into his arms. "We can always go for a visit."

I sighed and laid my head on his shoulder, my tears running down my cheeks once more. I squeezed Drake more tightly, glad that he was so willing to accommodate my desire to be close to my father.

Together, we watched Sophie bounce away in her Jolly Jumper.

When Sophie was finally drifting off for a nap in the afternoon, I felt Drake's eyes on me, waiting to see if I was still interested in a nap with him as well, but I felt too sad to make love. My newfound happiness that Drake was cleared of suspicion was dampened by the news my father would be leaving Manhattan.

I kept thinking how lonely and isolated I'd be with my father and Elaine out in Monterey. Heath and I were never close, and he was always off in Haiti or somewhere else involved in charity work, so we didn't get together much. Besides, his kids were in school, and I was afraid that they'd bring their sniffles and sickness to Sophie. I felt anxious about her health, given she was a preemie and had been born so early. She'd had her shots, but she was still vulnerable to the flu. I wanted to keep her as healthy as possible so I was reluctant to invite Heath and his family over for dinner.

After I put Sophie in her crib, Drake came up behind me and put his arms around me, but I shrugged him off and made an excuse about being too tired.

I felt bad, especially given how much good news we'd received, and said maybe I'd feel like it later that night.

Drake was disappointed but understanding.

He was so understanding of everything. Sometimes, I felt as if I didn't deserve him.

"I'm sorry," I said and squeezed his arm. "I'm a bit down because of the news about Dad."

"I know," Drake said and pulled me into his arms, squeezing me firmly. He rocked me back and forth. "I'll miss him and Elaine. But I completely agree that he should live in Monterey. He needs to be somewhere warm. It'll be good for them both."

"You're right," I said and sighed, and of course, tears sprung to my eyes. "I'm being selfish."

"You love him, and he's been so sick this year," Drake said and bent down, kissing me on the mouth warmly. "It's totally understandable."

We hugged once more and I stood there in Drake's arms, so thankful that I had found him. With him, I could admit anything and he understood and accepted.

"I love you," I said, my voice choking with emotion.

"I love you," he said, his own voice husky.

"I'm sorry," I said, pushing him away softly. "I'm too upset."

"It's okay," Drake said softly. "Maybe we can go and stay there for a few months. Neither of us have anything to do except look after Sophie. With Chris and Maureen getting back together and moving back to California, we'd all be in the same state at least. I could travel up to Silicon Valley to see Liam. We could spend time on the beach with your father and Elaine."

I glanced at him, our eyes meeting. "Do you really mean that? What about the Foundation and the Corporation?"

"They'll still be here," Drake said with a sigh. "Besides, I've had to take a year off. Now that I'm cleared of any suspicion, I hope that things will get back to normal, but it'll take a while. My reputation is still hurt because of my past, but at least people don't have to worry that I'm a murderer."

I nodded and smiled. "I'd love to go to California if you're willing."

He nodded "Let's go and watch the news. Who can say what they'll report next about the case? Even I'm excited."

He smiled down at me and I realized he truly didn't mind waiting until later, when I felt more like making love.

We walked arm in arm down the stairs to the living room where the news was still playing, showing images of the white tent where Richardson's body was found and the caption *Billionaire Financier's Killer Arrested.*

Even Drake was happy to watch the news, eating up every tidbit of information we learned. We plopped down on the sofa side by side, a whole mountain load of stress slowly falling off each of our shoulders.

CHAPTER 23 : DRAKE

The next week was a blur for both Kate and me, as we sat entranced and watched the developments in the Richardson case. Kate sat beside me, both of us glued to the television set while waiting for updates from Lara. She had her connections in the legal world and so did Ethan, so we got a few tidbits of information that were not generally known to the public.

Apparently, Jones didn't like me, had seen me at a few dungeon parties, and was jealous of Lisa's obsession with me. I examined images of him in the newspaper closely, but for the life of me, I couldn't remember him. I was only vaguely aware of male submissives, and never took note of them other than to acknowledge one of Lara's latest partners.

Jones had never been one of Lara's subs so I didn't recognize him, despite the fact he was quite distinctive, with his Mohawk hairdo and tattooed neck and shoulder. The tabloids went crazy posting images of him found on his website, showing his leathered-up tattooed body in various submissive poses. One was of him licking the boot of his Domme, while another was of him in chains, a mask and ball-gag in his mouth.

"I've never seen him before," I said to Kate as we read the Saturday paper together.

"He's a big guy," Kate said and shook her head. "He'd be hard to miss."

"Not my area of expertise," I said and turned the channel to see what the other local station was covering. "I haven't seen anyone mention that I'm no longer a suspect."

Kate sighed beside me and squeezed my hand. "My mother always said no news is good news," she said and met my eyes, hers filled with sympathy. "If they had decided to arrest you, you can bet it would be all over the news with gaudy headlines. But the fact that you're not a suspect? Not a mention."

I exhaled heavily. "How am I going to get my reputation back? I wonder if I should call Lara and see if she could release a statement about it so the news shows would actually say it out loud."

Kate shook her head. "I think you should stay under the radar for as long as possible. This will all blow over once the trial finishes. After that, some other criminal or freak will take center stage in the news, and people won't even remember Doctor Dominant."

"I hope so," I said and sat back, considering how long it might take to get back to the old normal, if that was even possible.

As to Jones, he was only too happy to deny that I was in any way involved with Lisa and recounted how angry Lisa was with every rebuff I made. Despite how he felt about me, it turned out Jones was the one sending the emails to Lisa, posing as Dr. D. It was all part of an elaborate fantasy that Lisa concocted involving me as her Dom. Lisa was undeterred and imagined that if Kate was out of the way, she could fulfill a need that Kate was no longer filling for me – be a true submissive in other words – and that I would become her Master.

She was confused, obsessed, and she manipulated poor Jones, who apparently wanted to be Lisa's footstool as well as her bum boy. He'd gotten in over his head with Lisa, letting her call the shots, and went along with her hare-brained plot to kill Richardson and use his income so they could afford to live the luxurious life that she felt she was entitled.

How she could keep it all up – the residency, the kidnapping of Derek, and the attempted seduction of me – was surprising.

She almost did get away with it, but she didn't realize that Derek's staff would check the cabin once a month. Not being used to having properties and staff, Lisa wouldn't know about those routine duties. Unfortunately, none of Derek's staff were concerned when he told them he went away to Malaysia after he sold the mansion. They were used to his freewheeling ways and wrote it off to his massive wealth.

Lisa impulsively attacking Kate, and doing so after renting a car in her own name, was proof that she wasn't thinking straight and that her hatred of Kate was so strong that she would risk it.

The next day while I was sitting in my office going over some financial reports from the foundation, I received a nice telephone call from Detective McDonald. I smiled when I saw the caller ID.

"Detective McDonald," I said, jubilant. "Just the man I wanted to hear from."

"I guess you've been watching the news and already know about the arrest of our suspect in the Richardson murder case."

"I have. I also spoke with my lawyer and she let me know a few details."

"Yes, Mr. Jones came clean as soon as he realized we had more than enough incriminating evidence about his involvement in the murder and his connection to the email account. He admitted that he and Dr. Monroe were carrying on an email exchange, with him pretending to be you. According to Mr. Jones, he thought it was just role playing, but he now suspects that Lisa was setting all of you up and that she was planning on killing Kate."

I shook my head and sighed. "Honestly, I hardly knew her back when we first met. We never spoke privately and I didn't remember her. It must have really bothered her that she was forgettable to me."

If I hoped to have an apology for the way the police detectives treated me during the case, I was mistaken.

"I want to thank you for cooperating with us during the investigation into your wife's attack. You were remarkably cool under pressure. I guess a neuro-surgeon has to be, given your line of work."

"We do," I said with a chuckle, guessing that was as much of an apology as he could give. "Oh, I wanted to ask. My wife and I are planning a trip to Africa in the summer. Do you see any reason why we can't go ahead and book flights?"

"The case isn't ready to go to trial so it won't be scheduled to start until the new year, based on how the lawyers are proceeding. You're free to go, but it would be a courtesy to let us know how we can contact you, in case we need any further information."

"Sounds good," I said. "Thanks again, Detective. I hope your case against Lisa Monroe goes well and that we don't have to meet again under anything but personal and friendly circumstances."

"Me, too, Dr. Morgan. Me, too."

With that, he hung up and I ended the call and put my cell phone down. I felt so good at that moment, I wanted to celebrate so I went to the living room and saw that Kate was on the sofa holding her phone in her hand. On the carpet at her feet laid Sophie, playing with some toys. Kate did not look happy.

She glanced up at me when I entered the room and I saw tears in her eyes.

I frowned and sat beside her, watching her face, which was flushed.

"No, Daddy, I understand," Kate said and nodded. She wiped tears off her cheeks. "You have to go somewhere you can enjoy yourself. It's just that we'll all miss you, and I was hoping you'd get to know Sophia more before you left. I thought you'd go in October, just before the cold weather really starts."

I stroked her cheek, and offered her a sympathetic smile. Obviously, Ethan was talking about the move to California. Maybe he had told her the date that they were leaving. I knew how much Kate was dreading saying goodbye, especially now that his health was so fragile. Before when we went to Africa, Ethan was healthy as a bull, the stroke he had only months later not showing up in anything but high blood pressure.

"Okay, we will," Kate said and turned to look in my eyes finally. "We'll drive you and Elaine to the airport. No, I insist. I want to see you off and I'm sure Drake does as well."

I nodded, even though I hated the thought of saying goodbye to Ethan. If Kate wanted to take them, and see them off, so did I.

"Okay, Daddy," Kate said, her voice breaking. "We'll see you then. Bye."

Kate ended the call and then put her phone into her bag beside her on the sofa.

"They're going to California?" I said and moved closer to Kate, knowing she'd need some comforting. "Monterey?"

"Yes," Kate said and leaned her head on my shoulder. "They're planning on flying out two weeks from Monday."

"So soon?" I said, and stroked her hair. "I had no idea they were going in the spring. I thought later in the year."

"So did I, but I guess they want to be there so Dad can be outside more and not just on his balcony. They had a realtor find a nice place on the ocean, beachfront, with a huge yard and deck. He's hiring a physiotherapist to come and work with him when he gets there. He's determined to be as mobile as possible."

"That's great," I said and squeezed her, pulling her more closely into my arms. "I know this is upsetting, but it's for the best. Plus, we can go for a visit anytime we like. There's nothing holding either of us here, unless you want to go back to finish your degree in September."

She shrugged and wiped her eyes. "I'd like that," she said. "I can finish my thesis anywhere and my target is by the end of next year. Maybe we could go for a month before we go to Africa to visit your father's grave. Sophie will be almost a year old."

"Sounds like a plan. I'll make the arrangements. I'm sure – I know that Ethan and Elaine will be happy to have us out there for a visit. Do you want to stay with them or should we get our own place for a month or two?"

Kate shrugged. "Maybe feel Elaine out before we decide. Dad said they got a five bedroom so there's lots of room for us and for Sophia to have a room. Plus, if Heath and the kids come, there's a bunk bed in a spare room."

"Would having Sophie around make Ethan happy?"

"I'm sure it would," Kate said and looked in my eyes. "We should stay with them," she said finally. "If things get too crowded, we can always find a place of our own. There's no reason we can't stay for a couple of months, but that may be too long for us to stay at their place."

"I'll find a rental close to theirs and we can go for a week with them and then take our place. That way, we don't overstay our welcome."

Kate smiled finally. "That sounds like a plan."

I pulled her against me and made a mental note to call a real estate agent I knew from selling my apartment in Chelsea. She'd most likely have contacts in California and might be able to hook us up with a realtor there.

I looked forward to going to California and staying for a while. Kate and I had a difficult year and now that Sophie was flourishing, I wanted us to leave behind the bad memories associated with the case. Maybe, by the time we returned from Africa, Kate would be ready to finish her thesis, and we could see where we stood at that time.

I felt quite negative about starting up my practice again in Manhattan. The case and my personal life had been far too public for my tastes. I doubted that I'd be doing much with the foundation or corporation for a while until memories of the case faded, and at least not until after the trial. I could see a couple of years of my absence from both being necessary.

I could start over somewhere new – somewhere fresh. Somewhere like California.

A plan began to formulate in my mind for a more permanent move to California. It made sense. Ethan and Elaine would be in Monterey. Liam would be close by in Silicon Valley with Maureen and Chris. If we relocated somewhere like San Francisco, we'd be close enough to be able to visit both Ethan and Liam when we wanted.

I liked San Francisco when I visited a few years ago. Besides the scenery and West Coast culture, there were fantastic hospitals. UCSF had a great Pediatric Neurosurgery program doing pioneering work in treating epilepsy and spasticity. And of course, SF had a vibrant artistic culture, in case Kate decided to pursue art instead of journalism.

I knew I could persuade her with little effort. I decided to pull together a plan and provide her with everything so it was easy for her to say yes.

As we sat together and watched the news, with Sophie babbling on the floor at our feet while she chewed on a favorite toy, I felt excited about prospects for the next year.

OVER THE NEXT TWO WEEKS, I did exactly that. I contacted Vince Markham, head of the Peds Neurosurgery program at UCSF, and indicated an interest in working with them, if they had any need of my skills. He was very accommodating, and invited me to come for a visit and meet the other faculty and staff in the program.

I talked to my realtor and asked her to start work on finding a rental for a few months in Monterey. I even checked out a few properties myself, book-marking them, even printing off the specs for a couple so Kate could see what we might be able to find.

I was excited, humming to myself as I worked away in the office while Sophie and Kate took a nap. Karen was coming by in a few hours to cook supper so Kate and I could go out and do some shopping. I planned to have a whole presentation ready for her so I could make my case.

I was sure she'd say yes. There was nothing keeping us in Manhattan any longer, with Ethan moving and my withdrawal from the Fellowship and my other business and charitable pursuits on hold.

Monterey...

As I sat and examined the dozen hospitals in San Francisco, I felt a sense of elation about the future that I hadn't felt for a while – at least since I first realized that Lisa was going to be a problem. I hoped Kate shared my enthusiasm.

Something told me she'd be as happy as me with the idea of starting a new life together in a place where the sun always shines.

CHAPTER 24 : KATE

The day I'd been dreading came all too soon for me – the day I had to say goodbye to my father and Elaine.

I knew it was for the best that he moved to California and live. He needed the warmth and the sunshine and the fresh air. Monterey would be exactly that. As a child, we had spent a few winters there, living in a house perched on a cliff overlooking the ocean. I loved playing on the beach, collecting shells, and watching the sea birds fly.

It made me nostalgic for the time when my mother was still alive and Heath and I were closer, playing together because we were the only friends we knew.

Now, my father would be moving away and leaving Drake and me – and Sophie – alone. Health and his family were always off doing missionary work in Haiti, and so I rarely saw them. Dawn and I were no longer friends.

There was nothing left here but Columbia and my thesis. Plus, showing my works at the Ballantine Gallery, but that would be short-lived.

I woke early that morning and laid in bed listening to the sounds of the apartment. The hot water radiators clicked and hissed. While it was getting warmer every day now that spring had arrived, the apartment was cold and we still needed heat on.

Light crept under the curtains at the window and fell across the bed. I turned and snuggled closer to Drake, who was sleeping with his back to me. He stirred and then went back to sleep, having stayed up much later than me to work on some mysterious project that kept him busy for hours on end. I

wanted to press him about it, but didn't because he wanted it to be a surprise
– whatever *it* was.

Finally, after about a quarter of an hour lying in bed awake, listening for
any sound on the monitor that Sophie had awoken, I got up and had a quick
shower, brushed my teeth and pulled on my robe. I'd get dressed later, after
we had breakfast and I dried my hair.

I padded into Sophie's room to find her awake and on her back, her pacifier in her mouth and her toy in her hand.

"Hi, baby girl," I said and smiled at her. She smiled back, around her pacifier, and shook her toy excitedly. "Time to get up?" I felt both my breasts,
which were hard as rock. "Time to eat, I think."

I picked her up and carried her to the change table and put a new diaper
on her, put her in a clean onesie, then took her downstairs, deciding to watch
the early news while I fed her. She was wide awake so she wouldn't be going
down for a nap for a few hours.

Before I could sit down, I saw something on the kitchen island – a card
standing upright. With Sophie on my hip, I walked over, curious to see
whether this was the surprise Drake had been working on for the past couple
of days. He'd been so secretive.

It was a card showing the UCSF campus in San Francisco.

I opened it and read the inscription.

*Drake, we'd be happy to have you as a visiting neurosurgeon. You can consult on cases
in the ER, if you would be willing, since we're always short on specialists who want to be
on call. That's all I can offer now, but we'd be glad to have you on board.*

   Cheers,

   Vince Markham, Head, Pediatric Neurosurgery

   University of California, San Francisco

I covered my mouth and put down the card. Beneath it were plane tickets
for two adults and a child in First Class, flying from JFK to San Francisco in
two weeks.

Beside the tickets, there was a sheet of paper with a real estate listing. A bi-
level house with a huge deck and yard overlooking the ocean in Monterey.
There was even a horizon pool that seemed to blend into the ocean and sky. It
had been rented for three months starting April 15th.

Sophie fussed, her hand on my breast. She was hungry so I took the sheet
of paper over to the sofa and sat down, putting it on the coffee table in front
of me while I got Sophie ready to nurse.

Once I had her nicely settled on the breast, I picked up the listing again
and examined it. Three bedrooms up, with two bathrooms, and a great room

with combined kitchen, living room and dining room plus another full bath-room on the main level.

It was lovely.

"What do you think?"

I glanced at the stairs where Drake stood watching me, dressed in his robe and slippers.

"You did all this?" I said, examining the listing sheet again. "We have it for April 15th?"

"I think we both deserve it, don't you?"

He came over and sat on the sofa beside me and took the sheet out of my hands. "It has a great pool, and a big deck. We can sit and watch the ocean, eat our dinner al fresco, and it's really close to where Ethan and Elaine will be living so you can take Sophie for a visit any time you want."

"And you're going to work at UCSF? On call in the ER?"

Drake nodded. "Yeah, I'll share call with a group of pediatric neurosurgeons. It won't be a full rotation and I won't have a practice, but it'll keep my credentials up. I'll get credit for the work I do, and so it'll be easier once I do finish my fellowship."

"That's wonderful," Kate said and smiled at me. "It makes this day a lot easier to bear thinking we'll soon be in Monterey, too."

"I know," Drake said and leaned over to kiss me, then he kissed Sophie's head. He stroked her light brown hair, which was starting to grow. "I figured if you knew you were going to be there soon, you wouldn't be so sad today."

"What about the case? The trial? Won't we have to be here for that?"

Drake shook his head. "I spoke with McDonald. He only asked that we keep him informed of any travel plans we have, but he thinks the case will be delayed for quite a while. I guess Lisa's lawyers are trying to postpone the trial as much as they can legally get away with. So, it's unlikely that we will even need to be in Manhattan at all."

"Thank God," Kate said and shook her head. "I really wasn't looking forward to having to attend and see her there."

"I wouldn't want you to go," Drake said and brushed hair from my cheek. "It would be hard for you. You don't need that kind of stress."

"Thank you," I said and smiled at him. "You're wonderful, do you know that?"

He smiled and leaned in, kissing me squarely on the mouth, his kiss tender.

"If I'm wonderful, it's only because I love you so much. You and Sophie. You're my world."

"You're our world, too."

Drake leaned closer, resting his forehead against mine. Sophie seemed amused by our show of affection and reached up to grab Drake's chin. He pulled away and kissed her tiny hand, taking it in his and kissing each little finger.

I felt an incredible surge of love at the sight of him doting on her, how tender and loving he was. He loved children – a man who had never been mothered much, or fathered much. He'd missed having a close family and always envied those who had them.

He'd spent his life preparing to one day be a pediatric neurosurgeon and a father and I knew he'd be the best father a child could hope to have.

He was everything. With him and Sophie, and now with the three of us moving to Monterey for the foreseeable future, I knew I would be happy.

Happier than I had ever been in my life.

WE FINALLY DRESSED and got ready for the trip with my father and Elaine to the airport. I no longer felt sad at the prospect. In fact, I felt excited for them both because I knew that soon, in a couple of weeks, we'd be joining them.

"Ready?" Drake asked while he pulled on his coat. "Ethan just texted that they're outside."

Drake had just finished getting Sophie all set in her car seat. I glanced out the window and sure enough, the limo was waiting outside on the street. All that was left was getting my coat and boots on. It had rained during the morning and was damp, so we bundled up before we went downstairs to the limo.

We trundled down the stairs and to the waiting vehicle, the side door open so Drake could get in and get Sophie's car seat fastened in properly. Then I followed and sat across from my father and Elaine, who were already seated.

My father looked excited and I wondered if he already knew about Drake's plans.

"You already knew," I said when I caught his smile.

"I did indeed," came his reply, humor in his voice. "Drake and I have been conspiring for the past two weeks to pull this off."

"You two," I said and shook my head, smiling at the expression of pleasure on both my father's and Drake's faces.

"We're so bad," Drake said. "We're plotters and planners of the highest skill."

Elaine laughed and caught my eye. "You won't believe how clandestine their activities have been since Drake decided to see if he could pull this off. The late-night telephone calls, the secret emails... You'd think they'd joined the CIA or something."

I laughed, happy to be able to enjoy the morning instead of dreading it.

"Have you seen the place we're renting?" I asked Elaine. "It has one of those horizon pools. Plus, a great view. It reminds me of our place when we were kids," I said to my dad, who was smiling to himself.

"That's what I thought," he replied. "It'll be perfect for you three. There's an extra room for an office, in case you want to paint or work on your thesis."

"There is," I said. "Drake will be working on call, so his schedule will be erratic, but we'll be close and I'll be able to come by anytime Sophie and I want."

"I can't wait," my father said, settling back in his seat for the drive to the airport. "It's going to be perfect."

"It will," I said and sat back. Drake took my hand and we sat together, the five of us, and watched as the streets of Manhattan passed us by on the way to JFK.

WE HELPED Elaine and my father through the baggage check and then sat in the comfy chairs before they entered the First-Class lounge. My father sat in a wheelchair, and would be one of the first to be boarded once the flight was ready.

"I was dreading this day for the past two weeks," I said to my father.

"I know you were, dear," he said. "Believe me, I was dreading it, too. But Drake called me up the next morning, after I called you with our departure date, laid out his plans and asked for my help and blessing. Of course, I said yes. We pulled a few strings here and there and voila. Teamwork paid off."

"I'm so glad," I said, bouncing Sophie on my knee. "If I didn't know we were following in two weeks, I'd be really depressed about all this."

"You had a spell of bad luck, but now that things have cleared up with the case, you three can move forward with your lives. You deserve it, given the past six months."

"We do," I said and reached out to take Drake's hand.

He lifted my hand to his lips and kissed my knuckles.

Finally, they called my father's flight and a customer service attendant came to help Elaine and my father board the plane.

We said our goodbyes, and I kissed Elaine and then leaned down and kissed my father goodbye. There were no tears in our eyes. Only happiness.

My father kissed Sophie when Drake held her down to him, and then Drake and my father shook hands.

"See you in a couple of weeks, Dad," Drake said.

My father winked at him. "I expect it. Take care of my baby girl and my little granddaughter, will you?"

"I will," Drake replied.

Then they were gone.

I waved at them as they went to the check in for the flight. Elaine smiled and waved and then my father did as well.

Finally, they disappeared down the ramp and Drake turned to me.

"That'll be us soon," he said and leaned down to kiss me.

"I can't wait," I said and smiled.

We sat by the window and watched the plane board, and then finally, taxi away from the terminal.

"Let's go home," Drake said.

And so we did.

~

CHAPTER 25 : DRAKE

Our last two weeks in Manhattan were extremely busy as we wrapped up the details of our trip to Monterey and packed our bags.

I had one last gig with Mersey to play, and we had plans for dinner at the O'Riley's on Sunday before our flight left.

We were lucky that Karen agreed to babysit for us late on Saturday, so Kate could attend the final performance. Karen planned to arrive in time so that Kate could make it to the ten o'clock final show.

I took my car and drove to O'Riley's for the last gig – maybe forever, and so I felt quite melancholic about the night. I parked and with my guitar in hand, I walked down the street to the restaurant, remembering so many other nights during the past decade that I walked down that same sidewalk, past the same alleys and street corners, all of it so familiar I felt as if I knew every crack in the sidewalk and hole in the pavement.

Dinner service was in the second seating by the time I entered the back door, and the cooks were busy plating food and the dishwasher had built up a good steam as I walked by. I said hello to those staff I knew and made my way to the office to say hello to Mrs. O. She was in her usual spot, going over receipts and smiled when she saw me, removing her reading glasses and standing up so she could give me a big hug.

"We're going to miss you," she said, her voice wavering. "You're like a son to me."

"You're like my mother," I replied, a bit choked up. "The mother I never knew but wished I had."

She tilted her head to the side, a sad expression on her face when she thought about my being a motherless boy after my parents split. "I'm glad we could be a family for you since you lost your own. Now, you have Kate and Sophie. Plus Ethan."

"I do," I said. "Where's Ken? Is he in the basement?"

"Yes," she said and pointed to the stairs leading down to the basement. "He's getting stuff ready."

I kissed Mrs. O on the cheek and left, making my way down to the basement room where we kept our equipment. I found Ken standing at a bookshelf filled with sheet music. He was thumbing through a book of music and turned when he saw me.

"Drake," he said and smiled. "You made it. Come here and look at this."

I went over to stand beside him, affectionately squeezing his shoulder. "What is it?"

"From one of our first gigs," he said and handed me the book of music. It was the Beatles, music from Revolver.

I flipped through the songs and smiled as I saw Ken's notation for the guitar on "And I Love Her."

"We have to play this tonight, when Kate's here," I said and showed Ken. "It's her favorite."

"Sure," he said and patted me on the back. "Anything to get you laid." He winked at me.

I laughed out loud at that. "We haven't practiced it for a while."

"I think we all know it well enough by now. We've been playing songs off that album for a decade."

We hauled the equipment up and into the bar, set it up and then when the other members of Mersey arrived, we warmed up for our first set. I was glad Kate was coming for the second set, because I was rusty, even if the other members of Mersey had been playing without me and weren't nearly as out of practice.

The first crowd was sparse and busy talking and drinking, but after a break, the bar was filled. I checked my cell to see if Kate had messaged me and sure enough, there was a text from her.

KATE: I'm on my way. See you soon. Love, me.
DRAKE: I do love you. :)

FINALLY, I saw Kate arrive, peeking her head in the doorway to the bar. She caught my eye and waved and I waved back, but we were almost ready to start so I watched as she slipped over to the bar.

The room was packed, and so she sat at the bar with Kevin and watched us play.

I felt a pang of sadness that Mersey would be getting a new bass player, but the guys loved the band and it was the only thing that some of them enjoyed. I doubted I'd ever play with anyone else, but decided to keep an open mind. Maybe I'd meet some other guys like those in the band and play again, but I was too focused on my term at UCSF to think too far ahead.

My last gig with the band went off without a hitch. We played all the old favorites – primarily the Beatles and Rolling Stones. When we came to play "And I Love Her," I took the mic and spoke directly to Kate across the crowd.

"This next song is dedicated to my beautiful wife and the mother of my wonderful daughter, Sophia. Kate, you are my life and my love. I do love you. Now and forever after."

She covered her mouth and I could see her eyes sparkling from across the room. She finally blew me a kiss and wiped her eyes. Kevin leaned over and squeezed her shoulder, smiling at her, and several in the crowed clapped as they heard the famous opening to "And I Love Her."

I sang that song with all my heart, for I felt every word. It was all true for me when it came to Kate.

She was everything to me – the true love of my life.

I'd spend the rest of my life making sure she knew that – that she felt it every single day. I almost lost Kate less than ten months earlier on a warm day in late June when the heat of summer had yet to set in and a woman crazed with jealousy and envy tried to kill her.

That event made me realize for the first time – truly realize – how happy I was with Kate. How she was perfect for me, and I believed, I was for her.

We finished the set to a round of applause and cheers, and even did an encore before leaving our instruments on the small stage and joining Kate at the bar for a drink.

"I'm going to miss you guys," I said after we found a table and sat together with a pitcher of draft.

Across from us, Johnny Mears and Cliff Walters sat side by side. Johnny held up his glass of beer.

"We'll miss you, brother," he said. "I don't know what we'll do without your voice. Have to get Ken to sing, I guess."

Ken sat up straighter. "I'll have you know that I sing almost as well as Drake. Besides, I already have a line on a new guy from Brooklyn. Was in a band that fronted for Bowie once."

The other guys raised their eyebrows at that. I turned to Ken. "You do? I thought you said--."

From the look on Ken's face, I knew he was joking. "Got you!" he said with a huge grin. "We don't have a replacement – yet. Gotta give us some time to mourn the loss first."

"Drake will miss you all," Kate said and held up her glass. "Here's to old friends and never losing touch."

"Here, here," Ken said and we all drank a toast.

Finally, I saw Kate yawn, trying desperately to hide it behind her hand, but failing.

"Time for us to go," I said and stood up, grabbing my jacket from the back of my chair. "My lady is tired and has a very busy day of packing tomorrow."

"And dinner with us tomorrow night," Ken said, his eyebrows raised. "Don't forget Sunday dinner." He turned to Johnny and Cliff. "You both are invited, too. One last meal together. How does that sound?"

"Sounds perfect," Cliff said and they both stood and we embraced.

Before Kate and I left, we stopped at the office to say goodbye to Mrs. O, who gave Kate a big hug and kiss.

"I can't wait to see that baby of yours," she said. "Drake said she looks just like you."

Kate turned to me and smiled. "She has her father's eyes, and coloring, but she has my face."

"Thankfully," I said with a laugh.

We said goodbye and promised to return for Sunday dinner, then made our way down the street to where my car was parked.

"That was nice," Kate said as we drove off. "You will miss them."

"I will," I said. "But I'm excited about Monterey."

We held hands while we drove through the streets back home. When we got inside the apartment, Karen was sitting on the couch watching television. The kitchen was clean and from the sounds of it, Sophie was sleeping in her crib.

"How was everything?" Kate asked, her voice soft.

"She was as good as gold," Karen said, smiling as she got her coat. "Didn't wake up once."

We said our final goodbyes to her, and I was surprised how attached I had become to her. She'd helped us out on many a night when Ethan was sick and when Kate and I needed some time to ourselves.

After I closed the door, I turned to see Kate standing in the entry watching me.

She had this faraway look in her eyes that I couldn't quite place.

I went over to her and pulled her into my arms. "What's that look, Mrs. Morgan? Penny for your thoughts?"

She said nothing. Instead, she slipped her arms around my waist and laid her head on my shoulder. She squeezed me and I held her even more tightly. I could tell she was very emotional and her soft heart made me melt.

Finally, she spoke, her voice soft.

"Sometimes, I have to stop and pinch myself to know I'm awake and not just dreaming."

I smiled and lifted her chin, kissing her warmly.

"I know the feeling," I said, my voice thick with emotion. "Let's go to bed," I said and rocked her in my arms. "We still have a lot to do tomorrow to get ready."

"Okay," Kate said and smiled. "Are you too tired?" she added. "I'm wide awake and a little keyed up..."

That sent a jolt of lust through my body for I knew what it meant.

"Keyed up are you, Ms. Bennet?" I said, my mind going to the lamb's-wool cuffs I bought her for Christmas. "Need an outlet?"

She nodded but said nothing else. She was leaving things to me, the way she used to before all this happened – before she became pregnant, before the attack that almost took her life and before new parenthood took away most of her energy, as was necessary.

I kissed the top of her head, signaling to her that I wanted to take control. Even though I knew it was what she wanted, she left it up to me to make the move.

"I want you to take off your clothes and lie naked on the bed for me, arms and legs spread."

I watched her vain attempt to hide her smile as she slipped out of my arms, obedient. I went to the closet in our bedroom and removed the wrist and ankle restraints and crossed over to the bed, climbing up and over top of her with them in my hand.

She blinked when she saw them and I knew what she was wondering – where is the blindfold?

"I don't want to cover your eyes," I said, my voice thick with growing desire. "I want to watch you respond to me."

She licked her lips and I knew she was beginning to respond to the idea I was planting in her mind and the response I was hoping to elicit in her body. I didn't need the restraints. She was going nowhere and she would do anything I asked of her. I knew that completely.

She still needed them to feel controlled, which she still enjoyed. She enjoyed feeling my power, even if she knew I'd never use it to harm her.

I carefully attached the cuffs to her wrists and ankles, then to the bed frame. She tested them to assure herself that they were in fact secure. When she finally turned back to look me in the eyes, I saw desire in them. She shivered, for the room was cool, her breasts all goosebumps, her nipples hardening. I smiled and after kissing her deeply, my mouth claiming hers, I began licking my way down her body. I started at her chin and didn't stop until I had her breasts in my hands, squeezing them together so I could move from one hard nipple to the other. She groaned and thrust her body up against me.

"Lie still," I commanded, and she relaxed, although her breathing had quickened.

"Sorry," she whispered.

"Sorry, what?" I asked, my voice firm.

She glanced at my face. "Sorry... *Sir*," she said, and I was just about to continue licking her nipples when I caught her lips quirk in the slightest smile.

I should have taken her at that moment and administered a spanking for her insolence, but I knew that her smile wasn't meant to be insolent. It was a sign of her pleasure that I was enforcing our old D/s rules. I realized at that moment that I would have to revive that part of our love life if I wanted her to be truly fulfilled.

"I can see I'm going to have to take you to a dungeon party, maybe display some rope technique so I can refresh your ability to obey."

"Sorry, Sir," she said quickly. "I'm out of practice."

"We're both out of practice," I murmured against her breast, my face pressed into its fullness for a moment.

It was at that moment, with Kate restrained and fully under my control, that I realized that I didn't need D/s anymore to be fulfilled sexually or emotionally. Whatever it was that made me need absolute control over my sexual partner before was small, almost so small that I barely felt it any longer. Almost losing Kate, almost losing Sophia, almost losing Ethan, finding out I had a son only to learn he could die – they brought it all into focus for the first time in my life.

I needed *Kate*.

I needed her – by my side, in my bed, in my heart. That was all. Everything else stemmed from her – Sophie, a real family, a home rather than an empty sterile house.

If I had her, I had everything.

I squeezed her breast and kissed it, then ran my hand down her back to her nice round buttock, which I squeezed lasciviously. I pulled her more tightly against me so she could feel my growing erection.

She groaned when I pressed it against her pussy, her eyes pressed tightly closed.

"Open your eyes," I said firmly. She did immediately and it was at that moment that I also realized that Kate still needed D/s. My control over her excited her, released her, freed her to feel everything. So, while I no longer needed D/s, she did and I would never deny her anything.

So, I didn't.

~

DINNER AT O'RILEY'S was what it always was – loud, filled with good-natured ribbing of each other, great food, and lots of everything, especially love.

Mrs. O held Sophie most of the evening, insisting on giving her a bottle when Sophie was due to be fed. The younger O'Riley cousins hung around Sophie, holding out toys for her to play with and talking to her. The rest of us went over our year, and past years together, reminiscing and generally appreciating what we had.

Kate enjoyed herself, Sophie was a model baby, and I got to say goodbye to the family that had been the only real one I knew until I met Kate and spent time with her family.

We returned home after a tearful goodbye on Mrs. O's part, with promises to come back again once we returned – if we returned to Manhattan.

Once we were finally home and inside our apartment on 8th Avenue, we stood in the midst of the boxes that were packed, labeled and ready to be picked up the next morning, before our late afternoon drive to the airport.

"I can't believe we're actually leaving," Kate said with a sigh.

"Was that a sigh of contentment or one of regret?" I asked, reaching for the car seat to take a sleeping Sophie upstairs to her room.

"Neither," Kate replied and handed the car seat over to me. "Fatigue. I've been so busy trying to wrap up our lives here, packing, planning, shipping, that I'm looking forward to two weeks at my dad's so we can unwind before we have to start unpacking our new place."

"Me, too. We haven't had a real holiday for a while. I'll put Sophie to bed."

Kate went to the living room and turned on the television while I took Sophie upstairs. I laid her down in the crib and covered her with her blankets. She sucked away on her pacifier and didn't even open her eyes once, worn out from all the attention she got at the O'Riley's.

Then, after checking my email, I went to where Kate was sitting drinking a glass of water.

"Well, Mrs. Morgan, are you ready for this?"

She turned to me and smiled. "As ready as I'll ever be. I'm sure there's something we've forgotten."

She changed channels and came upon a news story about the Richardson murder case. I was so glad that I was no longer involved in that whole business and felt a pang of regret for Derek. It was because of our mutual connection through Lisa that he was dead and that brought on some guilt on my part. Perhaps my texts to him about Lisa got him into trouble. He may have felt some responsibility to warn NYU about Lisa and that got him killed.

"Poor Derek," Kate said. "He was only trying to do the right thing in warning the department about her instability."

"When you run into someone like Lisa, it's always risky. These kinds of people leave a trail of bloody and broken bodies in their wake. None of us saw her for what she was until it was too late. We're lucky you and Sophie are alive."

Kate turned to me and then crept into my arms, straddling my hips.

"Mmm, Ms. Bennet, to what do I owe this development?"

Kate smiled and kissed me. "I was just thinking that we're so lucky you were extra cautious and hired that security company to provide me with a guard." She leaned back and brushed hair off my face. "If I had been alone, who knows if we would have survived? My guard had paramedic training. He saved my life, and Sophie's."

"He did."

We kissed and soon, the kiss turned to so much more.

"I need you," I said, my body ready, my heart beating faster.

"I'm yours," was all Kate said in reply.

Then I stood up, picking up Kate in the process, and carried her upstairs to our bedroom.

MONDAY WAS A BLUR, with Kate and I taking turns looking after Sophie while we finished preparations for our trip. The movers came and took the rest of the boxes we were shipping out to the West Coast. We checked our bags and carry-ons, and made sure we had the thermostat turned down low enough to save on energy while keeping the pipes warm.

I left one light on in the living room. One of the real estate agents from the company I used would come by and check on things on a regular basis, to keep with the terms of our home insurance.

Finally, with the limo waiting outside, we left the apartment and as I closed the door, I wondered when we'd return, and whether it would be to finish packing because we were selling or returning for good.

It was all up in the air at that moment but the prospects of starting over in Monterey felt right to me. This apartment had so many memories. It had been my father's gift to me when I was a student and needed a place to live. It had been Kate's and my first place together as a couple. It was where we welcomed Sophia into our lives. It would still be here if we wanted to return.

When I got to the bottom floor of the building, I stepped out into the cool late afternoon air and took in a deep cleansing breath. The first pink and orange rays of the sunset filtered down through the tall buildings surrounding us.

I glanced back at the apartment. As much as I loved this place and our life here, the past year had been one filled with so much stress – my fear about

Kate and Sophie almost being taken from me, worry about the police case going awry and being kept on the suspect list, Kate's PTSD and postpartum depression. My reputation was tarnished in the eyes of some of my colleagues due to the publicity surrounding the case and I had to pull back from involvement in my foundation and the corporation.

Moving to Monterey and starting over there gave me hope. While our old life was ending, our new life, filled with plans for the future, was just beginning.

I picked up Sophie's car seat and took Kate's hand, leading her to the limo where the driver stood, the passenger doors open and waiting.

"Let's go."

∼

EPILOGUE : KATE

California was just as I remembered it as a child – warm, sunny and most of all, laid back.

As soon as we arrived and left the plane, once we were on the road to my father's place in Monterey, I felt a weight lifted off my shoulders. Leaving Manhattan, while hard, was the best decision for us at the time.

The first week after we arrived and were settled in at my father's beach home, I sat beneath an umbrella and watched the surf. Sophie sat at the edge of the surf on the sand surrounded with beach toys – green and pink buckets and tiny shovels in bright pink and yellows. A tiny floppy beach hat was tied around her chin to keep it from blowing off and a mini pair of heart-shaped sunglasses, which perched a bit unevenly on her cheeks. She wore a one-piece hot pink and green pair of shorts and t-shirt for while the weather was warm, it wasn't yet warm enough for swimsuits. She was busy digging in the sand, generally throwing the sand around her, laughing as she did.

Drake stood beside her and watched, laughing when she did, not caring that the sand was going everywhere except in the bucket. She was still too uncoordinated to be able to dig with any success.

Liam ran in the surf with a boogie board in his hands. He had on a kid's sized wetsuit and was undeterred by the temperature of the water. Instead, he jumped on his board eagerly when a wave broke in front of him and rode it onto the sand near Drake's feet. Up on the cliff behind us sat my father's beach house. Huge, with a wall to wall deck, hot tub and full dining table under a broad awning. Beneath the awning sat my father and Elaine watching us. My father was in his wheelchair and was wearing a sun hat and glasses.

He waved when he saw me glance back.

Drake was so happy, standing there with his two children at his side. While I had been a bit homesick for the first few days we were in Monterey, feeling out of sorts due to the change in our lives, I was glad to be closer to my father, and of course, couldn't be happier that Maureen had a sudden change of heart and agreed that Liam could come to stay with us for the day at Ethan's house.

I guess it worked out well with Maureen's and Chris's plans to do some shopping for the day. Otherwise, who knows if she would have agreed?

I hoped that Drake would be able to show her, over the coming months, that he was as safe as anyone with Liam. Drake was a loving father, eager to establish a close relationship with his son. There wasn't anything Drake wouldn't do for Liam. He'd saved the boy's life, after all. Maybe slowly Maureen would realize that and agree to some kind of shared custody arrangement.

On Liam's part, he seemed such an easy-going boy. He never questioned anything and seemed only too glad to fit into our family, especially liking that Sophia was his little sister. He rode wave after wave in on his tiny board, the smile on his face broad. He looked so much like what I imagined Drake looked like when he was a boy. I only wish Drake could have remained that happy, but at least now, he could see his own son that way.

Drake plopped down on the beach beside Sophie and helped her fill up a bucket with sand. On my part, I went over to them and sat down on the other side of Sophie.

The three of us built a small sandcastle, and laughed as Sophie happily crawled into it, knocking down the battlements.

"Look what she did!" Liam called out when he saw her sitting in the middle of the fallen castle, her tiny fists filled with sand. "She destroyed it."

He ran over and sat beside her, laughing as they both knocked down one more turret Drake had so carefully constructed.

Drake turned to me and smiled. He glanced around at the beach, then up to the house behind us, waving at my dad and Elaine the way I had.

Then he turned to me, his smile fading into an expression of pure contentment.

He leaned over and kissed me, then turned back to his two children, who were busy patting down the sand around them in preparation to make another castle.

I could get used to this life. It felt good here. It felt like it could be a place I could call home.

Manhattan would always have a special place in my heart. It was where I grew up. It was where my family home had always been. I knew its streets and avenues, the familiar landmarks each associated with some event or time in my youth. California was new and wide open.

We'd build new memories there – memories of our lives together and with our children. Drake would have his work at the hospital. I would have whatever work I finally decided on – art or journalism. At that moment, I felt no pressure to do either, only a freedom to pursue both if I wanted.

I sighed and helped them build another castle, the bright California sun warm on my back.

THE END

ABOUT THE AUTHOR

S. E. Lund writes erotic, contemporary, new adult and paranormal romance. She lives in a century-old house on a quiet tree-lined street in a small Western Canadian city with her family of humans and animals. She dreams of living in a warm climate where snow is just a word in a dictionary.

Find S. E. Lund on the Web:
www.selund.com
selund2012@gmail.com

S. E. LUND NEWSLETTER

Sign up for S. E. Lund's newsletter and gain access to updates on upcoming releases, sales and freebies! She hates spam and so will never share your email!

S. E. LUND NEWSLETTER SIGN UP